Copyright

August, 2012 Edition

Cover Design by Andrew Pavlik

Edited by Catherine Adams of Inkslinger Editing

Dedication

To my parents, who always believed I could

CHAPTER ONE

When the dust cloud appears, we know they are coming.

My mama and I spy the cloud churning up the road at the same time. Her potato peeler clatters to the porch floor, sending goose flesh over my arms. I stare at the cloud kicked up by dozens of approaching tires and then back to my mother. There's no mistaking it. The fear is written on her face.

She grips my shoulder, hand already shaking. "Get in the cellar." Her face tightens. "Now."

Her rocking chair scrapes against the porch floorboards. She yanks open the screen door and runs into the house, yelling for my brother.

I stand up, my own hands trembling now. The advance of the dust cloud has me riveted, like an animal caught in headlights. It's what we've drilled for, prepared for, whispered about at night. And now they're coming.

My mama's frantic screams pierce my thoughts. "Riley, the storm cellar! Hurry!"

I shake myself out of my stupor and force my jellied legs to move. Running into the house, I spy my stepfather, Arn, at the pitted kitchen table. He slips round after round into his hunting rifle, his calloused fingers fumbling for more in the box that holds too few. He drops one. It hits on the floor and rolls under the table.

"Gawddammit!" he swears. His leathery forehead wrinkles as he searches frantically.

I run over, grab it and hand it to him. The bullet feels cold against my hot palm.

His eyes latch onto mine and a sadness creeps over his face. This frightens me more than anything. He grabs our pistol off the table and thrusts it forward. "You'll need this." His eyes say one gun won't be enough.

The revolver is heavy and solid in my trembling hand. I curl my fingers over the wooden grip, worn smooth with use. I let my index finger stray to the trigger, place my other hand under the grip like he taught me and aim at the dust cloud. I look up at him, unable to ask what I need to know.

In this moment Arn looks old. His sun-beaten face is carved by wrinkles and his forehead is dotted with sweat. The patched overalls sag on his too-thin body. Before this he was out milking the cow or mucking out the barn, mundane, boring tasks that I wish he could go back to now. Arn grabs both my shoulders and fixes me with frightened blue eyes. "You 'member what I taught you?"

"Is it the Breeders? It is, isn't it?" My voice breaks with the terror that's sticking to my insides and knotting my stomach. Arn says nothing. He doesn't have to. His face tells me everything I need to know.

"I can fight." The gun trembles, but I lock my elbows and grit my teeth. I want this chance to face the people who've been hunting us our whole lives.

Arn shakes his head, the lines around his mouth deepening. "Soon's they see you, they'd kill the men and take the women. Get in the cellar. I'll handle this." His weathered hand squeezes mine. It's the most affection he's shown me in months. I savor the roughness of his palm. Then, quick as it came, he drops my hand and goes back to slipping bullets into his rifle, his eyes marking the approach of our enemies.

From behind me: "Riley?!" My mama is near hysterics.

"Coming!" I sprint through the old farmhouse, the boards moaning beneath my feet. I skid to a stop at our bedroom and scan it for my brother. Both beds lay empty. Ethan's boots lie on their sides under his bed. His comic book is forgotten on the floor. He'd never leave it there on a normal day. But this isn't a normal day. Angry motors growl closer. How soon before they get here? Minutes? Seconds?

I burst through the back door. The storm cellar sits fifteen paces from the house, dug deep in the ground. When we moved in six months ago, my mama showed us the cellar that, when shut, folds neatly into the dusty landscape. We've taken pains to camouflage the doors, but will it be enough?

The cellar doors yawn wide, revealing the dark earthen hole. My mama crouches at the cellar's mouth, her hand-sewn cotton dress gathering around her knees. My little brother, Ethan, descends the ladder. His hand clutches her scarred one for a moment before he disappears into shadow. He's gone. An urge to sob washes over me. I bite it back and run over.

My mama turns, searching for me. From this angle she is breathtaking in her loveliness. Her shoulder-length black hair shines in the hazy sunlight, and her left cheek is supple and pink. She's a beauty queen, a *ten* as Auntie says. It's the other side of her face that marks the horrors she's seen. Red angry burn scars travel her neck and face. Her skin bunches and grooves like a pitted dirt road. Her left ear is only a ragged, red hole. Yet, I rarely notice her burned face. This is the way she's looked as long as I can remember.

I step to the edge of the cellar and peer at my brother. From the bottom of the hole, his eyes are wide as a jackrabbit's caught in my snare. His lower lip trembles. He looks five instead of eight. "It's okay," I lie.

My mother grips my shoulder and presses down. "Get in." Her voice is a choked whisper. She glances back at the dust plume. The gray cloud hangs huge, blocking out the horizon, a tornado set to tear our world apart.

I take a step back and narrow my eyes. "You first."

"I have to get Bell." She looks towards the upstairs window.

I grip her arm. "No! They won't take Auntie. She's too old."

My mama pulls me to her chest in a brief hug. Then she scrambles out of my clutches. I claw for her dress, but she's gone. "Don't go!"

"I love you!" she yells over her shoulder, her voice full of tears. The back door thwacks as she disappears inside it.

"Come back!" I yell, but it's too late.

I stare at the door, wondering if I'll ever see her again. I take a step toward the house, but the truck motors rumble so close they rattle my molars. They will be here in seconds. And what my stepfather says is true. If they see me, they will stop at nothing to have me and I can't put my family in danger.

Ethan whines, "Riley?"

I lower myself into the ground as tears streak the dirt on my cheeks. I draw the wooden shutters and the storm cellar plunges into darkness. Strings of light stream through the cracks of the rotting boards. This earthen hole reeks of damp soil and musty wood. A cobweb brushes my face. I cringe and bat at it as I step carefully to the bench where my brother is a small, dark shadow. Ethan crawls on my lap. He's all arms and legs now, too big to curl onto his sister's lap. His hands claw into my clothing, holding me so close I feel his heart flutter like a baby bird caught in his shirt. On a normal day I wouldn't put up with baby stuff, but today is different. Today we might lose everything.

"Shh. Shh," I murmur, until I remember we need to be silent. I grip Ethan to me with one hand and the gun with the other.

The engines shake the ground so hard I wonder if their trucks are parked on top of us. Dirt sifts through the cracks above. Brakes whine. Doors slam. Ethan trembles.

Husky voices raise the hair on my arms. They call out. I can't make out what they're saying, but I can guess the tone, which right now is friendly enough. Where's my mama and Auntie Bell? I can't just sit here. I slip Ethan off my lap. He moans in protest, his fingers grasping at my clothes, pleading. I pry them off and slip up the ladder. A rung creaks under my weight, but the men are too far off and their voices too loud to hear me. I climb up and press my eye against the knothole.

From this angle I can see the road and our front porch. Three trucks idle in our driveway. They're road gang trucks with big all-terrain tires and grates attached to the front for smashing everyone out of their way. A rusty blue F150 is pocked with bullet holes. A dark green Chevy has hooks welded to the bed rails and handcuffs slung through them. The handcuffs make me sick to my stomach.

A half-dozen men lean out of cabs. They wear leather road gear, buzzed haircuts and grimy goggles. A few have big crude tattoos. They glare forward, spit dust from their mouths and let their rifles drape loosely over their shoulders. They aren't aiming at my house. Yet.

"Riley," Ethan whispers behind me.

I wave one hand at him to be quiet, despite the dark. Then I turn back to the scene.

This gang's leader, a meaty man with a bald head and worn leather jacket, stands on the porch with Arn. The thug has his boot up on the seat of Auntie's rocker and he's leaning on his knee as if he were shootin' the breeze with a friend, but then there's the nine-inch serrated blade on his hip. He smiles crookedly, and even from here I can see he's missing half the teeth. His shaved head sports a crescent-shaped scar trailing from the corner of his mouth to his ear. His lapel winks in the sunlight. A gold star rests over his heart.

"Sheriff Tate," I mouth. This is bad. Real bad. He's the local arm of the Breeders. He delivers them girls and they keep him stocked in guns and ammo.

Sheriff Tate talks to Arn, though I can't hear. He steps off the porch and clomps toward us, with Arn at his heels. I drop back down the ladder, stand in front of Ethan and point the gun toward the cellar door. Their footsteps crunch closer. I can't breathe.

Ethan's hand tightens around my arm, a vice grip. *Please, God, don't let them find us,* I pray. *Please.*

Their boots crunch to a stop and veer right. Arn must be showing him our water pump. If the Sheriff takes another few steps this way, he'll be able to see the hidden cellar. I listen in the darkness, hoping against hope that he'll get a drink and go on his way.

The old pump creaks up and down as my stepfather draws water. This old farmhouse has its own windmill and well, which remarkably still produces fresh drinking water. It is why we can live out in this wasteland and not in town.

The Sheriff drinks and sighs in satisfaction. His heavy voice drifts through the cracks. "That's fresh. Didn't think clean wells still pumped 'round these parts. You sure got lucky." His voice is resonant, like a roll of thunder. Beside me, Ethan squeezes my arm until it goes numb.

"Yep. Yep. Lucky." My stepfather's worn voice catches in his throat. Let him hold it together a few more minutes. Please.

"So, just yer lonesome on the homestead?"

I hold my breath. Ethan shifts nervously beside me.

"Yes, sir. The boy I took in died a few years ago. Rancher's flu. Had a renter, but he cleared out some months back. Don't mind the quiet."

The men pause for an eternity. I glance down at Ethan. Even in this dim light I can see his face twisted with terror. If we get out of this, I'll give him the caramel I've been saving since Christmas to lift that look off his face.

"Awful big house for a stiff such as yerself. Mind if we give 'er a look? Couple crim'nals we hoping to strap in irons."

Liar! They're looking for girls. Everyone's looking for girls.

Arn blows out his breath. "Rather you boys be on your way. Got more milking to do."

The Sheriff clucks his tongue. "Uh–uh. Milking's a morning chore. Hiding something, are ya? We'll jist take a peek."

Sheriff Tate pushes a shrill whistle through his teeth. Boots *thunk* to the hard-packed dirt.

"Now hold on!" Arn yells.

I scramble up the ladder and press my shoulder to the cellar door. I steady my trembling hands. Ethan, the dull shadow beneath me, begins to cry. I flick my eyes away and swallow hard. I don't care what happens to me, but nothing can happen to him. I couldn't stand it.

My front door bangs open, and angry tomcat yowling cuts across the yard. I hop down a peg and fix my eye back to the peephole.

Auntie Bell bursts out of the house, screaming, her hair wiping around her like a great gray storm. Her arms flail as she barrels toward the Sheriff.

"You stinking, rotten pig eater!" She lurches, her hands hooked like talons. My stepfather grabs for her dress. The cotton shift pulls tight around her wrinkled body as she strains to attack.

She claws at the Sheriff's face. "You loathsome, dirty hair pie! I spit in your mother's grave!" Auntie kicks out wildly. One of her clogs flies off and smacks into the Sheriff's thigh. He stumbles back and drops his hand to his knife. He will kill Auntie and Arn, but I'll shoot him before that happens. I tuck my head to my chest and feel the adrenaline buzz inside me. The metal feels smooth under my trigger finger. I press my shoulder to the door.

Laughter explodes through the air. I slam my face back to the peephole so fast a splinter sinks into my cheek.

A crooked smile lights up the Sheriff's carved face. He thumps a meaty hand on his knee. "Batty, old witch," he says, cackling. He points at Auntie. "Ya got some fire left in them bones."

His hand leaves his knife and he waves off his men. "We ain't interested in a wrinkled ole cooz. We decent folk, not savages. You right to be careful, though. Some banditos would snatch her up, foul mouth and all." Auntie reaches through Arn's embrace and claws at the Sheriff. He clucks his tongue and laughs again, loud and nasty.

The Sheriff jumps off the porch. "Thanks for the drink. Take care now!" He waves real friendly like, hops in the lead truck and pushes a shrill whistle through his teeth. Motors flare to life. The line of vehicles peels out, spewing gravel against our house.

I can't believe it. They are leaving.

My heart pumps erratically as I try to breathe normal. A cold sweat trickles between my shoulder blades. I shiver and suck air.

Cold fingers wrap around my wrist. I jolt back, my foot slips off a slick rung, and I tumble. My flight through the air is short, the ground hard. The impact sends a snap of pain up my tailbone. I look up and make out my brother's big brown eyes.

"Damn it, Ethan. Don't scare me like that," I snap. Then I see the terror running over his face. God, I'm dumb. He still thinks his whole family's about to be murdered and I yelled at him.

I stand and squeeze him to me with one arm. "Sorry, little man."

He pulls away. "Did they leave?"

"Yeah, munchkin." I try to muss his hair, but my hand's not done trembling. "Safe for another day." I can't believe it. We got so lucky.

He sighs and slips his hand in mine. "Don't call me munchkin."

"You got it, munchkin." I stand aside while he mounts the ladder. Suddenly, I'm dead tired. The gun weighs a hundred pounds.

When we get in the house, Auntie Bell sits at the kitchen table. Her loose cotton dress sags against her bony shoulders. She's braiding back her long, gray hair as she mutters something about a dirt pie. My stepfather stands at the window, watching the dust cloud fade. He's got his hands in the pouch of his overalls, his thinking stance. My mama steps behind him, puts her hands around his waist and her head on his shoulder. Their love is so solid, like the beams that hold this house up. My stomach flip-flops with bittersweet longing. I am sixteen and the only boy I see is my eight-year-old brother. Love for me is like the sunset: beautiful from afar, but I can never touch it. Love is ancient history. I get safety instead.

When the dust cloud is only an image we'll see in our nightmares, my mama slips away from Arn and lights a fire in the old stove.

"Riley, get the bread out of the pantry, please." She grabs an opener and a dented can of beans.

"Nobody's gonna talk about what just happened?" I ask no one in particular.

My stepfather flicks his eyes at me and then starts tucking his guns in their hiding places. Auntie Bell mutters under her breath. My mama drops the beans on the pan. They sizzle and pop as their bodies dance on the cast iron.

"Riley, we're tired and hungry. Please get the bread." Finality settles on her rutted face.

I head for the pantry. I may be the most wanted thing in the country, but I still have to listen to my mama.

CHAPTER TWO

Today's the day, I think as I stride through the house. Outside I hear Arn swearing at our Jeep. *Yeah, right,* says the voice in my head. *He's never going to let you go.*

I push open the screen door and step out on the porch. According to Arn, this land used to be called New Mexico, though there's nothing new about it. For miles on either side of our yard, the scrubland, tumbleweeds and acres of dirt cover the landscape. Plant life consists of prickly cactus and squat, mean bushes that snag up my ankles. Animals are brown, wiry and should be avoided, unless you're eating one. And the people, we're made tough and prickly, too. I tell my mama this whenever she asks why me and Arn can't get along.

The sun looms orange and round in the east. At eight a.m., it's already sweltering. I squint down the road toward civilization. Our closest living neighbor is thirty miles east; the closest town, three hours after that. It's torturous living out in what Auntie calls "the devil's arse," but from what we hear, the roads north and east team with road gangs. My parents won't chance a townie life, and as my mama says, living where no one else would has its advantages. People leave you alone.

Out here we survive on what game Arn and I can trap and whatever plants my mama can coax out of her garden. Arn barters in town for the rest. If he is fixing the Jeep, it means he's going to town for supplies. This time I'm determined to go.

I jump off the porch, the one we spend hours on, rocking, shucking beans and counting the minutes with our eyes on the road. I sidle over to where Arn's legs stick out from under the rusted vehicle. My eyes trace over the mud-caked knees of his jeans, down to his boots with the hole in the right toe. A string of curse words float up from under the Jeep. I grip the rusty hood, take a breath and nudge his leg.

"What?!" There's a clunk. Then more curse words.

He's hit his head. Damn. Not a good start. I should turn around and eat breakfast with Auntie. Instead, I dig my toe into the dust and clear my throat.

"You going into town?" I say to his legs.

"What?" He wiggles out and pulls himself to a standing position next to the truck. He wipes oil from his hands onto a hankie and squints at me. His blue eyes sparkle on his dirty face like a glass bottle winking in a sand dune. "What'd you say?"

I run my finger along the top of the dented door. "I said, you going to town?"

Arn's salt-and-pepper hair is matted to his forehead in sweaty clumps. The soiled overalls match his sun-browned skin as if he's made completely of dust. Arn swipes at his face with the same rag he used to clean the oil off his hands. Some of it smears on his cheek. He regards me and then walks to the back of the Jeep. He squats and digs around in his toolbox.

"You're not coming," he says over the clanking of his wrenches and screwdrivers.

I kick at a loose pebble. It's fruitless, but something inside me has changed since the encounter with the Sheriff. I walk over and put my hands on my hips. "You're going to have to let me someday. What if you're not around to trade?"

He answers without looking, his eyes examining two wrenches in his calloused fingers. "You better pray Ethan's old enough." He drops one wrench back in the tool chest with a clang. He stands to get back under the Jeep. I take a step to block his path. His mouth tightens into a hard line.

"That's years down the road. I gotta learn to wheel and deal. I'll wear goggles and your leather jacket. No one'll know."

My stepfather sticks a hand in the pouch of his overalls and squints at me. He's trying to see me like the townies would. My black hair is cropped short like my brother's. Each morning I bind my breast with bandages until I can barely breathe. I wear boy's baggy clothing. Still it's obvious if someone gets a close look I'm not a boy. My Auntie laments what she calls my dangerous beauty. I'm too girly with curvy hips, slender cheekbones, full lips. The best I can do is pass for a bender, the feminized boys that are born instead of girls after we poisoned the planet. Benders can't have babies, so they're lower-class citizens. Passing for a bender does not help my chances in town much.

Arn puts a hand on my shoulder and moves me aside. Then he lies down next to the Jeep. "Nope. Not going."

"But, Arn, I—"

"Enough, Riley!" he shouts, gripping the side of the truck. His head and torso disappear beneath our jalopy. I've had enough fights with Arn to know this conversation is over.

I slump back to the house, a pain welling beneath my breastbone. I walk in the house, but instantly regret it. I want to be alone. The barn. It's my smelly sanctuary. Then I hear Ethan coughing from our bedroom.

Whenever the dust gets bad, Ethan coughs until his hankies are bloody. And the dust is almost always bad. I picture his thin frame hunched over, his body quaking with cough. Sucking on the caramel hidden in my nightstand might help him. I take a step to our shared bedroom.

"Riley Anne," Auntie bellows. A strange bashing sound echoes from our kitchen. "Your help … *oomph* … is requested. Hold still, you vermin!"

I want to ignore Auntie, but what is all that banging and scraping? I run in the kitchen.

What I find would be comic if it weren't so dangerous. Auntie Bell stands on a kitchen chair. In the cone of morning light from the open window, her loose cotton dress exposes far too much of her body. Leathery skin droops from her arms and breasts. Her face is lined like a dried lakebed. Her long, gray hair flies wildly behind her. She peers into the dark recesses of a cabinet, a broom in one hand and a butcher knife in the other.

"I've captured a bat." She whacks the cupboard with the broom. A fuzzy, brown blur flits out toward her face. She yelps and teeters in her chair. As her arms wheel through the air to regain balance, the butcher knife slices wildly close to her thigh.

"Auntie, Christ!" I run to the chair and steady it. The butcher knife clatters to the floor as she grabs hold of my shoulder. The bat flutters madly inside the cupboard.

I clutch her arm, feeling the thin ripple of muscle as she steps down. "You're gonna kill yourself! What're you doing?" I snag the butcher knife from the floor and tuck it into a drawer.

"I've got the bugger trapped," she pants. She points to where the bat knocks over my mama's dishes. "I'll fry it up for supper." She licks her thin lips. "It'll taste like chicken." Auntie takes another whack the cupboard. Inside the bat smashes into plates and cups.

I push her chair back under the table. "The bugger's got rabies. 'Sides, Arn's going to town. We'll have real chicken maybe."

She cocks her head and then sets the broom against the wall. "In that case, you can remove the vermin."

Great. What do I do with a bat? I crouch down, extend one arm and open the top cupboard. The bat bashes around inside for a moment. Then he sees his escape, flies out and flits around the kitchen. When he finds the open window and slips through, a tightness grips my heart again. His escape is so easy. I'm still trapped, bashing my body into closed doors.

A tear breaks through my guard and slides down my face. I pretend to itch my nose and wipe it away, but Auntie's eyes lock on me. She stops plaiting her hair and taps a weathered finger on the table. "Sit."

"I should check on Ethan." I don't want to discuss this.

"Sit," Auntie growls at me.

I sit and direct my eyes to the battered tabletop. Someone long ago scratched the initials J.R. on the wood. I wonder if J.R. is the man we found dead, half eaten by coyotes, in the side yard when we moved in.

Auntie grabs a dry crust of bread from the basket between us and starts gumming it. Then she leans toward me, her lips pressed in a thin, cracked line. "You got a bee in your bonnet and I want to know what it is."

I shake my head. "Nope. Fine. Can I go?"

Auntie narrows her eyes and puts one crooked finger on her chin. "Not fine," she says, slowly. "Definitely not fine. Heard you coaxing your step-daddy to take you to town. You know why you can't go."

Sure, I know why they say I can't go. I hear nothing but how they gotta protect me, how dangerous it is for me to leave this house, how I can't trust strangers. I also know we can't live this way forever. Someday I'll have to fend for myself.

"I know," I say, my head down.

"Then, what's the problem, punkinhead?" She lifts the hard crust to her mouth and sucks it. Arn's Jeep rumbles to life in the driveway.

I should mutter a response and hightail it to my room, but raw emotion crackles inside me like a storm about to break. The words tumble out before I can stop them. "I'm a prisoner here. This isn't a life. Nothing ever happens to me."

Auntie doesn't look at me. She sets the crust on the table and lays both gnarled hands on the dented tabletop. Her gnarled fingers curl into the surface until they look like talons. Her voice rolls out of her throat.

"You don't know because you've never had it happen to you."

"Auntie, I—"

She holds up a hand to stop me. Her eyes are burning embers.

"You don't know because no man has laid hands on ya. But I know." She thumps a finger to her chest. "Your mama knows."

I have made a mistake. I want to leave.

She rolls the sleeve back on her arm. I know what I'll see, though I'm afraid to look. "Look at it," she says, brandish her forearm.

I squeeze my eyes shut, then I look.

The brand is there, seared into the skin on her forearm. The dark, puckered shape of a cross with a round head, the ankh, a symbol of fertility. The Breeder's symbol. My mama has the same brand. I do not.

"After all we risked. After all we sacrificed—"

"Auntie, I'm sor—"

She holds up a hand. Her pupils have dilated to dark vacant holes. When she speaks, her voice comes from somewhere far off. "When the Breeders come for ya, there ain't no escape. They strap ya to a bed, and all ya hear is the thud of your heart and the cries of your friends as they wheel ya down to hell. Then the doctors come. You squeeze your eyes shut and pray you can forget. But you never do."

I drop my eyes and shake my head, more tears collecting at the crease of my eyes. I don't want to hear it and yet, a sick, curious part of me wants her to keep going. They never speak of the Breeders, as if it might call them down on us.

"Bell." It's my mama behind me in the doorway.

Auntie's eyes flick up to her, and the anger drops from her face. She picks up the crust of bread again. "Don't let me hear you complain again." Her gums make a wet sucking sound as she turns from me.

I scrape out of the chair, past my mama, and run to my room. I choke on the sob that's climbing up. I have to be alone.

When I burst through my bedroom door, Ethan sits cross-legged on the bed with a tattered comic book on his lap. His black hair hangs into his eyes. His bony elbows rest on his bony knees. I hate how skinny he is. The most recent growth spurt hasn't helped. Now he's two inches taller but no thicker. I've forgotten he was in here. There's no way I can cry in front of Ethan. I turn to go.

"Riley?" he calls at my back.

I can't play happy sister right now. Usually I can pretend, suck back my unhappiness and invent games of chase the pig or dig up anthills and let him watch in wonder as a colony comes spilling to the top. I can't do that today. I take another step out of the room.

The coughing fit hits. Ethan hacks like a frail old man. His bed rocks beneath him as cough after cough rolls through him. I slide my hand down my face, wipe off the mad and sad, and turn around. When he sees me, he smiles behind his cupped hand.

"Better catch those lung pieces so we can stick 'em back in," I say as I sit next to him. I look over; my moth-eaten bedspread is pulled tight. He made my bed and his. Of course he did. He'll do anything to keep me out of trouble. As the box springs shake with each cough, I try to think of something nice to do for him. For now, being here is all I got.

When the coughing stops, he looks up at me. "You okay?" He wipes at tears that have sprung up.

He's asking about me with his blue-tinged lips, flecks of foam at the corners of his mouth. I'll never be as good as my brother.

"Yep. You?"

He nods. "Were you fighting with Auntie?" His voice is raw from the cough.

"No."

His small, dark eyes narrow. "How come she yelled at you?"

"It's Auntie. She's … you know." I wind my finger around my ear and loll my tongue out of my mouth. It makes him laugh. The laughing makes him cough. God, I can't do anything right.

His eyes track to the window where his dad fixes the Jeep. "You're mad cause Dad won't let you go to town."

Ethan adores his dad and it bugs him that we don't get along. I understand. Two of the four people he loves snipe at each other all day, but even my peacekeeping brother can't mend the rift between me and Arn.

"Let's not talk about Arn." I pick up his comic book and flip through the pages. "Superman again? Haven't you read this like 800 times?"

"It's so cool." His eyes light up and his posture straightens. He turns to the middle of the book, crinkled with use, and points to Superman fighting a monster covered in knotty gray spikes. The dry desert behind them looks like what I see out our back window.

"Look." He points a dirty finger. "This is where Superman fights Doomsday. Isn't he awesome?"

Superman is Ethan's favorite. Whenever something bad happens, a man with rippling muscles flies in and rescues the townsfolk. Superman makes it all okay. I don't tell Ethan we have no Superman. No one will save us from the monsters that threaten us.

"Can you read it?" His elbow digs into my thigh as he scoots closer.

My mouth tenses as I look down at the little black words. There are some I know. Many I don't.

"Right here," he says, pointing to a word bubble.

I smile weakly and squint at the page. "Dooms ... day."

Ethan gives me a nod.

"Is he ... is he ..." I squint at the next word and try to sound it out. It has too many parts that swim around in my head, making the whole too hard to piece together.

I glance at the novel wedged under the mattress that I've been trying to read for over a year. Some massive thing called *The Stand.* I found it in the closet of our last house in a busted black safe. The little book with the bent cover must've been worth something a long time ago, probably something to do with the author's name scratched in red pen on the inside cover.

I close the comic book and set it on Ethan's nightstand.

"My eyes hurt." It's a lie and we both know it, but Ethan nods. "Come on." I stand up and offer my hand. "Let's go check the snares. If we're lucky, we'll get us a jackrabbit for supper."

We pull on patched coveralls, thin long-sleeved shirts, hats, thick boots. We're sweating before we walk out the door, but without the gear the white-hot sun would fry our skin. I snag the hunting rifle, the Winchester single barrel with the battered grip and oiled muzzle (*We keep our guns clean,* Arn always says) and sling it over my shoulder. I won't use it unless the coyotes are prowling. Guns ain't hard to come by, but bullets are. I got my hunting knife in my pocket. I hope to put that to some use.

I lead us through the yard. Ethan shuffles after me, his oversized boots—mine a few years ago—clunking through the dust. We tromp to the barn.

Its weathered sides lean left and the roof sags like a deflated piecrust. Arn says the main beams are so solid, it'll hold for thirty years. Looking at the rotting boards as I enter, I can't imagine it standing for another three.

I walk through the large, open doors and the air instantly cools. It's quieter here and even the smell, cow manure and musty hay, won't bother me for long. Bounty, our cow, moos at me as I walk by. I lean over the rail and rub the black patch on her forehead.

I lead us to the back of the barn. In a dark corner, a tarp-covered shape hunkers near Arn's workbench. I pull off the tarp and the air thickens. A four-wheeler with a cracked leather seat and worn, nubby tires winks at me beneath the dust. The four-wheeler is off limits. We can't afford to use fuel for a snare check. I run my hand over the bumpy leather seat and feel a pulling in my chest. One headlight stares out at me, begging me to unleash her.

Ethan slides up behind me. "We gonna take the four-wheeler?"

I can tell by his voice that he's uneasy. "Thinking about it." I grip the handlebars, the rubber warm to the touch.

"You know Dad says we can't."

I sigh and throw the cover back over the quad. "Fine," I grumble, "but you better not bellyache on the way back. I ain't carrying your big butt all the way home."

He pokes me in the stomach. "You're the big, fat bubble butt," he says, smiling.

I reach for him, ready to make him pay—through ticking mostly, but maybe a few pinches for good measure—but he's sprinting away. I charge after him, a smile spreading.

We head out past the dead fruit trees that mark where our yard ends and the scrubland begins. We tromp through the dried creek bed, the brown, broken dirt crunching under our boots. Ethan lags to watch a lizard dart under a rock. Flies buzz around my head, attempting to land and bite. With the human population on the decline, the animal population is on the rise. That is good for hunting, but swarms of bugs leave red welts up and down my arms.

Twenty minutes of sweating and tromping brings us to the game trail. I tread beside it, careful not to disturb the dry grass. When we approach my snare, I hear thrashing. Bingo. I run up and draw my knife. When the iguana hears me, the lizard scrambles around in the dirt, wiping his tail and kicking up a cloud of dust. My rope snare tightens around his neck until his eyes bulge. He's circled around the shrub I've used as an anchor, giving him inches to move.

When my shadow crosses him, his legs scour the dirt. He hisses and shows me his big pink tongue. I kneel beside him and grab a hold of his belly with both hands. He bucks and kicks, but my grip is strong. His sharp, spiny scales cut into my palm, but I grit my teeth and pin the iguana to the dirt. When I have him still, I draw my knife from its sheath. Ethan leans over my shoulder and looks down at the bug-eyed lizard.

"You gonna kill it?" His voice is thin. He hates the killing.

"Close your eyes." I don't like the killing. I just like it more than starving to death. I lift the knife. Its round dark eyes blink up at me.

"Sorry, guy," I murmur into the lizard's rolling eyes. His heart thrums under my palm. "Us or you."

Once the lizard is dead, I tie the rope snare around his long tail and then sling him over my shoulder. We need to hike it home fast. The smell of blood will get the coyotes on our trail soon enough. We jog back to the house, the blazing sun searing our heads until I swear my hair's on fire.

Ethan begins to wheeze halfway back. We stop in the shade of an angular cactus so he can catch his breath. In the lean slash of shade, Ethan lifts the rifle from the ground and raises it to his eye.

"Can I shoot the gun?" He looks up at me expectantly.

I look out over the dusty landscape. The dry land shimmers in the heat. The green cacti are the only color dotting the sea of brown. "Arn says you ain't old enough to shoot when he ain't around."

He sighs and peers over the gun, aiming at a rock formation. His fingers stay away from the trigger though. He's much more obedient than I am. A few years ago when Arn taught me to shoot, I pulled the trigger long before he gave me permission.

I put my hand on my little brother's shoulder. "You're holding the barrel wrong." I slide his hand into place.

"I can fire just once?"

I muss his hair. "Sure. What Arn don't know won't kill him, right?"

***

When Arn never returns from town, my words haunt me all night long.

CHAPTER THREE

We sit around the kitchen table as the first rays of daylight bleed into the horizon. It is seven-thirty. Arn has been gone for twenty-two hours.

When I awoke this morning, I found my mama at the table with her mug of weak tea. Her red, puffy eyes let me know she'd been crying. Yet, when I sat down with her, she smiled at me, her eyes dry. Somehow it comforts me, though I know it's just a show.

One by one we gathered at the table. The kitchen window looks out on the dry, gravel path where Arn disappeared yesterday morning. For an hour we have watched, not speaking as the dust swirls in little sand tornadoes across the road.

Arn usually returns before nightfall whenever he goes to town. The road is dangerous after dark. Marauders will run cars off the road, steal their goods and kill the occupants. Arn is smart, careful and a crack shot with his rifle. It's how he's kept us safe this long. I tell myself this as I watch the red and orange hues spread across the east.

Hundreds of reasonable problems could've befallen my stepfather. The old Jeep could've died, despite his deftness at fixing it, leaving him stranded. He could've had trouble trading for enough fuel. He could've been too tired to ride the four hours back home and slept in the safety of the town walls. Yet, those aren't the thoughts that run riot in my mind as we wait. I think about someone shooting him in the back because they wanted his rifle. I think about his mangled body lying on the side of the road. I think about Arn never coming home.

I glance at my family. Auntie's face registers no emotion, but her stubby fingernails click rapidly on the tabletop. Ethan's trying hard not to cry, but any minute the dam will break. My mama sits, her face a mask of muted sorrow. Her spoon clinks around her mug, stirring tea that has long since grown cold.

I can't just sit here. Bounty moos from the barn. Arn wasn't here for her morning milking. I push up from my chair.

"I'm going to milk Bounty." I don't wait for an answer.

My heart pounds as I reach the faded red doors. I yank them open and am flooded the raw stink of manure. Looks like I have shoveling to do. I pull my shirt over my mouth and walk into the dimness. Bounty greats me from her stall, blinking her big brown eyes and swishing her bristly tail back and forth. I put my hand on her neck. "I'm here," I murmur. At least I can help someone today. I dig out the milking bucket and stool.

My mind runs as my fingers pull on Bounty's udders. The warm milk zings into the metal bucket as my thoughts tumble around. If Arn is dead … It's gut wrenching to think. He can't be dead, but someone has to face facts. If he's dead, we'll all follow. He's the only one who can barter in town. We might be able to survive for a while on wild game I trap, but what happens if the game dry up? The canned food will last two or three months. The garden barely ekes out enough to make the labor worthwhile in this dry soil. We'd have to eat Bounty and the two pigs. And then there's medicine. Arn went into town to buy rubbing alcohol, bandages and disinfectant. I can't watch Ethan die of a little scratch that gets infected.

I tug Bounty's teat too hard and she shuffles against me, almost knocking me off the stool. I run a hand over her bulging belly in apology. Then I lay my cheek against her warmth. Arn will just have to come home. Any other possibility is unthinkable.

***

On the third day after Arn fails to show, my mama cries upstairs. The sound cracks me wide open. I stare at the ceiling and let hot tears trace my cheeks. My family is falling apart. Chores have come to a halt. Ethan straggles around the house and bursts into tears. Auntie Bell rocks on the front porch for hours. Nobody's eaten much in three days. I milk the cow, feed and water the livestock and then crawl back into bed. I stare at the cracks in the plaster ceiling and think about how to keep my family alive.

I drag myself out of bed, dig my feet into my boots and head to the barn. Bounty moos a greeting as I walk in, but I don't stop to rub my hand along her flank. I pass several empty stalls until I reach the big expanse Arn uses as his workshop. In the dim light, I examine his projects. The kitchen chair he was mending sits upturned, legs to the sky like a dead spider. A rough spear carved out of a tree branch rests against the wall. Oily car parts lie in pieces on the table. I notice a lumpy object covered with a cloth on the shelf above. Digging through Arn's things seems wrong, but if he's dead someone will have to.

I uncover a small block of carved wood that Arn has whittled into a rough figure. I turn the wooden doll until I can make out the strong chin, the bulging muscles, the S carved with Arn's careful fingers. Superman. Ethan's unfinished birthday present.

With tears in my eyes, I slip the wooden figurine back under the cloth. That decides it. If Arn's alive, I'll find him. There's no Superman. There's only me.

I walk to the tarp-covered quad. I pull off the cover and nearly choke on the dust. Three days ago I was going to take a joy ride. Today there's nothing joyful about the ride I'll take.

I sneak back to the house for supplies. My mama and Ethan are curled up in their rooms. Auntie rocks on the porch. She'll see me go, but by then it'll be too late. I grab my backpack from the hall closet and slip into the kitchen. I tuck in canned goods, crusts of bread and a big jug of water. From the closet I grab goggles, a bandanna and Arn's thick leather jacket. I've already got my hunting knife. I snag the rifle and a box of bullets on my way out the door.

My heart hammers hard by the time I get back to the barn. If I'd eaten much today, it'd be coming back up. I got plenty to worry about on the road: bandits, animals, running out of fuel and starving to death. Then if I make it to town I have to somehow find Arn without drawing attention to myself. Arn's stories about the inhabitants have nervous sweat pooling on my palms. Town is a den of thieves, rapists and murders. A girl like me is worth a lifetime's wages. This is not my brightest idea.

Back in the barn, I check the bandages binding my breasts and then slip on Arn's jacket.

His scent buried deep in the collar starts a lump of sadness in my throat. I tie the dirty brown bandanna over my mouth and nose and slide goggles over my eyes. Arn's battered helmet is a loose fit, but I strap it on anyway. I have no mirror to judge, but pretty sure I can pass for a boy. That is, unless they get too close.

The fuel in the quad's tank isn't enough for a return trip. If I do come back, I'll have to buy gas or steal it. Just one more problem on my list, but the alternative is giving up Arn for dead. I strap on my backpack and straddle the quad.

Visible through the open barn door is the house. I linger over the windows that mark my bedroom, my mother's room. My fingers tremble as I urge them towards the ignition. I touch the metal key, but can't force myself to turn it. From her stall Bounty moos and blinks her big brown eyes. I get off the quad, jog over to Bounty and throw by arms around her thick, bristly neck.

"Take care of them, Bounty," I whisper into her fur.

She shuffles and blinks.

I squeeze her once more, then hop on the quad before I change my mind. The engine's roar echoes through the barn, sending Bounty careening to the back of her stall. I don't look back. I hit the gas.

I peal into the hot morning air and fly across the yard. My eyes mark the patch of dust where I taught Ethan to ride the old ten-speed we found in the barn. I rush past my mother's little garden with the carrot tops just poking from the dry soil. I trundle over the spot where just three days ago Arn lay fixing his Jeep. I blink back tears. I look away.

The quad's tires crunch the gravel as I hit the main road. Auntie jumps up as I pass by the porch, her mouth formed into an O. She looks beautiful in her long cotton shift, her hair billowing around her. I raise a hand in passing. Then I turn my eyes away so her pleading eyes doesn't make me turn this quad around.

When I allow myself a look back, three people stand side by side on the porch. They lean into each other, their forms blur into one shape, a wall of mourning watching me go. Tears blear the lenses of my goggles. They think I'm foolish, rash, crazy. I hope to God they're wrong.

***

The open road stretches like a never-ending sea of busted blacktop. On either side, the scraggly hardpan and endless flat dirt never change. The sun has crept to her zenith and bores like a hot poker into my leather jacket. My shoulders and arms ache. My butt feel like someone's spent the afternoon kicking it. Three hours down. Two to go.

I crest a small hill and spot a splash of color on the horizon. A few more seconds and I make out a car. It's some snazzy thing, Camero or Viper, gone to rusty Swiss cheese on the side of the road. My shoulders tighten. Abandoned cars should be the state mascot there's so many, but this on looks drivable—odd since anything that moves is snatched up by somebody. I swallow past the tightness in my throat, let up on the gas and run my eyes over the car.

The hairs on my arms go up as my eyes fix on the lump cresting above the steering wheel. Someone's in the driver seat. Dead or alive? My insides go liquid. Most of me wants to let off the gas and turn around. Or crank the gas and fly past. But what if it's Arn? *Arn, Arn, Arn,* I think. I slow to fifteen miles an hour, my heart jackrabbiting beneath my leather jacket.

Wispy tufts of hair stir in the breeze, thin corn silk strands, white and fine. When I'm level with the car, I can see the dead man's face, blue and bloated. It slumps like a sack of grain as his forehead slowly fuses with the steering wheel. My eyes drag over the shriveled lips, curled back on a set of yellow teeth in a ghoulish grin. The only thing moving are the flies darting around his eye sockets.

Dead. So dead. I can't crank the gas fast enough. For an hour I see his shrunken face at the backs of my eyes.

As the sun marks four o'clock, a dark brown slash appears on the horizon. The town's outer wall blocks the road ahead. Arn's told me the battered wooden barricade is heavily guarded. I'll have to talk to a man and surrender my weapons before I can enter. If they're feeling generous, they'll give my gun back when I leave. If they're having a bad day, well, I might not make it out alive.

I pull up to the gate and squeeze the brake. The wall itself is enough to make me want to give up this whole plan. The thick wooden beams are topped with rusty nails, coils of razor-sharp barbed wire and broken glass that winks in the sunlight. The guard tower is twenty-foot wooden enclosure with a platform at the top. As I kill the engine, a burly man leans out of the tower and aims an assault rifle at my head. I throw my hands up.

"State your business!" he yells.

My voice catches in my throat and nothing comes out but a muted squeak.

The man shouts out again, his tone dangerous. "State your business or I'll blow off that foot!"

In the last second before I speak, I remember I'm supposed to be a man. My voice comes out choked and artificial. "I … I'm looking for someone."

The guard keeps the barrel aimed at my chest. Nervous sweat soaks my undershirt.

"Who you looking for?" he growls.

"My, uh, business associate," I yell up in my fake male voice. "Arn Meemick. Left three days ago with most of our supplies. Never returned."

"You here to shoot him?"

"No, sir. Just wonder what happened to my supplies." I blink the sweat out of my eyes and try to keep my breathing level.

The guard pulls his gun back and disappears below the tower wall. The gate creaks open.

As I hop back on the quad, I fight the urge to turn and drive in the opposite direction. *Arn, Arn.* I drive through the two massive wooden doors, big and scary as the gates of hell.

The guard blocks the road with his massive body. He's six-foot-four and muscled in areas I didn't even know possible, his arm awash in scrawling blue tattoos. Only someone brave or crazy would puncture their skin and risk infection for decoration. He's wearing cowhide boots and vest tied together with bits of electrical cord, the frayed ends splayed out like whiskers. And on his face—a grimace so unwelcome he could stop a stampede. He waves me over to where a dozen other vehicles sit inside the wall. I park the quad in between a rusted motorcycle and a truck with no doors. As I step off, he comes up.

The long barrel of his rifle is aimed at my chest when I turn. I throw my hands up. "I … I thought I was okay."

The guard spits a bit of wood he was gnawing at my feet. "Spread 'em."

This is it. He'll feel my breasts and it'll be all over. I could run or reach for the rifle strapped to my back, but he's already got the drop on me. I hold my arms up and try to quell their trembling. Stupid. I was so stupid.

He stands so close I feel puffs of his labored breathing hot in my ear. He smells of tobacco smoke and old leather as he invades my space. His big hands paw at my thighs. I squeeze my eyes shut and bite my lip. What will he do once he knows?

I keep waiting for him run his paws over my chest, but his hands slip off before progressing upward. I open my eyes.

He isn't looking at me. His eyes are fixed to the porch of the old Victorian house on the corner. Or rather, the fifty-something woman with shaggy gray-brown hair wearing a skimpy, black negligee. In her lacy underwear, she's nearly naked. White flesh spills out above the push-up bra, the tattered thigh-high stockings. Her lips are splashed red and dark bruises circle her flat, dead eyes. We watch as she begins a jerky dance. I turn away as she thrusts her hips back and forth, showing off the goods.

She's a sex slave. That house with the barred windows up top must be the brothel. When the Breeders have used up the women—the ones who survive—they ship them to their enforcers. Men like the Sheriff use them as sex slaves and pocket the money. A horrible life. Mine if I mess up here.

"Surrender your weapons," the guard murmurs. He holds out his hand, but his eyes stay on the woman. He licks his lips and I want to sock him, but at least he's not paying me any mind. I drop my rifle in his outstretched hand. He takes my gun, carries it back to the tower and comes out with a crinkled piece of paper. He pushes it into my palm.

"Lose your slip, lose your gun."

I tuck the paper, smudged with dirty fingerprints, in my pocket. "Thanks," I mutter reflexively, yet it's my own female voice. I freeze and shoot my eyes up to his face.

He's already walking back to his guard stand, one hand scratching his butt through his jeans. His eyes lock on the woman who's doing a strange jig. Her fearful eyes remind me of a jackrabbit caught in a snare.

I shake my head and focus on the plan. I remove my goggles and helmet in exchange for one of Arn's fraying straw Stetsons. I pull the brown bandanna to my chin. Peering at my reflection in a couple of truck doors, I figure I look as good as can be expected. Yet, when I step away from my quad, I feel buck naked.

I scan the parked cars for Arn's Jeep. The busted wrecks people call vehicles always amaze me. Most trucks or SUVs got no windows. Some got no doors. I spot a pick-up truck with the bed sheared off behind the back tires. I'm looking in wonder at a burnt-out car frame with new tires—when I see it. There, a few rows over, sits our Jeep. I almost clap at the sight of it. I run over and peer in. No blood splashes the torn and dusty upholstery. No signs of a struggle. No signs of Arn, either, but if the Jeep's here, Arn's here. For the first time since Arn's disappeared, I feel a little lighter.

The gate creaks closed behind me, slamming together with a decisive thud. I'm locked in. The fear falls back on me like a wet blanket. I've made it into town. That completes the only plan I had. As I swivel to take in the town, my stomach knots. Men. Everywhere I look are men—men on dusty sidewalks on either side of the main street, men going in and out of stores, men carrying brown packages or greasy car parts. Men linger outside the brothel to ogle the dancing woman. Every single one will attack if they know my secret. I'm a mouse in a basket of snakes. I shouldn't have come.

A gunshot cracks down Main Street. I throw my hands over my ears. But when I look, everyone is going about their business. I stand up, straighten my coat and pray my beating heart don't show through my jacket.

When I was little and the coyotes used to prowl around our shack, my mama used to whisper a saying in my ear. It comes back to me now. "Fear makes the coyote bigger than he is." Right now the coyote's pretty damn big, but I gotta do what I gotta do. I stick my chest out and strut like a man down the street.

A sassy piano tune starts up in the brothel. The off-key notes form into a song my mama used to hum under her breath at dishes or while mending. Behind the dancing prostitute on the porch, someone sings along real mournful and slow. *Are you lonesome tonight? Do you miss me tonight? Are you sorry we drifted apart?*

Arn loved that song. I bite down the jolt of raw pain, straighten my jacket.

When I pass the brothel's open door, I spy a half-dozen men lounging around the parlor in beat up recliners, sipping house gin. Three sad-eyed women in undergarments carry drinks on trays. One is missing an arm past the elbow. The other has a red, puckered scar that travels from her eyebrow to the corner of her down-turned mouth. In the corner a woman about sixty straddles a man's lap. Her breasts are bare, white, puckered and resting on her narrow stomach. Her sad, tired eyes meet mine as the man cups them in his calloused hands. I tuck my chin into my bandana. As I walk away, I send messages to her in my head. *I'm sorry about your life. Sorry, so sorry.*

My head down, I bump into a skinny man in a moth-eaten shirt. His gray hair straggles down his face in greasy stands. I smell the homemade liqueur on his breath. "Watch your strut, pard, or I'll cut ya a new grin."

"Sorry," I mumble. I race away before he can respond.

The town must've been a bustling main street before the world fell apart. I try to imagine it in its heyday, back when the cobblestone sidewalks lined the street like even teeth. The electrical cords overhead, long and black as snakes, used to pump light to the leaning streetlamps. The benches, now rusted iron frames, used to hold people eating flavored ice, laughing. The glass-front windows held shiny goods fresh off the factory line. I picture a red bicycle and a ruffled pink dress. Must've been real nice.

When I open my eyes I see it how it is now: everything broken, bent, brown. Half the storefronts are just crumbled piles of bricks. The other half still stand, but have boarded-up windows, graffiti splashed on the walls. One little shop's got a coat of dried blood splattered on the wall. Nothing new, shiny or nice to see here. I tuck my eyes and head forward.

I stumble up to the next building—a general store judging by the hand-painted sign reading *Stor* in sloppy red letters. The steps lie in a crumbled mess of broken concrete, so a plank serves as the ramp up to the hole in the brick they're using as a door. The clerk behind the counter looks up as I enter. He's narrow and wiry in his stained apron and cotton shirt. I cringe as he scans me. I find the first aisle and pretend to be fascinated by a dented metal teapot.

When I'm safely hidden behind the shelves, I scan the store. Four-foot high metal shelves runs in three rows. They're covered in a vast array of goods. Piles of scrawny carrots, potatoes and a single orange sit on a produce table. The factory-made goods are pricey and the clerks always keep them close by. The one or two factories that still operate are attacked with such frequency that nothing really gets made. Those dented cans and rectangular boxes with pictures of happy children were likely stolen from abandoned grocery stores. I stare at the smiling children on the boxes and my stomach grumbles. I wonder what those cheesy noodles would taste like.

I walk down an aisle of used household goods: cracked porcelain plates, tattered bed sheets, a stereo with a tin foil antenna. An elderly man with skin like leather lifts a pair of patched overalls to his skeleton frame. A man with a cowboy hat pulled low peruses the loose hardware aisle, sifting through bins of assorted nuts and bolts. No Arn.

I suck in a hot breath and approach the counter. The clerk's glasses, taped together at the center, slump down his nose. He pushes them up with a dirty finger and looks up from his ledger.

"Can I help you?" His eyes show no desire to help me.

I pull up my male voice. "I'm looking for a man. Name's Arn Meemick. He's five-ten, 140 pounds. Brown hair and brown eyes—"

He cuts me off with a wave of his palm. "Listen, son, every dirt farmer and cattle rancher from here to Tahoe fit that look-a-like. You here to buy somethin'?"

I knit my brows. "I'm sure you'd know 'im if I just describe 'im better. He was wearing jeans, a wide-brimmed hat—"

He slams both palms on plank counter. "This ain't the lost 'n found. If you ain't gonna buy something, git." He thumbs toward the open doorway and goes back to digging his nubby pencil into his ledger.

I stand, my mouth open. I've heard the Sheriff and his boys were rough and ruthless, but it'd never crossed my mind that common folk would be this heartless. When I tromp out, I pause once more at the door to shoot him a dirty look.

The man from the nuts-and-bolts aisle has his eyes on me. He looks away, but his eyes leave a burn on my skin. I tuck my head down and hurry out of the store. I gotta get Arn and get out fast.

I pass the doctor's where a man painted with blood writhes on an exam table. Two others sit in various states of messy disorder. No Arn. It's the same story in the armory, the livery stable and the inn. When I come to the end of the shops and the beginning of the houses, my heart sinks. I can't go knocking on doors.

A lump wells up in my throat. I can't leave without Arn and even if I could, I'm out of gas. I'd cry if I didn't think it'd get me killed. I rub my hand over my sweaty forehead and sniff back the tears. This was a stupid idea in the first place.

I look up at the one final building I haven't checked. It's the last place I want to look, but I take a deep breath and peer in. The building's a cement square with three barred cells lining the inside. The first cell's empty, but the second is occupied. A man leans lifelessly against the bars. Egg-sized welts decorate his face. His left eye is a swollen purple-blue lump. A dark trickle of blood meanders down his chin.

Even with his mangled appearance, I recognize him—Arn.

CHAPTER FOUR

I run up the steps and barrel through the jail door. I tear past the guard, who's sitting at a desk with his boots up. I skid to a halt at Arn's cell, drop to my knees and wrap my hands around the bars.

"Arn!" I yell. "Arn, wake up!"

Boot step up behind me. A giant hand yanks me backward. I fly through the air, my arms wheeling. I hit the concrete hard. My head bangs on the far wall and pinpricks of light burst before my eyes. As I'm shaking my head, trying to clear my vision, a shadow looms. The sound of a shotgun being cocked echoes around the room.

I throw my hands over my face. The world's fuzzy and far away, and when I look, the guard aims both barrels at my chest.

A voice from the other side of the room. "Don' shoot."

It takes me a moment to place the weak, garbled voice. Arn's struggling to sit up. He's alive. Thank god.

The guard doesn't lower his shotgun, but his finger inches off the trigger. With it still trained on me, he looks over his shoulder to where Arn pulls himself up the metal bars. The more I can see of him, the worse he looks.

"None o' your business, old man," the guard says to my stepfather. He turns back to me and nudges my leg with his steel-toed boot. "What the hell ya think you doin' barging in here? Want me blow yer everlovin' head off?"

I raise my palms up in a show of surrender. "Sorry." I point to Arn. "I … I'm here for him,"

The guard relaxes his grip on the gun. "Ya got bail, pal?"

I inch up on my elbows so my head's upright. The goose egg where my head hit the concrete throbs. "What's the charge?"

The guard lets the gun barrel tilt to the floor and wipes a hand over the sweat dotting his bald head. "Owes for the goods he stole."

I glance at my stepfather, who's upright but leaning against the wall for support. His left hand clutches his abdomen. There's more wrong with him than a busted face.

"Dat's a lie," Arn mumbles as if his mouth's stuffed with rocks. He spits dark brown flecks of dried blood on the cell floor.

The big guard, who reminds me of the bald guy from the cleaning bottles I saw in the general store, shrugs. "Don't matter. Sheriff already done sentenced ya. Ya stay 'til ya pay as the Sheriff say." He guffaws loudly at his rhyme, his big lips crinkling up in a grin. He looks at me, hoping I'm in on his joke. I'm not. The smile fades from his mouth, but he's decided I'm not a threat, either. He lumbers to the desk near the door and plops down in the metal folding chair. He lays the shotgun across the desktop and wipes more sweat off his brow. "So, you got bail?"

I ease up slow so not to disturb my pounding head. I give Arn a questioning look.

"Git outta here." Arn coughs and spits again. This time the floor is stained bright red.

There's no point in starting to obey Arn now. I pull myself up, walk over to the guard's desk and dig out my gun slip. My fingers tremor as I lay the paper on his desk. "I got a gun to trade."

The guard shakes his head and beads of sweat fling off the bald surface. "Can't make the deal, Neil," a goofy smile touches his lips, "but I can tell ya that ain't gonna be enough."

I put my hands on the chipped wood. "What about a four-wheeler in great condition?"

The guard shrugs. "Maybe. You gonna have to wait at this rate 'cause he's late." He grins sloppily now, despite himself.

"Huh?" I ask.

The smile slips and he waves a dismissive hand at me. "Never min'. Sit there 'til Warden come."

"Warden?"

"He'll tell you yeah or neah on that quad. Should be back in tick."

I sit on one of the dented folding chairs that are strewn haphazardly next to the cells. Arn and I don't speak, but he keeps nodding toward the door. I shake my head. He sighs and slides down to the floor, wincing and running a hand over his ribs.

Seeing him like this kills me. Who hurt him? The only one around is the guard, though he doesn't seem like the face-busting type. He's too busy picking his nose and eating it.

After about a half an hour, the guard stands up. He leans to one side, farts and then paws it away. He grabs a big key ring, the rifle and a tattered book with the picture of naked women inside the faded glossy pages. He points his finger at me as he heads toward the door.

"Going 'round back to drop a load. Don't try anything stupid or I'll shoot ya."

As soon as he's gone, I crouch down and grip the rusted rebar fixed unevenly in the concrete.

"God, Arn. What happened to you? You alright?"

Arn nods, though I see a wince of pain tighten his mouth before he covers it up. "Got some cuts and bruises. Couple busted ribs maybe." He sounds like he's got a mouth full of marbles. "Ri, you need to go. Don't mess with the Warden."

"No way I'm leaving. How'd this happen?"

Arn scrunches up the wall a little and winces again. "Made a fair trade. Got food, gas, odds and ends." He shifts and grimaces. "Turns out the shopkeeper and the Sheriff been running a scam. Shopkeeper takes your trade and then cries wolf. Sheriff's thugs lock you up. They split the spoils. Least that's what I reckon."

My knuckles go white around the bumpy bars. The injustice of this place and everyone in it makes my head swim.

"Don't worry. I'm gonna get you home. Mama will take care of you."

Sadness fills the eye not swollen shut. "Don't let 'em hear you talk that way."

I lay my forehead against the bars, the coolness soothing to my feverish skin. A slick unease is settling over me, sending shivers up my spine. This is why my parents never let me come in to town. It's more horrible than I could've imagined. I open my mouth to apologize when a lean shadow darkens the doorway.

"*Who* are you?" A venomous voice cuts the silence.

A shadow slinks into the room until he forms into one of the most frightening men I've ever seen. The man's black hair is greased flat to his skull. His button-down shirt is as white as Bounty's milk, a feat so impossible in this landscape I gape in wonder. His down-turned mouth drags up over sharp white teeth that match his white shirt. He can only be the Warden.

"Stand up," he commands. His acid-green eyes sear into me.

I pull myself upright. The Warden runs his eyes up and down my body. I fight the urge to shudder.

"Darrel says you have bail?" the Warden hisses. The guard trots in the doorway, pulling up his pants.

"I do." My heart patters in my chest. His eyes seem to see through me.

The Warden laces his long white fingers together. "What's the item of trade?"

"A quad," I say. "Yamaha. She runs like a dream."

His eyes narrow to slits at the word *she*. My stomach does somersaults.

He steps towards me, so close now I smell onions on his breath. "Pull down your bandanna."

I glance at Arn for help he can't provide. I focus back on the Warden. "Why?"

The Warden gives me a reassuring smile, yet he looks more like a jackal than a lap dog. "I like to see the faces of the men with whom I do business." He hisses the word *bizznezz* like a snake.

Somewhere in the distance a fly buzzes against a window. Down the street someone is shouting. The heat of the room intensifies.

I swallow hard. "What if I say no?"

The Warden snaps his fingers, a sound like stepping on a dry twig, and Darrel jumps up with the shotgun.

The Warden widens his smile. His polished white teeth remind me of fangs. "If you don't uncover, I'll know you're an outlaw. We don't tolerate outlaws." *Outlawzz.*

I picture the lizard I killed the day before. How did it feel when my snare tightened around his throat? Slowly, I reach up and slip my finger between the bandanna and my skin. Then I yank down, exposing my face.

The Warden recoils. "A bender."

He doesn't think I'm a girl. Relief floods me, then stops cold. Some think benders are filthy half-people. They're cursed at, kicked out of town, killed for being neither male nor female, but some mutated combination of both.

The Warden snaps a hand at Darrel. "Arrest him."

"No!" Arn tugs at his cell bars.

Darrel takes a heavy step towards me.

"Don't," I say, shuffling backwards. I back up till I hit the far wall. My eyes search for an exit, but the only way out is blocked by Darrel and the Warden. I look to Arn.

"He ain't done nothing wrong," Arn says, a mournful look falling over his bruised face.

The Warden reaches for the gun holstered at his hip. White flecks of spit sprinkle the corners of his mouth. "He's what's wrong." He points a thin finger at me. "He's an abomination. A poison in this nice community." The sound of his revolver sliding out of the holster echoes in the heavy stillness of the room.

My eyes snap from Arn to Darrel to the Warden. This can't happen. I might be able to dodge Darrel who's bulky and slow. Then I'll have to get through the Warden and his polished revolver. Even if I manage that, I'll have to get past security at the gate. And I'll still be without Arn.

"Don't—" is all I manage to say as Darrel grabs for my wrist. This time I won't be able to stop the tears.

A new voice cuts in from the doorway. "What's going on, fellas?"

Everyone turns. The man I saw in the general store stands in the doorway. His hands rest on his hips, inches away from the two big, shiny revolvers. He's tall and well built, not sickly and thin like ninety percent of the people outside. With his cowboy hat thumbed back, I can see his face. Even in my distress, my eyes linger on his smooth skin, strong jaw and sky blue eyes.

He strides in and tips his hand in respect. "Afternoon, Warden. Couldn't help overhear your conversation with this here gentleman." He points to me. "Guess I missed the memo 'bout benders being outlawed."

The Warden swipes back one of his slicked curls. He wags a finger at the young man like a naughty child. "Clay, this is not your business. Leave it alone."

Clay's boots click on the floor as he steps toward us, a dazzling smile on his face. "Now, see, here's the thing. Sheriff's off to see about a horse and he left me in charge. I know you won't go 'gainst Sheriff's orders."

Hatred creeps up the corners of the Warden's face, the crease between his lips showing those sharp, white teeth.

Clay ignores the Warden's grimace and points at me. "What's the kid here for?"

Eyes snap back to me. When Clay's meet mine, my face flushes. I got no words.

Arn answers from his cell. "Posted my bail."

"That so?" Clay stops and crosses his arms over his chest. His blue eyes deepen in hue the closer he gets.

I nod. I want to pull my bandanna up over my face to hide the blush that's coursing burning up my cheeks.

"Well then, let's get 'em on their way." Clay winds his hand in a hurry-up motion.

The Warden holsters his gun. He begins cranking his neck back and forth like a ruffled chicken. Black curls escape their grease mortar and bob back and forth. "This … this is outrageous. When the Sheriff learns of this—"

"He'll be pleased as punch we dealt with our neighbors without shootin' holes in 'em this time." Clay's face carries a hint of mischief. This boy, no more than eighteen, must be somebody around here.

The Warden stomps out the door, spitting curses. Clay watches, a smirk at the corners of his mouth.

I'm too shocked to move. Just a minute ago, I was being locked up. Now a handsome boy keeps smiling at me. I let a tentative smile creep onto my face until I remember how guarded I have to be. Clay's the Sheriff's right-hand man. One good deed and a handsome smile can't erase all the people they've hurt, all those women sent to the Breeders.

Clay's crisp button-down shirt tightens around the muscles of his arms as he stretches out his arm. "You got bail for this man?"

I wring my hands and force myself to focus. "I was gonna trade my quad."

His palm is smooth, clean. I wonder what he thinks of my grimy fingers as I dig the quad key out of my pants pocket and drop it in his hand.

He closes his hand over the key. "All set. Darrel, unlock the cell."

Darrel lurches forward and unlocks Arn's cell. Arn shuffles out and I slide myself under his arm for support. As we head toward the door, I gather the courage to meet Clay's eyes.

"Thank you," I say. "I hope I can repay this kindness." More blush. My cheeks will catch fire if I don't get out now.

He thumbs his hat at me. "Don't mention it, but I'd light out fast. That Warden's a devil."

I help Arn toward the exit.

He calls to us again. "I'd cover up your face. Not everyone's as open-minded."

I lift the bandanna over my mouth and nose. Beside me Arn spits another hunk of blood into the dusty road.

"Come on," I say, as he leans into me. "Let's get the hell out of dodge."

"Don't say hell."

I smile as I hustle him onward.

Amazingly, getting through the gate goes more smoothly then I could've hoped. I retrieve my gun with no trouble. The clunky vehicle turns over on the first try. When I finally see the town through the cloud of dust in the rear view, I relax a notch. I glance over at Arn, who's slumped over in the passenger seat. In the red sunset glare, his whole face looks bloody, though I know it's a trick of the light.

"Don't worry," I say, though I'm not sure he can hear me. "We'll be home in no time. Our luck's turning around."

He opens the eye that's not swelled shut. "Don't count your chickens. It's a long way home."

CHAPTER FIVE

Twilight slashes the western sky when I spot our house. In the dark, the dusty white farmhouse stands like a lone beacon. As the tires crunch onto our driveway, a kerosene lamp blazes to life in the upstairs. I kill the engine. Arn's already swinging out when I reach his door to collect him.

The screen door thwacks as my mama barrels out, her nightgown flowing behind her in the moonlight.

"Riley," she cries, her hands flying up to her mouth. Then her eyes land on my stepfather. "Oh God."

She runs through the yard barefoot. Gravel tears at her feet, but she doesn't bat an eye. She throws her arms around us, sobbing. She smells like home.

The door bangs again and Ethan stumbles out, rubbing the sleep from his eyes. He blinks, and then runs down the steps, smashing into us, almost knocking everyone over.

"Dad!" Then he turns his oval face to me. "Riley, you brought him home. I knew you would."

Tears leak from the corners of my eyes, but my hands are too full of my family to wipe them away.

Slowly we make our way toward the house, touching, hugging. Ethan asks a million questions which no one answers. Auntie's on the porch, clutching her shawl around her. She shakes her head at me as we pass. "Stubborn girl." She grips my arms and smiles.

My mama takes my spot under Arn and leads him to the stairs. When they get to the base of the steps, she turns and throws her arms around me again. "Thank you for bringing him home," she whispers and kisses my cheek. They limp up the stairs.

Ethan's cold fingers find mine. "Caught a rabbit while you were gone."

I lead him down the hall to our bedroom. "That's fantastic, little bud. Did you kill it?"

He drops his eyes. "I couldn't."

"What'd you do with him?" I drag my body down the dark hallway. So tired.

Ethan swings our arms back and forth lightly. "He's in a cage in the barn. I named him Superman."

I chuckle. "Superman, huh? Now we really can't eat him."

"I wanna keep him."

"We'll see."

I fall into bed with my clothes on. My last image is Ethan curling into his blanket, his dark hair falling over his sleepy eyes. Man, it's good to be home.

***

I wake to a sharp beam of sun dancing on my eyelids. I squint into the midday sun. Ethan usually has me up at the crack of dawn with his chatter. Either I slept through it, or he thought I needed the rest. Boy, is he right. My body aches like I've taken a bad fall down a rocky hill. The goose egg where my head hit the jail wall smarts when I probe it. My mouth tastes like a dirt road. Yet, the voices down the hall are laughing. All worth it.

I drag my body out of bed and down the hall to the kitchen. Arn sits at the table with a fresh bandage wrapped around his bare chest. His eye's still swollen shut and his jaw looks like someone put it on crooked, but his color has returned. He spoons weak broth into his mouth. His hand trembles when the spoon meets his lips, but he steadies it easily enough.

My mama strides around the kitchen, pounding fresh dough on the counter, chopping angled carrots. Her burned face is set in a calm contentment. Auntie knits in the chair opposite Arn. She's the first one to notice me leaning in the doorway.

"Up, I see," she says, her needles clicking. "Thought you'd sleep the day away."

"Hush, Bell. She needed her sleep." My mother floats over and hugs me. "Morning, angel. Hungry?"

I haven't eaten since the canned beans I scarfed on the road yesterday afternoon. My stomach growls. "Yeah. Is it lunch time?"

My mama drops dough balls on a tray. "We're pulling out all the stops. I'm making Auntie's famous bread, we got fried rabbit, and I found an apple in the back of the pantry."

"Rabbit?" I look for Ethan. "We ain't eating Superman, are we?"

She shakes her head, but her smile wilts. "I promised Ethan we wouldn't hurt Superman, but he's pretty upset we can't take him. I told him he has a few days till the move, but he's out sulking in the barn. Maybe you could talk to him."

I don't understand. "What?"

"I said he's sulking in the barn. When you're done eating, could you talk to him?"

"Not that. The other part. The part about us moving."

She stops slicing carrots into little orange circles. "Riley, you didn't think we could stay here after what happened? We'll never be able to trade in town again. As soon as Arn's well, we're leaving."

I stare at my mama with my mouth open. This had not crossed my mind. Of course she's right. We can't trade in town, but moving means traipsing through dangerous territory. Last time, it was nearly impossible to find a house with a working well outside of town walls. We'll risk being attacked, running out of gas, or starving to death. No wonder Ethan's in the barn sulking.

Arn raises his eyes to mine. The bruising under his left eye is a yellow green. He goes back to spooning the soup into his mouth. Auntie says nothing, but the furious clicking of her knitting needles speaks for her.

My mama offers me a calming smile. "It'll be fine, darling, as long as we're together."

As long as we're together. It usually brings me comfort. Today it falls flat.

"I'm going in the barn," I say, heading for the back door.

"What about your lunch?" she calls.

"I lost my appetite." It's a childish thing to say, but I can't help myself. I am jogging when I hit the back porch.

The barn's familiar animal scent greets me as I enter. Bounty moos deep in her throat. I detour towards her and stroke the soft fur along her nose.

"Hey, girl. Thanks for watching them while I was gone." She flips her ears back and forth, dislodging a few flies that buzz up and spiral around to her back. We won't be able to take Bounty. Arn will butcher her and the pigs before we leave. God, this day just gets worse. I turn away from her big brown eyes.

Ethan's squatting on the dirt floor next to the rabbit cage he's constructed out of old chicken wire. He's passing bits of carrot through the bars. Superman is a scrawny brown hare with long ears and a little cotton ball tail. He's too skinny to make a good dinner, anyway. I sit in the hay next to Ethan, my arms around my knees. My brother slides another carrot top through the wire into Superman's awaiting teeth.

Finally, Ethan looks up at me. "Are you gonna kill him?" he whispers.

I reel back. "What? No! I'm not going to kill your pet."

Ethan shrugs. "Mom says I can't keep him when we move, so I thought maybe she sent you out to kill him."

I shake my head. "She promised. You and your pal got a couple more days. Then we'll send him back to his bunny family."

Ethan slips his fingers through the mesh cage and strokes Superman's soft sides. The jackrabbit is surprisingly calm at my brother's touch.

"He bite?" I ask.

Ethan shakes his head. "Not me. When I got him out of the snare, he was bucking a lot and scratched my arm, but I calmed him down."

I stick my fingers through the wire and stroke Superman's rump. He twitches a little at the initial touch, but doesn't jump away.

I lean into Ethan's skinny frame until our shoulders touch. "It'll be fine, you know. As long as we're together."

Ethan looks up at me through a dark lock of hair. "You sound like Mama."

"Well, it's true." I twirl a piece of hay around my finger. "As long as we're there, you'll be safe."

"It's not me I'm worried about," he whispers.

I mull this over. The worry I have every night for my family weighs so heavily on my chest I can't breathe. How big that must feel for a little boy? I put my hand on his boney shoulder. "You knew I was coming back, right? I wouldn't leave you."

Ethan looks at me, his round, dark eyes shining in the dimness. "Promise?"

"Of course." My chest tightens at the thought of Ethan watching my dust cloud recede as I drove away. I ruffle his hair, trying to lighten the mood. "Besides, who'd make fun of you for picking boogies and wiping them under the bed?"

"Shut up," he says without emotion. He smiles with his mouth, but not his eyes. So serious, my little brother.

I stand up. He gives Superman one more carrot and then stands, brushing the hay off his pants.

"I wish there was a way to keep Superman," he says, sighing.

"Maybe you can fold him in your suitcase like this." I scoop him up and turn him upside down, so his knees are at my face and his head dangles toward the ground. When he giggles, his belly shakes beneath my arms. He nearly kicks me in the face as he struggles to right himself. In a month, he'll be too big for me to do this any more.

When he starts tickling my ribs, I nearly drop him on his head. Instead I roll him into a pile of hay near Bounty's stall. When we walk out, he slips his hand into mine.

"Maybe you can talk to Dad for me. You saved his life. He owes you."

I tug a piece of hay out of his hair. "Nah," I say, shaking my head. "After all the crap I've put Arn through, I bet he figures we're 'bout even."

***

I dream I'm back in town searching for Arn. I run up the dusty street, but my legs droop like useless sandbags. In the dirt, I claw through the scrub on my belly. My heart pounds up into my throat. Someone's after me.

I feel eyes on me, sending shivers up my arms. The deserted street is empty. The hot sand burns my hands as I dig forward. I have to get away. I have to find Arn.

A hand circles my leg. I scream and claw through the sand, but the hand snags my pants and drags me backward. I wheel around, unable to breathe.

Greased, black hair, watery green eyes the color of bile and a mouth full of jagged, white fangs. The Warden has found me. I gasp and struggle, but his fingers are tentacles circling around my legs, dragging me to his mouth, which unhinges like a copperhead's. He will swallow me whole. Every part of me screams. My fingers claw through the dirt, but it's no use. His fingers scratch up my legs and cut into the soft flesh of my stomach. He drags me towards rows and rows of sharp, white fangs.

"Help!" I scream to the empty hills. I turn back, but my attacker is no longer the Warden. It's Clay. "Help me!" I plead.

I lock onto Clay's blue eyes. I watch in horror as a sulfur green seeps into his blue irises. Clay opens his mouth and reveals rows of dripping fangs.

I wake up screaming.

My room is dark. My heart pistons out of control. I place my hand to it and try to breathe. Across the room Ethan lies under a mound of tattered blankets. There's my boots where I left them beside my bed. On the nightstand, Ethan's comic book flaps in the breeze from the window. I lie back in bed and try to relax.

My brain begins to separate nightmare from reality, but my skin still crawls with sweat. I stare up at the vein-like cracks in the plaster ceiling. *I'm fine,* I tell myself. I clutch the sheet around me. I don't feel fine.

A puff of night air traces my sweat-drenched skin, sending shivers up my arms. My comforter lies in a wad on the floor. I stand up and cross our window to get it. Outside there's a delicate crunch of gravel.

What was that? I hear it again. Footsteps on the gravel outside. My pulse skyrockets. I take a step toward the open window and peer into the darkness.

Sheer, ratty curtains hang limp over the opening to discourage bugs; through them I scan the moonlit yard. The dead apple trees are dark gnarly slashes in the distance. The outhouse is the rectangular shadow to the right. I clutch my arms around myself and shiver. If the coyotes are prowling this close, we're going to have a big problem. I reach around for my hunting knife on the nightstand. When I'm turning back to the window, I see the moving shadow.

It's a lean, dark figure slinking from the outhouse to the barn. It's too tall for a coyote. Only one thing can make a shadow like that and he walks on two legs.

The fear in my dream is nothing compared to my fear now.

"Riley." A voice behind. A rough hand that slides over my mouth. I jab an elbow backward. My attacker *oomphs* and the hand falls away. I turn and raise my knife.

Arn's hunched over, his hands wrapped around the bandages that circle his middle. I've elbowed him in his broken ribs. I start to apologize, but he snaps his fingers to silence me.

"Get your brother and get in the cellar. Don't come out no matter what you hear."

The gun in his hand paralyzes me.

"What's going on?" Ethan asks groggily from his bed. He's propped up on an elbow looking at us.

Arn doesn't answer. He strides to Ethan's bed, leans down and hugs him. If Arn is hugging, this is serious. I can't think with the terror screaming through my head.

"Take him now, Riley." Arn slips out of the room and down the hall.

"What's happening?" Ethan sits up, alarmed. His eyes trail his father.

"Get dressed," I say, grabbing my own boots and coveralls.

There's a low whistling sound, then a crash as our front window shatters. Something explodes, rumbling the floorboards beneath us.

"What was that?!" Ethan presses his palms to his ears.

I snatch Ethan. He's weightless as I tear out of our room. I shoot a glance toward the front room. The window lies in jagged pieces on the floor. Arn's got the kitchen table flipped over and hunches behind it with a rifle to his chest. My mama crouches at his feet, slipping rounds into another rifle with trembling fingers. Auntie sits with her back to the table, the revolver clutched to her breast.

I can't think. I can't breathe. I just run. I'll drop Ethan off and come back for them. It don't matter what Arn said. They need me.

I hit the porch, barely feeling the boards under my feet. When I jump into the yard, headlights blaze from our driveway. Half-dozen men are clustered behind three trucks. They're armed. They're going to kill us all.

I skid to a stop at the storm cellar. Ethan's crying when I set him down to pull open the doors.

"Riley," he sobs. "What's happening? Where's Mama?" Snot runs in strings from his nose.

There's no time to comfort him. I point to the hole. "Get in."

He shakes his head, tears flinging off in every direction. "Not without you."

"Get in!" I yell.

He cries harder, shaking his head. His eyes are wide.

Gun shots crackle behind me. My panic chokes out all thought. I gotta get back. I pick Ethan up and carry him down the ladder. He cries and struggles, but somehow I get him down without dropping him. I dump him on the bench and run back to the ladder. His sobs fill the dark hole. I'll calm him down when this is over. I gotta get back.

I scramble up the ladder. Two rungs from the top, a shadow blots out the light. I peer up. With the headlights streaming behind him, it's hard to make out a face. For a moment I think it's Arn. Then the shadow turns his head and I recognize the square chin and short, dark hair.

Clay?

I stop climbing for a moment, confused. He's one of the men sent to kill my family?

I scan his face, looking for answers. He opens his mouth to speak, but shots rattle in the distance. He steps back and he's gone. As I'm reaching for the next rung, I hear a loud squawk. Too late.

The heavy wooden door falls over the entrance, plunging us into darkness. Then I hear him slide the board through the handles.

He's locked us in.

CHAPTER SIX

I slam into the cellar doors over and over. My shoulder blazes with pain, and splinters pierce my skin, but I pay no heed. Barking sobs like a tortured dog's escape my throat.

More gunshots clatter above, then shouting. My mind runs as I pry chunks from the doors until my fingernails break and warm blood spills down my hands. With only two rifles, a handgun and a box of cartridges, my family stands against a dozen well-armed men.

They don't stand a chance.

I scramble down the ladder, falling off the last rung. I bang into a shelf, knock over something that smashes, but I don't stop. Ethan, sobbing, reaches out for me as I run past. I shake him off. My hands scramble over the shelves, tossing out canned goods, changes of clothing, a jug of water. Dry goods tumble off the shelf as I fling them out of my way. I need something to wrench the door open, a shovel, an ax, anything. In the dark, my hands come up empty.

Overhead something explodes.

My sobs turn into keening that fills the cellar. I fumble for the ladder and pull myself up. Bashing my shoulder against the locked doors won't help, but I can't stop. I smash into the wood until I see stars.

Above, everything quiets. I stop bashing and press my ear to the crack in the door. The truck engines flare to life and rumble away.

Quiet. The only sound is my brother's muffled sobbing and the throbbing of my heart. It's over. Images of my family riddled with bullet holes dance in the darkness before me. I pound my fists into the boards and scream.

Eventually Ethan pulls me off the ladder. He leads me to the bench. I curl onto the wooden surface. In the dark, I can pretend I don't exist. That I've died, too. The thought gives me a little comfort. When you're dead, you don't feel pain.

***

Little streamers of light trickle through the boards above. I open my eyes and watch the dust motes slide lazily through the triangles of light. Then I remember my family. The hurt hits my chest like both barrels of a twelve-gauge.

As my mind wakes, pain lights up my body. My shoulders feel like they've been run through a meat grinder. I lift my hands—shredded knuckles, splinters dug deep under my bloody fingernails. Ethan shifts next to me. We lay on the hard-packed earth, his back to my chest, my body curled around his. I brush his bangs off his face and swallow back the sobs. I can't wake him. Maybe in his dream everything we love isn't destroyed.

In the dim daylight, the storm cellar looks like a tornado hit. I've torn everything off the shelves. There's the broken glass from a jar of peaches. Clothing litters the dirt floor where I flung them.

I stare up at the locked cellar doors, as fresh tears dampen the corners of my eyes. What's up there? Part of me wants to crawl into a ball and never face it. A sob escapes my throat and Ethan stirs. *Stop it*, I tell myself. Even though my whole world's been blown to pieces, I have to pull it together. For him.

I stand up and pain rockets down my spine. I walk to the ransacked shelves. I slip cans back up into their dust rings on the shelves, pick up glass shards, fold the clothes. Beneath a pair of coveralls I find a rusty ax. I ignore the pain from my busted hands as I grip it and climb the ladder.

Ethan sits up suddenly. "What're you doing?"

I look down at him and try to smile. My face is unresponsive, so I give up and begin hacking at the crack between the doors. "Getting us out."

Ethan watches me. "What do you think happened, you know, to Mama and Dad?"

"I'm sure they're fi ..." My throat squeezes. I look down at my little brother. "I don't know." I swing the ax over and over until my hands are screaming.

It takes a half an hour to bust the doors open. When I can barely grip the ax and my head throbs enough to blur my vision, the last of the wood gives way. I push open the mangled doors. Sunlight floods my face. Squinting, I climb out of the cellar and look around.

The stillness sends goose bumps over my arms. The yard is empty. Our farmhouse is silent, the back door open. Across the yard, the barn door thwacks in the breeze. A crow perches on the roof. When it sees me, it caws and flings itself into the air. Arn says crows are a bad omen. I watch the bird slash upward and feel like throwing up.

I peer down the hole at Ethan. "Stay here." I don't wait for him to protest. I steel my will and stalk toward the house with the ax.

The first porch step creaks as I walk up. I freeze. Someone might lurk inside the darken doorway, waiting to ambush me. I grip the ax handle, take a deep breath and slip through the doorway into the dark hall.

I stand in the hallway and listen with the ax clutched to my chest. There's no sounds, no sign that anyone's inside, but I can't shake the feeling that lurking behind a door someone waits to kill me. My hands tremble as I step into our living room.

Small beams of light sift in through bullet holes in the front wall. A vase is shattered and lying on the floor, yet the couch and Auntie's Victrola look undisturbed. I tiptoe forward and something crunches beneath my heel. I pick it up. It's a shotgun shell. I set it on my mother's sideboard table, clutch the ax to my chest and creep toward the kitchen.

When I see what's become of the kitchen, I can't help gasping.

The place is unrecognizable. The table is flipped on its side; the table top, a splintered mess of bullet holes. Glass shards from the exploded front windows litter the ground like jagged snow. The cupboards are open and their contents in pieces on the floor. I pick up a shard from the green ceramic mug that my mama drank tea out of every morning. I set the pieces on the counter with trembling fingers. Then my eyes trail toward the front window. What waits outside?

More glass on the porch. Auntie's rocker rests on its side in the empty flowerbed. But no bodies. Then my eyes find a trail of blood that streaks the porch boards and continues down the steps.

The sick panic cripples me. Whose blood paints our porch? I lean my head against the window frame and close my eyes. I can't do this. I can't search for the bodies of my family. My trembling hand smears tears across my cheeks. But, I can't leave them out there for the coyotes to pick apart. I wipe my face with my sleeve. My stomach's lined with lead as I pull open the front door.

The screen door dangles crookedly by one hinge. There's the streak of blood and one bloody footprint. I lean down and examine the smeared red stain. My mama's? I look up through the yard, expecting a body. Big tire tracks cut through the dirt where the trucks peeled out last night. Here and there, the dust is tinted deep brown. I've killed enough rabbits to know a bloodstain. A stray boot lays about fifteen yards from the porch. It doesn't look like Arn's. Hopefully one of those bastards took a bullet. Hopefully more than one.

With no bodies and no sign of what happened to my family, I turn back in. What if they're wounded and hiding upstairs? As I stalk toward my bedroom, the fear of being watched settles on me again. I know that if they wanted me, they would've come down in the cellar and taken me. Unless Clay didn't tell them we were down there. But why wouldn't he?

I pull up to my bedroom and listen. Nothing but my breath, hot and fast. I push the door open with my toe, the ax held high. The door gives a loud *screech* as it opens.

"Riley?" A voice behind me.

"Ahhh!" I brandish the ax.

Ethan's face twists in fear.

"Jesus, Ethan!" I drop the ax and put my other hand to my beating heart. "Thought I told you to stay in the cellar."

He steps beside me until his hip's touching mine. He's carrying a rusty kitchen knife. He peers down the hall with frightened eyes. "Where's Mama and Dad?"

"I don't know, but let me handle this." I push him towards the back door.

He digs in his heels. "I can't stay down there no more. What I'm thinking about can't be worse than what's up here."

I know what he means about pictures in your head. Mine's flooded with horrible possibilities. I take his hand and together we slip quietly up the stairs.

The upstairs hallway is tensely quiet. The scuffed wood floor sighs under our weight. With shaking hands I push open two bedroom doors. Nothing. Everyone's gone. My eyes linger on the soft-bristled brush on my mother's dresser. Will she ever use it again? I stumble out of her room before the ghost of her presence suffocates me.

We head downstairs and slump on the couch. Neither of us says a word. I can't think. I can't feel. I sit in a trance. An hour passes before Ethan's stomach rumbles. It's noon and we haven't eaten or drank anything since dinner last night.

Somehow I find the strength to stand. "Canned beans okay?"

He nods and then goes back to staring at light trickling through the bullet holes in our living room wall.

I drag myself to the pantry, but when I get there, something's wrong. The shelves are bare. I run a hand over the planking, my fingers brushing past a circular rust stain. This pantry was stocked yesterday. Today it's bare. Where did it all go? There's no cans on the floor. I peer into the kitchen and then back at the shelves. It takes my deadened brain a few beats to realize what's happened. They took our food. Every canned good—the dried fruit, bread, flour, rice, carrots, apples. All gone.

The bastards stole our family and now our only chance at survival.

The livestock. Banging out of the pantry, I stumble through the kitchen and out the front door. I break into a run around to the barn. I push open the barn doors.

"Bounty?" My voice breaks.

The minute I'm not greeted by her mooing, I know she's gone. And why wouldn't they take her? She's a commodity, useful, tradable. Just like my family.

I fall to the barn floor and lay in the dust. The sobs run though me for what seems like hours. Until there are no tears left. Until I'm hollow.

Sometime later Ethan's small hand slides over my back. His trembling voice cuts through my stupor. "Riley, I ... I found Dad."

By the sound of his voice, I know Arn's gone. Empty of tears, a dark numbness covers me. I take Ethan's hand and he leads me through the barn and around back. There, in the shade of our dead apple trees, is Arn's motionless body. His blood paints the ground beneath him a deep, muddy brown. His legs and arms are extended at odd angles. Someone dragged him here and left his body for the coyotes.

This is all my fault. I led his killer right to him.

As we approach, Ethan begins to shake. I stop and put my hands on his shoulders. "You don't have to do this," I say, looking into his eyes. "I can bury him myself." Can I? I'm not even sure I can take another step.

He shakes his head and wipes at the tears that trickle into the dust on his red cheeks. "He's my dad. I need to bury him."

Today, my brother becomes a man, though I would trade all I had in the world to keep him a boy.

We arrange Arn's body so it looks like he's sleeping. It gives me some comfort to see him lying back, eyes closed, arms over his chest, like he's fallen asleep in the shade. We get shovels and spend the rest of the day pouring our pain into the dirt. We bury Arn as the red sunset bleeds out across the horizon. Neither one of us cries. The grief is too big for tears.

***

The next days are a fog. I lie in bed and stare at the ceiling. Ethan pushes food at me that he's brought up from the cellar. The opened cans go uneaten. I close my eyes and my dreams are splashed with horrors. I open them and the horrors are the same, except awake I can feel pain.

When I'm awake, the guilt eats at my insides like acid. All of this is my fault. I went into town and pissed off the Warden. I led them back to our house. It doesn't matter that I rescued Arn. He'd have been better off in jail than under six feet of dirt. And now my mama and Auntie are gone. They are likely dead or wishing they were. And Ethan? I get to watch him starve to death. When he brings me the meals that I keep refusing, I can't look him in the face.

The only time I feel alive is when I think about revenge. I think of hurting the motherless bastards who did this. But mostly I think of Clay. I picture myself standing over his crumpled body and aiming my gun at his chest. I thought he was a good guy. He was just setting me up so they could follow me home and take everything. Why Ethan and I are still alive is a mystery, but I assume it's a minor setback. He'll be back to finish the job, and when he does, my hunting knife will find its last victim.

That night I have another nightmare. My mother cries in the distance. I run through the desert looking for her when something shakes me.

"Ri, wake up."

I swim up out of the nightmare and open my eyes.

Ethan's gaunt face hovers a foot from mine. His black hair hangs lank on either side. Seeing him like this brings the stab of pain to my chest. I roll away and face the wall.

"Let me sleep."

He shakes me again. "Someone's here."

I sit up, heart pumping. "Who's here?" I grab my hunting knife. When I stand, the room spins. God, I'm weak. I shake the dizziness away and let anger wake up my limbs. I stalk to the front room.

An engine grumbles outside. I blow through the front door and stride onto the porch. At my feet is a package wrapped in white paper. On the road I spot a leather-clad biker on a black motorcycle. The helmet's face shield is down so I can't tell who's out there. The biker watches as I pick up the package.

There's charcoal scrawl on the white paper. *A peace offering—Clay*

I drop the package, jump off the porch and run toward the motorcycle. The sand sears the bottoms of my feet as I tear toward the bike, but I barely feel it. I sprint with my hunting knife gripped in my fist. He watches for a moment, revs the engine and takes off. By the time I hit the road, he's a cloud of dust in the distance. I pick up rocks and chuck them after him.

"Come back and I'll kill you!"

He's gone. All I can do is choke on the dust.

My adrenaline spent, my legs barely carry me back to the house. Splotches of light dance in my vision. I mount the porch and kick Clay's package into the dirt. Then I stumble up the remaining steps, slump onto the couch and pass out.

The sound of sizzling wakes me. The delicious aroma of cooking meat sends my stomach twisting. My mama cooking bacon? Then I remember.

I drag my useless body into the kitchen. Ethan's at the stove tending whatever's smelling so wonderful. I walk over to him and see two prime cuts of beef sizzling on the skillet.

"Where'd you get that?"

A smile forms on his face. "From the package. Who's Clay?"

I recoil. "We can't eat those!"

"Why not?"

"They might be poisoned." I grab the nearest fork and stab the delicious steaks. Warm red juice drips down my hand as I open the belly of the stove. I toss the steaks into the fire.

Ethan cries, "Stop! What are you doing?"

I slam the stove shut and stand in front of it. "Clay's a monster." I look Ethan hard in the eye. "He killed Arn. We can't trust him."

We watch through the slats in the stove door as the steaks crinkle in the fire. The delicious aroma turns to a charred stink. Ethan bursts into tears beside me.

"What's wrong?" I say, standing over him as he sinks to the floor.

He buries his head in his hands. I crouch down beside him and put my hand on his bony shoulder. He shrugs it off.

"Listen," I say. "I'm sorry about the steaks, but it was for your own good."

He lifts his head and glares at me. "Since when do you care about me?"

I lean back, hands up in defense. "What're you talking about?"

He pulls at his hair in frustration. "You've been sleeping for three days! You won't even look at me! You said you wouldn't leave me, but you already have."

I didn't think it was possible for me to feel worse. The one person in the world I have left to care for, and I've turned my back on him. I put my hand on his shoulder. This time he doesn't shrug it off.

"I'm sorry." If I can get through this without crying, it'll be a miracle. "It's just real hard."

He sniffs. "I know."

"Yeah, you do. But I gotta get over it. Get my ass in gear, as Auntie would say."

He wipes his eyes with the back of his hand. "She'd say you were being a lily-livered dirt eater." He frowns, remembering.

The memory of Auntie's strange sayings lingers bitterly on my tongue. I stand and my legs buckle. Ethan grabs my hand and helps me up.

I throw my arm over Ethan's shoulder and press my face into the top of his head. "We'll eat lunch and then set some snares. A couple of rabbits and we'll be all set." He looks up at me, his face searching mine for reassurance. I squeeze his shoulder. "It'll be okay."

What a terrible liar I am.

CHAPTER SEVEN

The next day there's three unopened aluminum cans in a small pyramid on our porch. I squat down and examine the rippled cylinders. The labels are long gone, but the cans are in good shape, no dents or weird bulges. Food from another time. I wonder how long ago these were made. I'm about to chuck them in the trash when Ethan appears behind me. He looks longingly at the cans.

"Those can't be poisoned, right?"

I shrug. "Maybe there's poison on the outside of the cans."

He disappears, returns with Mom's rusty tongs. "There," he says, picking one up. "Now we can't get sick." He smiles at me. "Let's eat."

His feet thud smack on the wood floor as he runs into the kitchen. I hear him open drawers and digging out utensils. I stand on the porch and stare down the road. There's no motorcycle, no sign that Clay is lurking around. Something glints in the distance behind a large pile of rocks. Is he watching us? I stare in that direction for several minutes until Ethan calls from the kitchen that the food's done. The smell that trickles past my nose is enticing, but I can't stand the thought of eating something Clay's brought us. On the other hand, what choice do I have? My snares haven't caught anything, and the canned goods in the cellar won't last more than a week. We either eat Clay's offering, or we starve.

I sit at the table with Ethan and spoon manufactured chicken noodle soup in my mouth. The soup is thick and savory and I can't help but enjoy it a little. As I roll the slippery noodles around on my tongue, I think about Clay and what he's playing at. Why would he want us to trust him? If he wanted to capture us, he could pull up with a band of armed men. What could he gain from being kind? Maybe he just likes torturing his prey before he pounces and bites their heads off.

The next day, there's a homemade apple pie sitting on the porch. Ethan watches me with desperate eyes as I cradle the pie and bring it to the table. We hover around it and stare at the sugary apples peaking out through the slats of toasted crust. My stomach somersaults.

"Please don't throw it away." Ethan tugs on my elbow.

Though I'm desperate for the taste of that pie in my mouth, my pride can't allow it. I push the tin towards Ethan. "Eat it all." I leave before I can change my mind.

I head to our bedroom and pull on my coveralls, long-sleeved t-shirt and boots. I gotta do something other than sit and sulk at my inability to provide. At Clay's ability to do it so easily.

"Hey, pie face," I yell. "Let's go check some snares so we don't have to depend on treats from terrorists."

Ethan meanders in, smelling of baked goods. The wide smile on his crumb-covered face deepens the hurt mounting in my gut. Clay brought him that happiness.

"Put your boots on," I grumble.

The smile slips off Ethan's face, but he does what I ask. God, no matter what I do I feel like a loathsome, hairy dirt pie.

The sun bakes our heads as we tromp through the yard to the snares. The dust kicked up gets Ethan's asthma going again. We take a break in the shade of a rotted cactus husk and stare out over the crumbling landscape. The sea of brown stretches as far as I can see. Life was nearly impossible with three adults working their fingers to the bone. Now it's just me and the kid. We have four more days of canned goods in the cellar. Without the gifts from Clay, our only hope is the snares. Rabbits are plentiful, but the coyotes get to them before we do. And leaving isn't an option. Even if we had somewhere to run, we got no fuel. I tuck my chin to my knees and try not to think about what it would feel like to starve to death.

A buzzard spins in lazy circles overhead and Ethan tracks it with his eyes. "You think buzzards see color?"

I glance at him. A dark lock of hair falls in his eyes and he blows it up with a puff of air. A hint of a smile sits on his face as he watches the bird. When he sees a buzzard, he thinks about the wonderful things the bird can see. I think about the carcass that bird's about to eat. Ethan deserves to survive. It's my job to make sure he does.

When we find the first snare, it's empty. I tuck my hands in my pockets and hide my disappointment when Ethan looks from me to the empty wire loop. In my pockets my hands clench and unclench.

The next snare delivers. A fat brown gopher lies strangled to death in my wire. Its paws have dug four deep ruts in the dry earth. Its tongue lolls to one side of his matted brown muzzle. I loosen the wire and lift him up by his hind legs.

"Gotcha," I say to the gopher. Then I turn to Ethan. "I'm gonna reset this snare. Go check the one over the hill and yell if we got something."

Ethan nods and clomps over the rise.

The snare wire is kinked and it takes me a while to straighten the noose and secure it on the game trail again. Just as I'm driving the anchor back into the ground, I hear a scream.

I sit bolt upright. "Ethan!"

I drop everything and run. The rise of the hill blocks my view, but then I hear a sound that sends gooseflesh over my arms—the distinct growl of a predator.

"No," I whisper as I sprint up the hill and dig out my hunting knife. How could I have let him go alone?

When I reach the crest, I spot Ethan. Four coyotes—snarling mongrels with their hackles raised, their bloodstained mouths contorted in fanged smiles—circle him. They'd picked up the scent of the rabbit in our snare, but Ethan stumbled upon them. Now their eyes glint as they circle another treat. They close in. This can't be happening. I sprint faster.

Ethan hears and throws me a desperate look. His arms are extended, his palms out, as if he could shoo them away. He's complete unarmed.

The ground blurs. My heart pounds. Twenty yards to go.

The alpha, a mangy mongrel with a blood-flecked muzzle, must sense me coming. He lurches. In a flash of yellow teeth, the coyote bites Ethan's outstretched arm.

"No!"

I close the last few yards in giant bounds and barrel into the pack, my knife out, teeth gritted. I charge past the three coyotes in the back and head straight for the alpha that's trying to drag Ethan away.

Time slows. The ugly scene is crisp as lock onto my prey. Face contorted in terror, Ethan's free hand digs into the coyote's scruff. The coyote's tail is a taut brush behind him. His ears are erect triangles marking my approach. The frothy saliva runs from his fangs into my brother's bloody arm. There's a low, guttural growl, deep in his throat.

I fall on him. The only sound is the beat of my own heart as I jab my hunting knife home.

The serrated blade slices into the coyote's mangy hide. I bury it to the hilt in fur. With a fierce yelp, the coyote jolts and skitters sideways. He drops my brother's arm. Blood gushes from the animal's haunch. The coyote looks to his wound and then to me. He growls, flashing bloody fangs, but then limps sloppily over the ridge. His pack follows.

They're gone. Ethan.

With my blood still thrumming in my ears and the prickles of heat flooding my veins, I drop beside my brother, now pale and covered with dust.

"Ethan," I say, reaching for his bloodied arm, "are you okay?"

Of course he's not okay. His arm is a torn mess of shredded skin, blood and coyote drool. His face drains of color and his eyes well with tears.

"He ... he bit me," he stammers. He looks like he's going to faint.

I cradled him and take off running. I keep my eyes on my brother's pale face. He has to be okay.

By the time I reach the house, my lungs feel like deflated balloons and a stitch digs like a knife into my ribs, but none of that matters. I know what an infection means. With no antibiotics it means a horrible agonizing death.

I am stumbling through the yard when the figure blocks my path. A muscular man in clean denim, a faded t-shirt and cowboy hat. My eyes mark the silver revolvers at his hips. Clay.

I skid to a stop. "Get out of here!" I yell, though it comes out raspy from my aching lungs. I want to dig out my knife, but my hands are full of my brother, who's … unconscious? Is he breathing? I flick my eyes from Ethan, back to Clay.

Clay sees Ethan's arm and his face darkens. He whistles low. "That's a nasty bite. Let me lend a hand."

"No." My voice is slick with hatred. "Get off my steps before I make you." My words sound strong, but my arms feel like limp noodles. If I have to fight Clay now, it'll go poorly. I don't care. I'll die before I'll let him hurt Ethan.

He wrinkles his blue eyes as if weighing his words. "Really," he says. "I can help."

"Help what?" I'm stalling. My eyes skim our dusty yard for an exit, an answer, something. "Help capture us?" Ethan moans and more blood runs from his arm onto his shirt. I have to get him inside. Now.

"Listen," he says, looking at me sheepishly, one thumb hooked in his belt loop, "I'm not here to take you in. When I locked you in the cellar, I was trying to keep you from getting shot up."

He offers that smile now, one he's probably given his parents a million times to say, *Trust this face. Would I lie?* I don't care how charming he is. All I can see is an image of Arn's body drug out for the coyotes.

"My parents and Auntie are dead because of you." I feel my pocketknife pressing against my thigh, waiting for me.

Clay's forehead furrows and he turns his eyes away. When he looks at me again, his voice is almost too quiet to hear. "Your ma and auntie aren't dead."

Suddenly the world feels smaller, heavier. "What'd you say?"

He blows out a breath. "They ain't dead. We … they took 'em into custody. Nothing I could do."

Not dead. My mother and Auntie Bell aren't dead. But what's happening to them? Were they sold to the Breeders? The thought of them going back there feels like an iron fist around my insides.

Clay takes a few steps sideways. He takes his hat off and tucks it to his chest, a cowboy's act of contrition if I ever saw it. Then he nods down at Ethan's arm. "He needs disinfectant or that'll fester. Coyot' bites are nasty."

"I know that," I say, taking a few steps toward our back door. I walk slowly past him, never taking my eyes away.

He gestures toward the bike sitting in our driveway with his hat. "Got a first aid kit on the bike. It's not much, but I got antiseptic and bandages." He brings his hat back to his chest and smiles.

Arn in the dirt, left to die.

"We don't need your help." I run up the steps and lock the door behind me.

***

Ethan's arm worsens.

I wash the wound with water, but it's not enough. The four slashes, deep bloody valleys with peaks of shredded skin, swell and puss. While Ethan moans and rocks on the bed, I scour the house for soap, disinfectant, anything. I pull apart every cupboard and closet. I come up empty handed.

In the barn I knock over empty gas cans, dig through drawers and fling empty bottles from shelves. I find nothing but fat centipedes and oily rags. My heart won't stop thudding in my chest. What if there's nothing? Desperate tears threaten, but I dig my fingernails into my palms and keep searching. I gotta find something. I gotta.

I save Arn's workbench for last. There's too much pain hovering around his worn table, the notes tacked above in his slanted scrawl, his projects never to be finished. I walk to it slowly, feeling the waves of sadness wash over me as my eyes touch all the things that he never will.

My vision's drawn to something smooth and shiny on a top shelf. My hand closes around the brown glass dropper. I lift the three-inch bottle up to the light. Brown liquid sloshes inside. Half a bottle of iodine. Jackpot.

I run back to the house. When I barrel into Ethan's room, he's a sweaty moaning mess. I slide up to his bed and push the hair out of his eyes.

"I got it, bud," I say, unscrewing the bottle. "Hold still."

He moans, but stops thrashing. I fill the little dropper with iodine and drip it into his wounds. Such a little fix for such a huge problem. I pray it'll be enough.

Ethan calms a little, though his arm still throbs. I find myself rubbing his sweaty back and singing verses of "You Are My Sunshine" and "Rock-a-bye Baby," songs my mother would sing on nights when we were fitful or the thunder rattled the walls. The words feel heavy in my mouth.

He falls into a feverish sleep. Exhausted, I stumble down the hall.

Night has crept up in all the commotion. I stare out the ragged hole that was our front window to the quiet of our yard. The cool twilight air that pulses in feels good on my face. Somewhere an owl gives a mournful hoot and the insects buzz in harmony. I run my hands over my arms and slump on the couch. The familiar smells and sounds help me to breathe.

I've spent most of the day alternating between beating myself up for letting Ethan check a trap alone and picturing Auntie and my mama in chains. Now in the dark, my thoughts fly to them. Are they crouched against a concrete wall in one of the jail cells, waiting for the Breeders to collect their prize? My mind supplies chains on their ankles or collars around their neck. The horror of that thought haunts me. I hug myself and shiver. I gotta free them. But how?

My eyes trace the scattered remains of our life strewn around the living room. There's shards of a ceramic vase, the desert flowers my mother lovingly picked shriveled to husks on the floor. My eyes trace past shreds of our tattered wallpaper. A picture frame, knocked off a sideboard, lies broken on the ground. I pull myself off the couch and pick it up with tender hands.

The cherry wood frame, dented at the corners, holds the treasure I was seeking. The glass is gone, but the drawing remains. I lift the paper delicately out of the frame. It's a piece of butcher block with a ten-year-old's pencil scrawl. To anyone but my mama, it would've been trash, but she framed it and set it on the sideboard. Looking at it now brings a tightness to my throat I can't swallow down.

The pencil drawing shows five stick figures, each with giant circular heads and grins that cover half their faces. For my mama, I drew a triangle dress and her clutching what looks like a bean with a face—my best effort for baby Ethan. For Arn, I sketched his overalls as uneven rectangles over his stick body. Auntie's figure has a long rope braid down her back. And for myself, the biggest grin of all plastered on my little circle head.

My family as I saw it at age ten. I drew this at the kitchen table of the house we lived in six years ago. A thunderstorm crackled overhead and I tried to clamber on my mama's lap. She kindly pried me off and set the pencil and paper in front of me.

"Draw something happy," she'd said, caressing my cheek. "It'll keep your mind off the storm."

I hold the picture delicately to my chest. What I wouldn't give to go back there, under the flickering sky with my mother's hand at my shoulder and the *clack clack* of Auntie's rocking chair, the slow steady rhythm that meant all was right with the world. How could I have known then I had everything I ever need? That it would all be taken from me?

What can I do now to keep my mind off the storm?

***

The sharp knock on our front door wakes me. I bolt upright and dig in my pants for my knife. Nothing. I scan the room, lit with morning light, for a weapon and spy the fire poker in the stand near the hearth. Hefting the metal rod over my shoulder, I tiptoe to the front door.

Through the bullet holes in the wood, I see a figure on the other side.

"Go away!" I yell in my deepest voice. "We don't want any."

"Now, I highly doubt that."

Clay. I turn the knob and yank the door open. He stands on the porch in his clean cowboy best—short-sleeve button-down shirt, jeans, boots and his hat. In his left hand he holds a basket of apples, rolls and wrapped bacon. In his right hand is a bar of antiseptic soap. He lifts a dimpled reassuring smile.

I raise the poker as if to strike.

"Jesus!" He jumps back. "What's a fella gotta do to prove he's worth havin'?"

As I'm brandishing the poker, Ethan slides up behind me.

"Are you Clay?" His smile is wide and inviting.

"He was just leaving," I say through clenched teeth.

"Oh." Ethan's face falls. He pulls his wounded arm up and clutches it to him. The wound looks awful. The skin around the bite is puffy and oozing. The iodine is long gone.

I look at Ethan's arm and then at Clay, who's eying the poker, waiting for me to strike. I have no choice. The poker thuds heavily against my thigh as I bring it down.

"Come in," I say, stiffly. "Can we get you some breakfast?"

Clay scans my expression and then takes a tentative step forward. "Sure," he says. "Just put away the brainin' stick, will ya?"

I hand him the metal rod. "Take it. I'll start the stove."

Ethan leads Clay to the table and begins peppering him with questions as I try to figure out what the hell I'm doing. Mechanically, I open the stove, toss in the kindling and dig around for a match. When the flame ignites, the yellow-red tongues eat up the starter twigs until they are crumbled black husks of their former selves. Then there's nothing left to do but make breakfast for my enemy.

CHAPTER EIGHT

I sit across from Clay as he eats bacon off my mother's blue china plate. The three of us ignore the bullet holes shot into the table. Clay is telling some story to my little brother, who laughs and then chomps a rippled slice of bacon between his teeth.

I can't laugh. I don't even know what he's saying. I pretend to eat and watch the words form in his mouth, but all I think about is Clay sitting in Arn's chair. It makes me want to go find that stove poker again.

"Riley, did you hear that?"

"Huh?"

"Did you hear what Clay said? He said Mama and Auntie are still in town. He can take us to see them if we want." Joy dances across Ethan's face.

I stop eating and stare up at Clay. "Can I have a word with you outside?"

Clay gives a wary smile and drops his napkin on the table. "Sure."

I lead him out onto the porch and shut the door tight. On the porch the air is searing, a perfect match for how I'm feeling inside. Clay clomps out, leans his hip against the rickety porch railing and offers me his smile again.

"I mean it, you know. I can take y'all into town. We'll have to be caref—"

"You can get the hell out of here right now," I say, trembling. I point to his motorcycle. "Just go. I had enough of your lies."

"I'm not lying. Your ma's in town. Won't be for long, so if you want to see 'em, we need to shake tail."

I clutch my hands together until my knuckles are white. "It's just another trick. Another way to get us into town so you can finish what you started."

Frustration deepens the lines between his eyes. He shakes his head slowly back and forth. "You're really irritating, you know that?"

I stare at him with my jaw dropped. "Me?"

"Yeah, you." He grips the porch rail and it rocks under his weight. "What do I have to do to prove I'm sorry? I saved y'all during the raid, I brought you food, medicine. What do I have to do?" He flaps his arms in frustration.

I cross my arms over my thrumming heart. "You can start by bringing my stepfather back to life."

He winces and drops his head. "Wish I could." He grips the porch railing and stares sadly off toward the barn. "I didn't want anyone to get hurt. When they told me we were going on a raid, I had no idea we were coming here." He points to my bullet-riddled house. "Then I saw you and your brother in the yard. I locked you in to keep you safe. By the time I got back, your pa was toe up. Nothing I could do." Clay lifts his sorrowful eyes from the dirt to meet mine.

"Do you think feeling bad is enough? You were a part of this whether you shot him or not."

He digs the toe of his boot along a crack in the porch floorboards. "That's why I'm trying to make amends. I may be Sheriff's number two, but I don't like his politics. I don't mind rustling criminals, but I can't abide this. Taking you to see your ma is the only decent thing I can think of to make up for what I did."

I dig deep for more fury, but the wellspring runs dry.

Then it dawns on me. If Clay's not our enemy, he might be useful. A plan hatches. I look down the road toward town. "You said you want to help us, right?"

Clay stands straighter, thumbs in his belt loops. "Yeah."

"Good." My mind's still reeling. I take a few steps across the porch, swivel on my heel and face Clay again. "Where they keeping my family?"

Clay's eyes widen and he shakes his head. "Now hold those flyin' horses of your'n. There's one thing you gotta understand."

"No," I say curtly. "There's one thing you gotta understand. I'm getting my mama and auntie out of there 'fore the Breeders come. I don't care what I got to do. I'm not letting those monsters take 'em."

Clay rubs a hand over his head, mussing short brown hair. "Sorry, chief, but Breeders are coming tomorrow. And don't nobody get in their way."

I stare out over the dusty landscape of our yard until my eyes light on my mother's garden. "Then we go today."

He shakes his head. "Now wait a minute—"

I point my finger at his chest. "You want to make up for what you did? You helped lock 'em up. You get 'em free."

He screws up his mouth and begins worrying the chipped paint on the porch rail. "I'd be strung up or kicked out with nothin'."

I shrug and wave my hand at the desolation that used to be our family farm.

Clay rubs his smooth palms over his face. "Ah, God. This is crazy. You understand what you're asking me to do?"

I nod.

Clay blows out his breath. "Fine. I'll help *you* bust 'em out, but Sheriff can't know I had a hand in it."

For the first time, I let a smile slink up my face. "Deal."

Clay stares at my expression for a lingering minute. With my hate no longer clouding my judgment, I realize how reckless I've been with my secret. My breasts are bound tight, but I've done nothing to disguise my voice or the rest of my features.

Clay punches my arm. "God, you sure do got balls for a bender. Wait, do benders have balls?"

I give him a cold stare.

He waves his hand dismissively, a blush climbing up into his cheeks. "Never mind."

***

In the back of the Jeep, the ruts in the road feel like craters. Ethan and I lay across the back seat, covered in a large canvas that's got us both sweating. Clay's driving. Every time the Jeep slows, I expect the townies to rip off our cover and arrest us.

Everything that matters is stuffed in two sacks in the back of the Jeep. Changes of clothes, my mother's quilt, Auntie's knitting needles, the Superman figure Arn was carving, Ethan's comic book, any spare food and water. It's amazing how items that used to mean the world to me I tossed without a thought. It's easy to know what matters when what you really love is stripped from you.

The Jeep jerks and Ethan and I rock back and forth and nearly knock heads. Laying pressed together like this, it's hard to see his face, but I feel his hand tighten around my arm. I give him a squeeze, but that's all I can offer. My stomach's in knots. Questions run in my mind till I'm dizzy with them. What will we have to do to free my family? How will we pull it off? What happens if I can't get back to Ethan? Our whole plan's paper-thin and it all hinges on Clay. Clay who I didn't trust, who I'm not sure I do. As the sun pokes through the holes in the canvas blanket, I wonder if this will be my last day breathing free air.

We rock to a stop, gravel crunching under the tries. I hear the guard holler down. We're here.

Clay shouts a friendly hello and the gates creak open. For him, there's no identifying himself, no weapons confiscation. He's a good ally to have. If only I knew for sure he was our ally.

Insides the gates, I feel the weight of what we're doing pressing down on me until I can barely breathe. I focus on listening and trying not to move.

"Stay here. I'll be back after dark," Clay whispers from somewhere above.

I want to answer, but the Jeep rocks as he jumps out. He's gone.

Three hours goes slow when you're cramped in the back of a Jeep, trying not to make a sound.

Darkness falls. The light filtering through the canvas is a dusky gray. Ethan's fallen asleep on my arm and I can't feel my fingers. Every few minutes male voices shout, guns fire. Waiting makes me crazy. Where the hell is Clay? I'm about to slip up the canvas and attempt a peak when there's a hand at my back.

"Don't move," the voice whispers.

We're done for.

The canvas slips back and there's Clay, washed and dressed in clean jeans and a fresh button-down shirt. The pearl snaps on his breast pockets wink in the twilight. I feel the rivers of sweat on my face and neck. I'm a hot mess. It doesn't matter what I look like. Clay thinks I'm a bender, and besides, after tonight, I'll never see him again.

As I untangle myself from Ethan, I glower at Clay's sparkling appearance. "Nice to see you had time to get a change of clothes. Did you have a bath? A massage?" I wipe the sweat from my brow.

"Shh," he puts a finger to his lips and then and holds up a bandanna, a wide-brimmed cowboy hat and a brown coat. "You'll be hot, but least you'll be covered."

I clench my teeth to keep the sarcastic remarks from slipping out. I put on the clothes. Then we both look down at Ethan.

"I told him to stay in the Jeep," I say, looking at his curled form, his hair lying in damp strands across his face. His mouth twitches in a dream. I hate leaving him, but I don't want him where I'm going. I brush a strand of hair from his face. "Let's get this over with," I say to Clay.

He nods. "Follow me and try to act like you belong."

In the twilight, little gas lamps flicker on either side of the street, a few more in the windows. The noises of the day have quieted. A few drunken calls spill out from the brothel. A woman cackles from an upper window. Besides a handful of stragglers, the streets are mostly empty. All respectable persons have gone home. Down the road lamps glow in the windows of the well-to-do. Right about now, my family would be cleaning up from supper. Auntie'd be knitting in her rocking chair on the porch. Ethan and I would dig out the molding deck of cards and invent a few games until the light grew too dim. My mama would rub the kinks out of Arn's shoulders. I blink the painful image from my mind and turn my eyes to the task at hand.

We stroll down the road, the same one I traveled not more than a few days ago. Clay saunters, smiles, stops to chat. The men lift their hats to Clay. I stand stiffly at each exchange, hoping no one notices me. Hoping I don't run into the Warden.

A toothless old man crosses the street and makes a beeline for us. He extends his wrinkled hand and for a moment I think he'll snatch me. I flinch, but he limps past and starts pumping Clay's hand like a dying man at a water well.

"I jest want ta thankee again fer the help, son," he says, through the few teeth left in his mouth. "Thought I was up a crick with that charge. Not a dime in me pocket when I got pinched."

Clay lifts his reassuring smile. "Don't mention it, Hawk. Glad to help."

The withered man's face glows with gratitude. What did Clay do for him? Probably something like he did for me at the jailhouse. It eases my frayed nerves a little to remember how he put himself on the line.

Hawk finally lets go and we continue past the brothel. My stomach knots as I peer in the open doorway. A few weary men hunch over the bar. One unfortunate old woman in ratty underwear and too much makeup slings drinks. Her eyes are like dull hunks of coal. Clay puts a hand on my shoulder and shakes his head. Thank God. I couldn't stand seeing a townie with his hands on my mother. I'd do something we'd both regret.

We stride past the darkened doctor's office, the general store, the armory. Clay never slows. My stomach flip-flops as we come up to the jail, but Clay doesn't turn. I glance in as we walk by and see Darrel's dirty boots up on the desk, his head back. The Warden is nowhere to be seen.

When we run out of shops and hit the residential end of the street, I'm confused. I shoot Clay questioning looks, which he ignores. When he continues past the rest of the homes, with their dimly lit windows and smells of cooked meat, and heads straight for the last house on the road, the stately white ranch with the wrap-around porch, I grab his arm.

"This is the Sheriff's," I hiss.

He removes his arm from my grip and scans the road. With his face set all calm, he nods. "Thanks for the tip, hot shot, but I think I know where I'm going. Duck behind there and wait for me." He points to a slanted wooden outhouse. "I got to send the guard on a little errand."

I scowl, but bite my tongue. If I make a scene here, it will be the end of me. I slip behind a battered outhouse several yards from the Sheriff's white picket fence and watch from the shadows as Clay slips through the gate into the lion's den.

From my dark hiding space, I can see everything. Gas lamps light the front rooms of the Sheriff's house. I note the smoothly carved furniture, the shiny upright piano in the sitting room, the polished silver tea set on the table. I scan the windows for my mother and Auntie, but see no one.

Clay strides up the gravel path and greets the guard at the front door. They chuckle about something I can't hear. Clay motions back toward town and the guard nods, picks up his rifle and crunches down the street. When the guard's out of sight and the road quiet, Clay waves me forward. I slip out from behind my hiding spot, feeling more nervous than ever. My skin crawls beneath my layers of clothing. What are we doing?

He leads me around the side of the house. We trot past the little backyard with patches of clipped green grass and four apple trees heavy with red fruit. Beneath the trees is a weathered wooden swing. I imagine the Sheriff wiling away the hours, rocking beneath his apple trees. He probably needs to relax in between butchering families in their sleep.

Clay steps up to the back door, grabs my arm and pulls me in. Our bodies are so close, I can smell the sticky sweetness of his aftershave. My eyes rest on the curve of his jaw, the stubble on his chin. My cheeks flush beneath my bandanna. I shake my head and focus.

"Here's the plan. I head in and make sure the coast's clear. You slip down the basement real quiet. I'll send 'em down to you. When you're ready, head out the back gate. They'll be a ride waiting."

"What about Ethan?"

"He'll be there, too. Okay?"

I nod.

Clay looks up at the house. "Let's get started. We only got an hour."

Clay puts a key in the lock and cracks open the back door. I follow on his heels. To my right is the basement stairs. I tread carefully into the dark basement. I don't dare fumble for a lantern, just plunge into the cool darkness with my hands outstretched. When my feet hit the concrete floor, I shuffle forward and almost smack into a pole. I wrap my arms around the cool metal beam. It gives me something solid to hold onto when most of me feels like dust picked up in a twister.

Footsteps overhead, whispering. I can't tell who's speaking, but I hear a female voice. My mom? God, why won't they hurry up? My heart thuds against the metal pole.

A beam of light trickles down the basement stairs. Someone's coming. Please God, let it be my family.

A foot appears, then an ankle, followed by a white cotton dress that's frayed at the hem. Auntie. In the lamplight clutched in her outstretched hand, she looks twenty years older, all wrinkles and sagging skin. She's wearing a clean cotton housedress and a head rag over her hair. I want to run to her, but my arms feel anchored to the pole. I watch her expression as she searches for me in the darkness. Her eyes adjust and lock onto mine. She shuffles to a stop; her hand flies to her mouth. "Riley?"

My arms aren't anchored anymore. I throw them around her.

I clutch her bony frame and she strokes my hair, murmuring sweetness like she used to do when I was little. She smells like fresh baking and wood smoke. I don't want to stop hugging her, but I can't help but keep one eye on the stairs. My mama. Where is she?

Auntie follows the direction of my eyes and shakes her head. She runs her hand over my hair and tries to get up the courage to tell me. She doesn't have to. I can see it on her face.

"Where is she?" I ask, my voice trembling.

"They took her this morning."

Pain slams into my chest. This can't be happening. She was supposed to be here. Hot angry tears spring to my eyes.

Auntie pulls me to her. Some tears escape down my nose before I wipe them roughly away. Auntie pulls back and traces a tear with her crooked finger.

"If I know your mama, she'll give 'em a fight. She'll be right as rain until you can get her."

I gaze up at Auntie's face, wanting to believe, but I can see the truth in her face like when I was eight years old. She found me crying that I'd never get married. She held me and said the right man would come along. I shouldn't worry my pretty head about it. When I looked into her face even then, I could tell she was giving me the words I wanted to hear, not the ones she believe. She's doing that now.

"What will happen to her?" I ask, afraid for the answer.

She twists her mouth down and shakes her head slightly. Then she takes hold of my shoulders and peers into my face. "You get to her. You do what you have to and get her out. And quick, darlin'. You have about a week before …"

I stiffen. "Before what?"

Auntie shakes her head. "Just get to her. I know you can."

"How? I don't even know where she is." I set my chin on Auntie's boney shoulder. She snakes her arms around me. She pets her hand over my hair again and again, stroking in time with her words, spurring me on. "That youngin' up there can sniff out where they tucked her. He's a good 'un. Useful. Looks like you already got him in your pocket if he'd risk bringing you here."

"He's only helping because he feels bad about what happened to Arn. He said he'd help get you out. That's all." I hate the childish tone in my voice, but I can't stop thinking of my mama in the clutches of monsters, their sharp teeth snagging at her flesh. I shake the image away.

Auntie stops stoking and pulls me back. Her hands clamp tight around my arms. "I'd bet a truck bed full a squealing piglets that's not the case, but no sense in all this talk. You got to go. Sheriff's due home any minute." Auntie takes my hand and leads me back to the stairs.

I pull back. "You're coming with me."

Auntie squeezes my hand. "Sorry, turnip, the old lady's staying put. Got too many bunions and my arthritis is flaring up. Road'd just make 'em worse."

I shake my head. "No, Auntie. You're coming."

Auntie grips my arms at the wrists. "Since when do you tell your Auntie what to do? You'd have to drag me kicking and screaming and I don't think you've got the taters to do it." Her grip softens. She leans forward, a reassuring smile spreading up her face. "Sheriff's taken a liking to Auntie's famous bread. He doesn't mind if I swat at him or call him a dirt pie. I got my own bedroom and three squares and all I got to do is cook and clean up. Not a bad way to spin my last yarn."

"I can't just leave you here. He's a murderer."

Auntie takes me by the shoulders and gives me a dead-eyed glare. "Listen up, young lady. I'm staying."

I tuck my chin to my chest and pick at the hem of my jacket. It's hard to say what I really mean. "But I need you, Auntie."

She hugs me again. I smell the wood smoke in her silver hair. "You don't need me, nor nobody. You got Auntie's spunk. Jesus, you broke into Sheriff's house for the love of Pete. You can get your mama from those bastards."

I stare at the concrete floor, but she lifts my chin until I'm looking at her.

"Don't even think about your old Auntie. I'm not done yet."

"I'll get you out as soon as I find Mama. I promise."

"Alright, punpkinhead. Now, go. Tell Ethan I love him."

I hug her once more and she kisses my forehead. She leads me to the stairs and I shuffle up the steps and feel my way to the back door. In the small span of darkness, she's a million miles away. Leaving her feels wrong. I stand in the foyer and look back down.

The front door bangs open. Loud footsteps thud on the wood floors. I freeze. The hulking shadow striding through the front door forms into my worst nightmare. It's the Sheriff. I'm trapped. All I can do is watch from the shadows.

He sits on a fancy chair near the front door and pries off his boots. Then he looks around.

"Clay? You here?"

Clay appears from the hallway and strides towards the Sheriff.

"Right here, Pa."

CHAPTER NINE

Clay is the Sheriff's son.

The realization smacks into me like a wind-whipped barn door. Stunned, I take a step back and bump into a table with a vase perched on top. It wobbles. Shatters.

The Sheriff draws his gun. "Who's there?"

Run. I stumble over shards of vase and fumble for the door. Boots pound toward me. I yank the door open. Night air floods my face. I'll make it out. Then a meaty hand grips my collar and yanks me back.

I tumble into the kitchen, knock over a chair and spill onto the tile. I slam to a stop against the cabinets. When I look up, my eyes find the barrel of a gun.

"Looky here," the Sheriff says with a sneer.

The Sheriff looks like a bulldog that's been in too many nasty fights. He's got a dozen scars carved around his jowly cheeks and bald head. There's a wicked crescent-shaped scar from his ear to his jaw, as if his sneer runs all the way up. He wears a white cotton t-shirt stained yellow at the pits and ratty blue jeans. My eyes trace over the holey socks with his toe peaking through. As he smirks at me, I can see the gaping hole where half of his teeth used to be.

"Bin a long time since we had ourselves an intruder," he says, eying me. "'Bout time I got to shoot sumbody."

My eyes flick from the Sheriff to Clay, who's appeared over his father's shoulder. He gives me fretful looks, but says nothing. The Sheriff reaches for me. I flinch. He rips the bandana off my face.

"Huh." He examines me as he uses the barrel of his gun to scratch a bug bite in his chin stubble. When he leans in close, his breathe smells like raw meat. "Gonna ask you once, bender, what the hell you doin' in my house. If I think you're tellin' tales or I plain don't like yer answer, I'm gonna kill ya. But outside." He smiles. "Don't want blood on my tile. Travertine. Nice, ain't it?"

My heart pounds out all thought. I glance at Clay for answers, but all he's giving me are agonizing looks. My mouth flops open and shut like a fish. I can't speak.

The Sheriff shakes his head. "Alright then, outside. We'll make quick work of ya and I can get in for my soak."

I tighten up, ready to fight off the meaty hands that reach for my jacket. Clay clears his throat.

"Uh, Pa, I need to … talk to ya. Can this wait? I'll run the bastard down to the Warden."

I stare up at Clay. Behind his father, he lifts his shoulders in a little shrug. Then he straightens his face as the Sheriff pushes up on his haunches and turns.

"Okay, take 'im. I wanna git in the tub anyway. Give me a whistle when you git back." He hands the revolver to Clay and pats him on the back.

"Sure, Pa." Clay grabs me by the arm and hauls me upright. "Let's take a walk." His voice is ice cold.

With his hand around my bicep, Clay pulls me forward and I struggle against him. His hand tightens. "One move, you motherless bastard, and I blow your ever-lovin' brains out your ear." If he's pretended to hate me, he's sure doing a good job.

Clay pulls me out of the house and down the porch. My eyes flick to his face, a mask of disgust. I keep waiting for him to smile, wink, but nothing. I'm about to give up hope when he yanks me into a dark alley. In the dirty crevice, his grip loosens from my arm.

"Jesus, we're in a hot mess." He leans against he building and rubs his hand over his face. "Goddamn. So much for plan A."

I pull away from him and step back until there's a good five-foot gap between us. I glare at his shadowed figure. "You never said he was your pa."

"Yeah, well, he is. Didn't think you'd be too keen on going with me if you knew."

"Well, yeah," I say, my voice too loud.

Holds a finger up to silence me. Then he nervously scratches his chin stubble. "Listen," he says, gazing back at the house, "just because the Sheriff's my pa don't mean our deal's off." He sighs deeply. "I … I'm still in."

"In for what?" I ask, flapping my hands. "Our master plan failed. We're done."

He glances back toward the house. In the glinting windows, I can make out the shadow of his father clomping up the stairs. Clay sighs heavily. "We don't got a choice now. We'll have to head out. He's seen you."

"We?"

He looks back toward the pristine house and grinds his teeth. Finally, he nods. "Yeah, I'm coming."

I search his face. His eyes look tired, his jaw tense. The stubble on his cheeks and chin make him look twenty-five instead of eighteen. "Why?"

He blinks and looks up at me as if coming out of a dream. "What? Get you out?"

I shake my head. "Risk your life for strangers. That," I say, pointing to the house, "is your flesh and blood."

Clay's eyes search the night sky as if the stars contain some answer. He laces his fingers behind his head. His answer is slow in coming. "I don't know. My pa … he's been good to me." He swallows hard. "But, he's not a good man. He wants me to be his second. I can't. Not after last month …"

I frown. "What happened last month?"

Even in the shadows I can see the sorrow running through his expression. "Nothing," he says sharply. "I'm just not as tough-minded as my pa. That's all."

"Not as psycho, you mean."

His brow darkens. "He's still my family." His eyes flick to the little squares of light at the front of his house. "I'll disappoint him if I stay."

I know what that's like. I've let down my parents more times then I can count, and a man like the Sheriff probably isn't as nice about failure. Clay's answer is not great, but we need him. I walk to the edge of the shadows and look down the road that has once again plunged into silence. "Coast's clear. We should go."

Clay gives me a tentative smile and then steps beside me. "I won't let you down."

I don't turn. It's enough that he's so close I can hear him breathing.

We jog in the shadows of the sleepy houses. We skirt around Sheriff Tate's white picket fence. My eyes lift to the dark windows of the house. What will Clay leave behind?

When we reach the high wooden stockade at the back of the Sheriff's yard, Clay runs his hands along the solid wooden structure as if searching for something. He must find what he's looking for because he stops and beings working an object in his hands. Metal glints in the moonlight, a tiny padlock. He spins the combination like he's done it a hundred times. He pops the lock and the little door opens, notched so neatly into the wood that no seams show. I would never have known it was there. We slip through to the other side of the fence. There's our Jeep, idling with the lights off. In the driver seat, Ethan can barely see over the dash, but he's never looked prouder of himself. Arn taught him to drive the Jeep around the yard, but how in the world did he get out of the front gate and around back? There's no time to ask.

I grab the dented driver's side door and yank it open. "Move over."

Ethan pouts. "Ah, man. I wanna drive."

"I should drive," Clay says over my shoulder.

"No chance." I turn back to Ethan. "Move before they start shooting."

"Where's Mama and Auntie?" he asks, as he scrambles into the backseat.

"Auntie's fine, but wants to stay. We're going to get Mama."

Ethan eyes me, but doesn't ask.

I jump in and Clay slides in the passenger seat, his face pale and slack.

"You sure you want to do this?" I ask.

He nods, but keeps his eyes on the dashboard. He doesn't look back when I pull away from the wall.

The only thing that marks our exit is crunching gravel. We take the two-lane highway out of town. I drive with white knuckles, expecting headlights to appear behind us any second. It's a half-hour before my shoulders relax.

Hitting the open road with the night air in my face makes me feel a bit better. I glance at my two traveling companions. Ethan sits in the back, his head lolling from side to side, fighting sleep. Clay's scanning the pitted black top, his mouth twisted down, deep in thought. It dawns on me that all three of us are driving away from all we've ever known.

"Thanks," I say to Clay. With the night wind lashing around the Jeep, I wonder if he's heard me.

"Welcome," he mumbles.

"Which way?"

"West," he says, pointing. He tucks himself into the passenger seat and closes his eyes.

I drive into the night. The rutted blacktop is a mess with potholes, car husks, animal carcasses. My eyes are drawn up to a stretch of wind turbines in the distance. I trace the smooth white structures upward. Mom told me they used to provide electricity to this region. Now their tall, ivory forms remind me of bleached bones in the moonlight. When the wind stirs, the spinning blades moan wearily. I shiver and pull my eyes back to the highway.

Clay shifts beside me. His cowboy hat's tipped over his eyes. His fingers twitch over the black stock of one of his revolvers in his sleep. What's he dreaming about? How furious his pa will be if he ever finds out he helped us escape? He's agreed to leave every luxury in the world. Until I can figure out why, Clay's presence will always make me uneasy. He thinks I'm a bender and if he finds out my secret, turning me in would pay him enough to start a whole new life free of Daddy's expectations. Even a remotely honest man might jump at the chance for those riches. No, Clay can't know I'm a girl.

A tire bites into a deep rut and the Jeep jostles Clay awake. He bolts upright, his hand tightening on a revolver. His face slowly registers where he is. He looks over at me with tired eyes.

"Want me to drive?" he asks. He rubs his eyes with the palm of his hand in a way that I would find irresistible if I didn't have to keep from growing attached.

I shake my head. "Not yet, but I need you to tell me where I'm going. Where's my mama?"

Clay stares, red-eyed over the moonlit road. He shakes his head. "There's no use. You'll never get in."

I veer around a stretch of blacktop that's completely fallen away and then meet his eyes. "I'll get in."

Clay snorts. "Sure. Let's just break into the Breeder's facility, shall we? Brilliant. Even my pa wouldn't mess with those sons-a-bitches."

I grip the steering wheel with white knuckles. "It's your pa's fault in the first place. If he hadn't sold my mama to the Breeders, we wouldn't be in this mess."

He doesn't meet my eyes when he answers. "I ain't sayin' it's right, but she was of fertile age. They pay good money." He looks off into the star-filled horizon. "'Sides, if you don't, they come burn the town down."

I shiver in the darkness, thinking about the Breeders again. I picture men's bodies with grotesque animal features—slitted snake eyes, forked tongues, arms that extend to scorpion pinchers. I shake the image out of my head. Those are just old wives tales. They gotta be.

"Have you ever seen a Breeder?"

He shakes his head. "Don't want to."

I drive around a charred car frame and fight off images of my mama being tortured. "We're going to the hospital," I say, my jaw tight.

Clay pinches the bridge of his nose and sighs. "Are you gonna be this difficult the whole time?"

"Yes."

"Fine. I'll take you to the hospital, you'll see it's locked up tighter than a bull's ass during mating season and then we can go. It's 300 miles west in what's left of Albuquerque. We'll stop at my friend Bennett's, fuel and water up. Get a decent night's sleep before heading out."

I straddle a crinkled car muffler between my tires. "We stay one night and then on to the hospital."

He shakes his head. "We need time to come up with a plan."

"One night," I say. Suddenly, my eyelids droop and my vision's doubling. The Jeep jostles as I pull to the shoulder. "You can drive. I'm tired."

We slip out of our doors and walk around the Jeep. As I'm almost to the passenger side, I spot the eye shine in the distance. Three pairs of copper coin eyes glow in the moonlight. A black and white tail twitches up at our scent. It's a mother skunk leading two kits on a hunt. One of the kits, curious and alert, sniffs toward me. The mother yaps once and the kit trots back in line.

As their bushy tails recede into the darkness, I ache for my mother. I used to think her rules were the source of all my problems. Now I have all the freedom want and feel completely lost.

"You coming?" Clay removes his hat and runs his hands through his wavy brown hair.

I hop in the passenger seat, close my eyes and hope Clay will take us where we need to go.

***

When the Jeep lurches to a stop, dawn is spreading out in reds and oranges on the horizon. Next to me, Clay rubs his red-rimmed eyes.

"We're here." He pops out of the Jeep and walks toward the house in front of us.

At first glance the red farmhouse reminds me of home. The simple one-story ranch sits alone on a few acres of dirt. There's a windmill in back for water and an outhouse in the side yard. When I look closer, the differences are clear. The yard could double as a junk heap. On either side of the walkway, rusted car parts, worn out shoes, a crooked bike tire and loads of other junk, discarded and forgotten. A beat-up barn cat with one eye slinks out behind a stalk of scrub grass and darts under the rotting porch. The stink of human waste wafts from the outhouse.

Clay hops up on the porch and knocks on the door.

"Where are we?" Ethan leans forward and brushes the hair out of his sleepy eyes.

"Bennett's. Stick close to me. If I say run, bolt to the Jeep."

Ethan furrows his brow. We watch as Clay peeks in the broken sidelights beside the front door.

I pull the bandanna up over my mouth and nose to disguise my face. I have to pee, but I'll hold it as long as I can. Catching me peeing would uncover my secret for sure. The smelly outhouse might be my only bet. The dozens of flies buzzing around the back promise an interesting experience.

The front door bangs open. A naked man stands in the doorway. His emaciated frame reminds me of a skeleton wrapped in beef jerky. He points a double-barrel shotgun at Clay's chest. The cocking of the barrel echoes around the front yard.

"Who's goes?" the naked man growls. His look is wild, almost rabid.

Clay holds up his hands and takes a step back. "I—I'm looking for Bennett."

"Who in Sam Hill are you?" The wrinkly old man keeps both barrels pointed at Clay.

My hand reaches toward the driver seat, but Clay took his revolvers with him. Damn. I reach around the seat for some sort of weapon.

A figure steps behind the old man and puts a hand on his shoulder. "It's okay, Pop. Clay's a friend."

The old man spits a wad of phlegm on the porch, but lowers the shotgun. The young man steps around his father and pats Clay's shoulder.

The young man, who must be Bennett, is bare-chested and I'm worried nudity is a rule here. Luckily, his lower half is clad in a pair of jeans more holey than Mama's colander.

"What you doing here?" Bennett smiles and whacks Clay a couples more times on the back. "Wasn't expecting you."

Bennett is a little older than Clay, probably in his early twenties. He has most of his teeth and a thin, wiry physique. He's got long, dirty-blond hair that trails down to his bare shoulders and a crooked nose that looks like it's been broken a few times. I notice a heavy limp when he shuffles around the porch. Nearly everyone falls prey to some injury or illness by the time they reach their third decade. Bennett seems friendly enough though, clapping Clay on the back, but something about this whole scene makes my skin crawl.

Clay tucks his hands in his pockets and rocks back on his heels. "We're just passing through. On my way to Albuquerque. Thought I'd stop by and say howdy."

Bennett hitches up his jeans that have slipped down his hips. "Albuquerque, eh? Big daddy got you taking stock to the Breeders?" Bennett leans around Clay and scans the Jeep. I stiffen as we lock eyes.

"Naw. Just some friends who need a lift into the city." Clay waves us out. I stiffen. After seeing this place, I want to stay in the Jeep the whole visit.

"Well, bring 'em in," Bennett says, waving us into the house.

Clay gestures again and, when we don't move, glares at us while Bennett's back is turned. I guess staying in the Jeep isn't an option. Ethan and I slink toward the house. When I step on the porch and Bennett sees me, his smile falls.

"What's with the mask, *extraño?*" he asks me, his eyes narrowing.

Any good feelings evaporate. I shrug.

He turns to Clay. "You bringing fugitives into my home?" His tone slips from friendly to dangerous.

Clay offers up a smile and turns to me. "Cut the act, Riley. Smell's not that bad." He nods toward the outhouse. "What you got in that outhouse, Ben, a maggot farm?"

Bennett doesn't answer. He keeps his cold eyes locked on me.

I got no choice. I slip my bandanna down and offer a weak smile. Bennett scans my face. He's not happy with what he sees. I keep my eyes on the guns at Clay's hips.

Finally, Bennett limps into the house. "Y'all hungry?"

Clay leans towards me and whispers, "Stop acting nuts. These are good people." He disappears inside.

Ethan puts his hand in mine. He looks up at me for reassurance. I got none. I follow Clay into the house with a lump in my throat.

CHAPTER TEN

The smell inside the house is a strange mixture of body odor, feces and mildewed air. The floor crunches as we step. Dirt, eggshells, and bits of garbage I can't name litter the floor. In one corner a stack of decaying newspapers is piled so high if it topples, it would crush a small child. In the other corner, a horse saddle is splattered with dried blood. Alarm bells go off in my head as we follow Bennett in through the hallway.

The steady buzz of flies greets us as we enter the kitchen. They're everywhere—on the dirty plates piled in the sink, on the broken eggshells that litter the floor, on the gelatinous smear on the table. I notice a swarm of them on the floor and realize they're clustered on a dead rat's bloated stomach. I swallow bile. Is this what Clay was expecting? A similar look of disgust flashes on his face before he can politely cover it up. Bennett says nothing about the mess. He pulls out a couple of the battered chairs, one with three legs that I perch on carefully. While we sit at the garbage-strewn table, he selects a cast-iron skillet from the dish pile and brown speckled eggs from a basket.

He holds up the eggs. "Over easy? Scrambled? How you like 'em?"

"Over easy, but don't go out of your way, Ben. We've got supplies in the car." Clay swats a fly off his arm.

Bennett cracks eggs into the skillet with deft fingers. "Least I can do. Things are tight 'round here, but we've always got good laying hens. God, I eat so many eggs one day I'll turn sunny side up." Bennett's laugh is hollow and tragic. I can count his ribs from the table.

The old man shuffles in and plunks in a stool to my right. Thankfully, he's pulled on some ratty long underwear. His chest is still bare and he's even thinner than Bennett. His ribs ripple down his chest like a washboard and his collarbone juts out like jar handles. The pure desperation in this place weighs on me heavy. I glance between Ethan and the door. Should I signal him to bolt? His attention's drawn to a skinny hound under the table. The dog gives Ethan's hand a pathetic lick and then slumps lazily at his feet.

Clay seems to have recovered from his shock and tries to strike up a conversation. "What was it, Ben, six months since you left the crew? Never did hear why."

Ben hunches over the skillet. "Pop got pneumonia last spring and almost didn't make it. I came home to take care of him. Then I fell off my horse in July and was laid up pretty bad. We damn near starved to death 'til I could get back on my feet. Been slow going since. We're getting back to it, though. Right, Pop?"

The old man says nothing, but I can feel his eyes glaring at the side of my head. I pretend to look out the busted window, then realize he's not looking at me. His eyes are locked on Ethan. My shoulders tense. I lean forward to pick up a fork buried in papers on the table and block his view.

Clay continues. "Sorry to hear. You know we'd take you back quick as a lick. Sheriff always said you were a crack shot and a hard ass." Clay smiles at this. Bennett comes over and slides some eggs onto his plate.

"Can't leave Pop and he sure ain't a townie. Won't leave the homestead. Right, Pop?"

The old man says nothing, but continues to stare at my baby brother. I picture punching this frail, old man in the face. It sounds cruel, but his creepy cataract-filled eyes keep tracking Ethan as he strokes the dog or twirls the rusty butter knife found on the kitchen table.

Clay picks up his fork. "Well, we 'ppreciate the hospitality. Won't bother you long. We need some fuel and water, which we'll pay for. Maybe a little shut-eye?"

Bennett sits next to Pop, hunches over the plate and shovels big scoops of yellow into this mouth. Between bites he says, "I can bunk with Pop and you can have my room. Be happy to have ya. Right, Pop?" Pop doesn't answer.

I nearly choke on my eggs when I finally grasp what Bennett is saying. I'll have to share a room with Clay and Ethan. This cannot happen. Clay might notice something fishy when I sleep in my coat and jeans. I try to think of a solution while a fly rubs his feet together on my fork. It's going to be a long day.

After breakfast, we spend hours helping Bennett do his chores. He limps around, showing us what to do. His left leg is pretty well useless, but somehow he works through it, tending his straggly garden, hauling bails of hay, cleaning out his horse stable of the skinniest horse I've ever seen. Clay, meanwhile, tosses heavy bags of feed and slings a shovel like he's been doing it all his life. When he takes off his shirt in the barn and shows off his muscular chest, my cheeks grow hot. I keep my eyes on my pitchfork.

As I'm spreading hay into the horse stall, Clay saunters over to Ethan, who's sprinkling chicken feed in the coop. Clay's hand casually rubs my brother's mop of hair. They could be brothers with their dark hair and easy smiles. Ethan turns his on Clay now, a smile normally reserved for me. I feel a pain beneath in my ribs. I skewer an innocent bail of hay with my pitchfork to stifle the feeling.

Working in ninety-degree weather in a coat and jeans has me so hot black blobs dance in my vision. With the fresh hay spread, I need a break. I walk over to the shade of the chicken coop where Ethan has sought out shade. He sits cross-legged behind the coop with a chicken on his lap. He's stroking the thing like a dog. I shoo away the skinny bird. She scuttles off, throwing up feathers and squawking at me.

"These chickens look sickly. Don't touch them." I feel bad for my crankiness. Is it the heat and or my burning jealousy?

"They're nice," he says. Then his eyes slide to the slanted shadow on the porch. "Riley," he whispers, "that old man keeps staring at me."

I follow his eyes to Bennett's father, who's leaning against the porch rail. Why is he so fixed on my brother? Ethan's a cute kid, sure. People sometimes marvel at his blue eyes or the way he asks a question that everyone's thinking. But this old man's not watching him with wonder or fascination. He tracks him like a hawk tracks a rabbit.

I squat down next to Ethan and whisper, "If you notice anything, if you even get a strange feeling, we're out of here. I don't care how much Clay trusts Bennett. We can find Mama without him."

Ethan nods and lets his fingers stroke a passing hen before he remembers my scolding. "Gives me the creeps, Riley. That's all."

"Me, too," I say. "Me, too."

When the sun sags low in the west, we call it a day. It's been over a week since I've done a full day's chores and my muscles ache. I'm sweaty and gross under my heavy coat, but there's no bath in sight. It doesn't matter. No one here would notice body odor over the thick smell of waste and decay inside the house.

Bennett sets out crusts of bread and muddy water and then limps to bed. Even with help, the farm work has wrung him out. A wave of pity washes over me. Their life is punishingly hard and working their fingers to the bone might not be enough. Somehow Arn made life on our farm manageable. The image flashes into my head of Arn's lean figure standing on the porch after a long day's labor flashes into my head. The sadness sticks in my throat. I swallow it down with a gulp of cloudy water. I gag and set the glass down. The water's vile, a taste between wet shoe and rusty pipe. How did Ethan gulp down so much when he came in earlier? It probably made him sick. That's why he's already in bed.

Clay slumps into a chair next to me. The hairs on my arms start to tingle and I realize this is the first time we've been alone together. *Stop it.* I focus on trying to identify the lumpy brown mush smeared on the tabletop.

He gulps his water, makes a face and then looks at me. He points to the coat. "You wore that thing all day? Jesus. Bet you're dying under there. You can take it off. Ben doesn't care you're a bender."

I shake my head. "Just like wearing it."

"It was a hundred degrees today. You gotta be soaked." He takes another gulp of water. "Aw, hell, that's nasty." He sets the water glass down with a *thunk*. "Taste like horse piss."

I look down at my water and watch the brown flecks swirl in the glass. I should get more fluids after how much I sweat, but I can't bring myself to gag back any more. Maybe I'll sneak out to the Jeep and drink some of the water there.

Clay pushes some junk out of the way and rests his elbows on the tabletop. His arm sits inches from mine. I can feel the heat of his skin, smell his musky male scent. Despite all my scolding, my body is responding to his presence in ways I haven't felt before. My cheeks flush. My heart pounds.

Clay looks at me and our eyes meet. How are his eyes so blue? "It's okay, you know," he says. "Bennett's a friend. And 'sides, I wouldn't let them hurt you."

I'm flustered and nervous and I want him closer to me. And ... no. I got to do anything but feel how I'm feeling toward Clay right now. I curl my fingers into my palms until my nails bite into the soft flesh there. "I can take care of myself," I say a little colder than I intended.

Clay arches back on his chair, the smile dropping from his face. "I know, tough guy." He looks as though he'll speak to me again, but a wave of fatigue settles on his face. Rubbing his eyes, he scrapes out of his chair. "I'm going to bed. Don't wake me when you come in."

Clay stumbles into the spare room. In his wake, I feel cold and alone. The orange light drains out of the room. Only the hound sits with me the twilight and he's snoring under the table. I stare at Clay's water glass, the dirt smudges from his broad hands around the base. He must have calluses sprouting on his smooth palms, and if I'm aching with chores, what must a townie kid be feeling? Not once did he complain. He acted like there was nothing he'd rather do than help Bennett. Then there's me, the world's most awkward girl. It doesn't matter that I have to keep my gender a secret. Even if I could tell, no one would line up for the job of dealing with my mess for the rest of his life.

I put my head in my hands, but command the tears to stay where they are. No sense in crying. Pushing Clay away is for the best. The less I get attached, the easier it will be to sever ties once we find my mama. After that we'll have to go our own ways. Naturally.

A stupor falls over me. My eyelids droop and the air thickens. It's time to stop torturing myself and go to bed. I shuffle to Bennett's bedroom. Ethan is curled into a ball on the mildewed mattress in the corner. Clay lies on the floor, his mouth open, sawing logs. I slink in, climb on the mattress and wedge myself between Ethan and the wall. His slight wheezing and the fatigue in my limbs knock me out before I can punish myself again.

***

Something's moving in my room.

I try to open my eyes, but my lids feel weighted with sandbags. Fatigue pulls me under, but I fight. Something or someone's here. I can feel it. I force my eyes open and blink into the dark. At first, there's nothing. Then a shadow slinks along the wall.

Ethan or Clay? Too big for Ethan, so it must be Clay. Before my lids slip closed, the figure steps into the square of moonlight cutting through the window. It's Bennett. What's he doing in our room?

Sitting up, I startle him. He whips his head in my direction. "He's awake," he whispers, pointing.

Rough hands grab my wrists. They're wrenched behind my back.

"Hey!" I shout, groggily. "Stop!"

Scratchy twine pinches my wrists as my hands are bound. What's happening?

"Let me go!" I arch up from the bed. Someone slams his body against mine. My face hits the mattress as hands grip my shoulders. The old man uses his body weight to hold me down. I struggle to breathe as terror grips me.

Bennett leans down until his face is a foot away. I fight to keep my eyes open, though the fatigue is heavy. Why is it so hard to wake up? The muddy water, the foreign taste. Those bastards drugged us.

"Get off!" I yell, though it's muffled as the old man presses me into the mildewed mattress.

"Knock this 'un out again, Ben," the old man grumbles.

Bennett shakes his head. "Used up the last of the tranquilizer. Don't matter, though. We're all set." Bennett heaves something onto his back—Ethan, drugged and hog-tied.

"You sonovabitch, put him down!" I scream.

I throw myself upward and buck off the old man, who crashes into the wall, sending plaster dust raining down. I try to stand, but the tranquilizers are too strong. My mind's forgotten how to control my legs. I topple to the floor.

"Goddamn, Pop, hold him down!" Bennett sets Ethan on the floor and grabs hold of my legs just as I get them working. Rolling to my side, I kick out and land a blow to his ribs. He buckles, but recovers fast. He snags my pants and wraps both arms around my legs. I flop against him like a fish.

"Pop, get up and hold this bastard! Jesus! He's gonna wake Clay."

"Just kill 'im," the old man shouts.

Bennett clutches my legs to his chest. Unable to find more twine, he wraps the blanket around them and pins them down. I growl. I spit. I fight against my bonds, but they're knotted tight. The panic settles on me like a lead blanket. They're going to kill us?

Bennett hefts my brother's limp body onto his shoulder. The old man tries to lift me, but I squirm so much he can't get a good hold. He looks at the unconscious Clay instead. "What 'bout your townie?" he asks.

Bennett looks back at Clay's motionless form on the floor. "I told you, Clay stays here. He don't need no part in this. Once we get our money, we're gone."

My eyes trace Clay's body, begging him to wake up. "Clay'll find us," I say, my voice breaking. I won't cry, though. I bite my cheek until I can taste blood. "He'll kill you."

Bennett looks down at me as if surprised I'm still here. "We'll have our dough and be half way to Jacksonville by the time those tranqs wear off. He can tackle the Riders if you're really the treasure ya think ya are."

"The Riders?" I ask, afraid for the answer.

Bennett nods. "Riders pay decent money for benders, but better for boys. That sweet-faced brother of your'n out to fetch us a nice price."

I tuck my head into the dirty mattress as tears well up. I've heard of gangs like the Riders. They buy boys and use them for … disgusting things. I glance at Ethan's fragile frame and then back up at Bennett, hoping see a glimmer of human compassion behind his eyes. Bennett's eyes are like dry pebbles. He won't look at me.

"Why're you doing this?" A sob wavers at the back of my throat.

"Money's all. Gotta get out of this God-forsaken hole." Bennett takes a dirty bandanna from his pocket and brings it over to my face. "Shut up, now." He gags me and slips a burlap sack over my head.

I let the tears come. They soak into the rough burlap pressed against my cheeks. Bennett lifts me. I struggle, but his farmer's hands are strong. He limps outside, his uneven gate rocking me back and forth. Then he tosses me onto a hard surface. I shift around until I get the feel of it with my arms and back. It's the trunk of our Jeep. A few moments later, a body slides in next to mine. Ethan. I curl myself around him as Bennett closes us in and the engine flares to life. We bump down the road, toward unknown horrors and all I can do is close my eyes.

***

Shards of light press at my eyelids. I moan, blink and squint into the brightness. A shadow slides in and blocks out the sun. My eyes adjust and find Bennett's hooked nose, sunken cheeks and pocked skin. I search his face for compassion and find none.

During the night, the gag has worked its way out of my mouth. My tongue tastes like sweaty sock, but I'm able to speak again. "If you let us go," I croak, "I'll give you all our supplies."

Bennett shrugs. "Already got those."

He grabs my lapels and hauls me to a sitting position. From the back of the Jeep, I can see we're parked on the shoulder at the crossroads of two well-driven highways. There's nothing in sight but hard pan, scrub brush and a few buttes off in the distance. A vulture circles around a blazing noon sun. I've been out for hours. We could be anywhere.

Bennett's my only hope. I think of Ethan and a pathetic quality seeps into my voice. "You can't do this. Do you know what they'll do to us?"

Bennett doesn't meet my gaze. He offers a plastic jug of muddy water.

I shake my head, thinking of the tranquilizers.

"It's clean," he says and he takes a swig. A large gulp spills out of the corners of his mouth and into his dirty hair. He flings the water off with a shake of his head. He offers the jug back to me.

It's hardly clean, but must not be drugged. I'm so thirsty I can't turn it down. Bennett pours the musty water in my mouth. It washes away some of the stickiness in my throat, but leaves a foul aftertaste.

He starts to walk away.

"Bennett, let the boy go. Just him. He's too young for this."

Bennett glances at Ethan, still unconscious on the bed of the Jeep beside me. "He's worth double what you are." Then he walks around the Jeep and out of my view.

If only he knew what I was worth. Then it hits me.

"Bennett," I shout as he's walking away. I can't think about what I'm about to do or I might not do it. "I'm a girl."

The silence around the Jeep presses down on me until I can't breathe. What have I done? It doesn't matter. If it will save Ethan, nothing else matters.

He stops dead in his tracks. Then he swivels on his heel and marches back.

I'm trembling a little when he steps up and peers at my face. I bite my lip and let him look.

"Prove it," he says slowly. The old man wanders up behind him, glaring at me with beady eyes. They both stare at me like I'm some sort of new, exotic monster.

"I'll prove it. Just let him go," I say, a lump forming in my throat.

Bennett reaches for me and I flinch. He runs a hand over my damp shirt. My stomach lurches at his touch. I want to bite at the hand that runs over my chest. Instead I close my eyes and wait for it to be over.

"Breasts," he says as he fondles mine. I see his face turn up in sick glee.

He's reaching in to pull off my shirt when his father elbows him and points to the horizon.

A dust cloud boils up over a dry hill. The Riders, whoever they are, will be here in minutes. And I've just told my captors my secret.

Bennett runs around to the front of the Jeep and pulls out his gun.

I struggle forward, the ropes on my wrists digging roughly into my skin. "Let the boy go! All you need is me. Let him go!"

Bennett never looks at me. His face is lit with joy like discovering a wad of silver buried in his back yard. I've made a mistake. He won't free Ethan. He'll make a fortune off both of us. And I'm running out of time. I scoot over to Ethan and nudge him with my foot. "Wake up! Ethan, get up!" He moans, but I can't wake him.

I tug on the cord at my wrist. It's tight, but if I have time to work on it, I could probably wiggle it loose. I pull until my skin's raw, but I'm nowhere close to free.

Then a truck, welded together from pieces of others, chugs toward us. In its wake are two skinny tan horses, with a rider each. I count my adversaries—two in the cab, two on horseback. Four men. Even with free hands, my odds aren't good against four armed men. I work on the twine at my wrists as the men jump out, slam doors, or sling their legs over their horses.

The Riders are the strangest group of men I've ever seen. They're clad in animal-hide loincloths and shapeless moccasins. They have dark brown braids adorned with feathers or with bones coiling down their backs. Their arms, chests and faces are streaked with stripes of ashy gray, brown and dried blood in alternating patterns. A phrase flashes through my head—war paint—though I've no idea where it came from. The two on horseback could be twins, though one's taller than the other. One Rider, emerging from the truck, has a thin bone—a coyote rib perhaps—shoved through his nostrils. Another wears a necklace of white squares. The closer he strides, the more sure I am they're human teeth.

In contrast to their basic dress, they could be an armory ad. The squat leader with a small belly sagging over his loincloth has an antique shotgun slung over his bare back. The second man, with a network of slashing scars running the length of his chest, carries a bulky semi-automatic rifle in his bear-like hands. I haven't seen one of those in a long time. The twins each hold wooden spears.

They're men gone wild. One of the primitive cultures that slunk off into the desert and stayed there with their sick religions and rituals. Some believe in human sacrifice, but not before raping and torturing their victims as much as they like. My eyes trace over the fine points of their spears, the necklace of teeth that are too small to be adult. I pull furiously at my bonds until my skin shreds.

The Riders approach warily, sniffing the air, heads cocked, like a pack of animals ready to attack at any sudden movement. I half expect them to curl their lips up and growl. The leader lets his eyes slip over Ethan and I. Luckily my chest is still covered.

"I've got a girl," Bennett says, nearly jumping up and down with glee.

Every eye turns to me. I try to shrink into my surroundings and focus on freeing my hands. My wrists are raw now, bleeding.

The leader sniffs toward me, as if he could pick up my scent. He turns to Bennett, his voice rolling out slowly, like he hasn't used it in a while. "The Good Mother frowns on lies." He glares at Bennett. His eyes trace over the delicate face of my baby brother. His lips curl up. "We'll take the boy." He waves his hand dismissively at me. "Bender, you keep. Bender's pleas do not appease the Good Mother."

What does he mean appease the Good Mother? Is that their god? The leader walks up to my brother and lifts up his sleeping head. "Yes," he moans in pleasure, his brown body rocking against the Jeep. "This one's cries will wake Good Mother to our troubles. She will bless us."

His cries? This is not happening. I want that man's soiled hands off my brother. I got to get my hands free. Got to.

"I ain't kidding." Bennett says, a frenzied look creeping up in his eyes. He points at me. "See for yourself."

The leader draws back his hand from where it cupped Ethan's face. He looks as if he'll scold Bennett again, but he turns slowly. Three lines of ash mar each cheek, and a pink scar slashes through his upper lip, a sore festering in the corner of his mouth.

My heartbeat picks up at every step he takes. The others come now too, crowding behind their leader, leering with brown, cracked teeth, their painted faces. Behind me the rope around my hands twangs loose a notch. It'll be wide enough to pull free any minute. The leader's rifle hangs loosely on his back like a child's forgotten toy. If he's got ammo in that gun, I might have a chance.

The leader leans in until I can smell the animal fat in his greasy, black braid. His calloused fingers reach for me and I cringe. He grips my chin and wrenches my head from side to side. If my mouth weren't so dry, I'd spit on him. I grit my teeth and keep working on the twine.

"No benders," he says to Bennett.

"She's got breasts," Bennett says.

The leader pokes at the sore on his mouth with his tongue as he looks me over again. He grabs my shirt and pulls me to him.

"A woman would make the Good Mother pleased," he says, nodding. "Oh yes. Very pleased indeed."

My heart is thrumming in my chest. I can smell excitement on him like a thick musk. He tugs up my shirt, revealing the dirty cotton binding on my breasts. His fingers trace my skin. His panting pulses against my neck. The sick longing on his face is unmistakable.

My right wrist slips out of the twine. I'm free! I wait as the leader leans toward me, his fingers reaching for the cotton binding on my chest. I force myself to look away from the Rider's spit-flecked tongue that circles his dark red lips. *The shotgun*, I think. *In a minute it'll be mine.*

He flicks out a small knife of whittled bone and slips it under the binding on my breasts. I feel the coolness of the blade against my stomach. I turn my eyes skyward and wait to be exposed. The bottom of the bandage frays against the blade. I close my eyes.

A gun blast crashes through the desert.

As if in slow motion, a bullet removes half of the leader's head.

CHAPTER ELEVEN

Warm blood splatters my face. The leader's hair blows up as part of his scalp curls over his forehead. Blood spurts like a fountain, drenching his hair, his neck, pattering on the Jeep. And the grayish clumps that can only be … I squeeze my eyes shut. The leader falls like a sack of cement, sending a cloud of dust up around his twitching body. I stare at the blood that pours into the dirt.

The place breaks into chaos.

The horses bolt into the distance, kicking up dust. Three Riders swivel and draw weapons. The semi-automatic rifle strung across Bear Paws's shoulders gets tossed to the dirt as he lunges for his leader's rifle. Just as I thought, no bullets. I might have a chance to grab a gun with everyone's eyes on the horizon, but that would mean coming out of cover. I can't do that until I know who's shooting.

The landscape falls deadly silent as we wait. From where I lay in the Jeep trunk, I can see boulders, shrubs, and buttes off in the distance. Who is shooting? We wait, barely breathing.

Someone begins shuffling quietly through the dirt. We turn to see Bennett and his father backing up. If they wanted to make a quiet break for it, they're too late.

"The Good Mother will destroy those that harm her people," Bear Paws says in a low rumbling voice. Bennett raises his hands and starts to explain while his pop pulls his rifle around. Bear Paws is faster on the draw. He aims his antique rifle.

A gun explodes. I throw myself to the Jeep floor. Bullets ping the side of the Jeep and rattle over us. I curl myself around Ethan until the firing stops. There's a watery moan. Then silence.

I raise my head until I can see the bodies. Bennett and his father lie on the ground. The dust beneath them puddles with blood. Before I can process this, I catch movement out of the corner of my eye. I swivel toward it and see our unknown shooter. Clay, his cowboy hat tucked so low that his face is all shadow, pads toward us. The silver revolvers in his hands glint in the sun. His face is a mask of deadly calm.

I've never been so happy to see him.

He steps into the clearing between the vehicles, completely uncovered. What is he doing? They'll see him and he got nowhere to hide. The Riders are busy turning out Bennett's pockets, but they'll look up soon enough. Clay doesn't wait for them to turn. He calls out.

"Heard you slimy bastards like making boys cry." He thumbs down his safeties with a decisive click. "Let's see how you like me."

Three Riders snap around, raising their weapons, but their movements are slow like they were moving underwater. Clay fires so fast, his hands are a silver blur. The dual shots crack through the canyon like twin smacks of a bullwhip.

A bullet sinks into the taller twin's neck with a thud. He lurches back, eyes wide. He gurgles, clutches his throat and falls to his knees. His clawing hands can't stop the blood pouring through his fingers, splattering the side of our Jeep, coating his chest. He falls into the sand, in a red, muddy puddle.

So much blood. My breathing hitches and my hands tremble. But Clay's here. For a moment, I think it'll be all right. Then Bear Paws raises his rifle to his shoulder and fires at Clay.

Everything seems to happen at the same time. My hands fly up to my mouth to stifle the scream. The bullet zings toward Clay, who snaps toward the sound, his eyes narrow, his revolvers gleaming. The sleeve of Clay's shirt ripples as the bullet zips past, fraying the fabric. Clay dives toward an outcropping of rock and disappears behind it. Bear Paws drops behind our Jeep and issues a sting of foreign curse words below me. One of the twins gurgles his dying breath. Then silence descends, heavy like a blanket.

The only sound is my hot breath in and out in quick succession. No one moves. One of the Riders, the smaller twin perhaps, whines below. I slip a quick peek over the side of the Jeep and peer down on my enemies. Bear Paws hunches against a tire, his rifle clutched to his chest. He blinks sweat out of his eyes. His tongue darts out and licks at his lip in nervous pulses. The smaller twin sponges clots of blood off his dead brother's neck with part of his loincloth. He begins praying in a language I can't understand. No one pays me any mind.

Clay's crouched behind the boulder, still and silent. Why doesn't he shoot? Maybe he's worried he'll hit us. Or maybe he only had two bullets.

Bear Paws takes a deep breath, heaves up and aims, squinting with one eye over the stock. The gun cracks. Clay's rock cover explodes, sending pebbles and dust in all directions. No response from Clay. Bear Paws drops back down and reloads.

Silence. A crow caws from the ridge. Why won't Clay fire?

Someone's shuffling around at the base of the Jeep. My eyes flick to the ground where the smaller twin crawls forward on his hands and knees. Something in his hands glints in the sun— truck keys. His eyes flick between Clay's rock cover and the truck. He's going to run. I'm elated, but then it dawns on me—he knows my secret. If he leaves now, he'll just be back with more guns and ammo.

With one more glance to his dead brother, he scrambles up and sprints to the truck. He throws his arms over his head like that one gesture will keep him from being shot up. I can't let him escape, but I can't run into the open without catching a bullet in the back.

Bear Paws yells after him. "Juto, you bastard! Get back here." But Juto isn't stopping. He'll soon be kicking up dust as he peels away.

I can't think. I just act. I hurtle over the Jeep tailgate and jump into the dust. Bear Paws sees me and levels his gun in my direction. I scramble, choking on the dust I kick up. Behind me, a gun fires. I wait for the bullet that will punch through my guts, but nothing. Patting my body for holes, I look back over my shoulder.

It wasn't Bear Paws's rifle that went off. He clutches his shoulder, his mouth dropped open in surprise as blood blossoms under his hand. Clay stands behind his rock, smoke curling from the barrel of his gun. There's a devilish gleam in his eye.

Bear Paws shrieks and shakes a fist at Clay. "You will be punished! No one harms the Mother's children!" He drops down behind the Jeep again.

Twenty yards away the truck starts up with a grumble. I got to go.

I run up to the rust-eaten truck with no back windshield and mismatched panels welded together in lopsided squares. Juto sits on the cracked leather driver's seat, looking small and out of place in his blood-splattered loincloth and smeared body paint. He's swearing at the gearshift he grinds into first. The truck sputters and jumps forward. He doesn't see me.

You have no weapon and this man has at least thirty pounds on you! It's too late for plans. I yank the door open and stare up into Juto's very surprised face.

"Wha—"

I grab his arm and drag him out.

Without time to brace himself, Juto tumbles out of the cab. I slide over as he falls with an *oomph* into the dust. The truck lurches forward. I climb into the driver's seat and slam the door. It's warped and won't close properly.

Hands claw at my door. "Let me in, you dirty bitch," Juto says, pulling at me through the open window.

I fight off his fingers and reach for the button to roll the window up, but it's long gone. Juto leans through the open window, his dirt-flecked upper lip curling in rage. His fingers dig into the collar of my shirt and drag me toward him. I claw his face, racking my nails through the paint on his cheek. Lines of blood bubble up where I've scratched him. He shrieks, high-pitched and feminine, and pulls away. The truck keeps bounces forward on its own while I dig around the cab for a weapon.

Juto yanks the door open with a loud screech. He'll drag me out and kill me. My hands scramble over the dash, into the glove compartment. Nothing. His hand cinches over my bicep hard enough to bring a cry of pain to my lips.

"I'm going to take what you did to my face out on your body. Good Mother will hear you howl and be much pleased." He grins. Some of his front teeth have been whittled into points. His eyes are feral black pools.

The truck chugs over a pothole and we bounce back and forth. Juto's grip on my arm loosens. He wobbles backward. This is my chance. I lean back and kick him squarely between the ribs. Juto claws the air as he falls out of the cab and into the dust with a thud. I jam my foot to the gas.

The trunk rocks wildly as if I've run over a boulder. But a boulder doesn't crunch like that. I step on the brake and lurch to a stop, my face banging into the steering wheel. Squinting in the rearview, I see the crumpled mess of blood and mangled bones. I've run him over. I slam the truck into park and jump out. I walk to my enemy, smelling blood and burnt rubber.

I've seen roadkill before, flattened rabbits, blown-apart coyotes, lizards that are sizzled lumps on the pavement, their eyes pools of jelly around their bloody mouths. It doesn't prepare me for this. Thick ropes of dark red blood pool out both sides of Juto's mouth and ears. His chest is a concave bowl and there's tire tread running the length of his stomach. A bloody rib angles through the war paint on his chest, stark white against the mess of red and brown. His hands clench and unclench once. Then they settle on the hard pan.

He's dead. I killed him.

My ears ring and my mouth tastes like blood. I killed a man. I look at the blood streaming from his ear and pooling under this neck. There's a dark stain on his loincloth. I killed him. I gotta look away. I can't stop looking.

Slowly, I remember the shootout behind me. Clay and Ethan. I run sloppily back, my brain feeling loose.

The Mexican standoff is still going on, neither shooter willing to break cover. Now the men are taunting each other.

"Infidels' howls will please the Good Mother," Bear Paws shouts from behind the Jeep. "Come, let me please her."

Clay's voice floats up from behind his rock. "Still so holy, you sick sonovabitch? I can shoot all day. Come try me." I want to believe him, but how many bullets can he have?

Bear Paws wipes his forearm across his brow and hugs the rifle to his chest. "I think I remember you, infidel. Didn't we buy a pretty pet from you a while back?"

There's a long pause. "No."

"Yes, yes." Bear Paws smiles wickedly. "Last month. You had the boy who wet himself—"

"Shut up!" Clay yells from behind the rock. "Shut your mouth!"

Bear Paws smiles vilely. "Good Mother was much pleased with him. His cries were long and loud. All the way to the end."

"I said," Clay shouts, standing, "SHUT UP!" He strides around the rock, lifting his revolvers.

I clutch my face. Is he crazy?

Bear Paws stands, fumbling to raise his rifle with his injured arm. He lunges for the hood of the Jeep to steady his shot. Clay strides forward, his face contorted in rage. Bear Paws squints one eye and curls his finger over the trigger.

"Clay!" My voice is drowned out by the sound of a rifle discharging.

The bullet wings out, the hot lead zipping close enough to ruffle Clay's collar. Clay doesn't flinch. He strides forward, his teeth bared.

Bear Paws's eyes widen. He scrambles to reload, his right hand useless and blood-crusted. Clay runs the last few steps and springs around the Jeep. Bear Paws slips a bullet in the chamber, but Clay kicks the rifle away. It whirls end over end into the dust. He tackles Bear Paws. They roll, a tangle of arms and legs and grunts and I can't see what's happening. I run over. Can I help?

Bear Paws throws a few wild punches that do nothing to stop Clay. He grabs Bear Paws by the shoulders, hefts him up and throws him against our Jeep. There's a loud *thunk* and the Jeep rocks back and forth. Bear Paws slides weakly to the ground with a moan.

Clay straddles the crumpled man, his lean shadow trailing out behind. He presses the muzzle of his revolver to the Rider's forehead.

"Don't! Don't!" Bear Paws throws up his shaking palms. "I say sorry. You can have whatever you want."

"Not enough," Clay growls. His eyebrows angle down dangerously. "No goddamn Mother to hear your cries today. You're going straight to hell. And I'm the one to send you there." He thumbs down the safety on his gun with a sharp click.

Bear Paws clutches his hands together beneath his throat and looks up at Clay with wet eyes. He begins to mutter a prayer.

Clay's lip curls back from sharp white teeth. "How dare you pray after what you done." He narrows his eyes. "This is for Kody."

When the gunshot crackles over the desert, I close my eyes. When I open them, there's nothing but the Jeep and Clay and a bloody mess of bodies on either side of the dusty crossroads. It's over.

Somehow I make it back to the Jeep, though my head's thrumming like an engine and everything's doubling in my vision. I walk past Bennett and his father. Both lie in muddy red pools. Their lifeless faces stare up at the sky. I can't look. I keep my watering eyes on the Jeep. Ethan's in there. I gotta get back to him.

Clay stands above the Rider, a bloody mess against the side of our Jeep. I don't look. I can't take any more blood. I climb back in the Jeep next to Ethan (who's completely undisturbed, thank God or the Good Mother or whoever) and tuck my head in my arms. The urge to throw up returns. I breathe through my nose and try to sort through what just happened.

Clay was amazing. And scary. The way he dispatched Bear Paws ... I'd hate to have that directed at me. And who is Kody?

When I look up, Clay stands at the edge of the tailgate. His face is pale and distant. His voice rolls out of his throat as if he were just coming out of a dream. "The little man? He alright?" His hat's down low over his face so that his features are covered in shadow again, but his hands tremble slightly as he rubs a revolver on his shirt and tucks it in the holster.

I put my hand on Ethan's chest. "He's still out."

He tucks both guns into their holsters. He looks at me, his face tight. "You okay? You look really pale."

I nod, though I feel anything but okay. "All in one piece." I look up at him and note the tremble of his hands, the paleness of his cheeks. "What was that back there? The Rider said something about—"

"Nothing," he says sharply. Then his tone softens. "He's a lying, thieving sonovabitch, but he won't hurt anyone again."

I bite my lip. I don't believe that was nothing.

Clay's eyes stray to Bennett and his father. He walks over, crouches and lays two fingers on their necks. Each time he shakes his head sadly. Despite all they've put us through, he's sad they're dead. I can't feel sad. They would've sold us into torture and death.

Clay frowns, his hand on Bennett's arm. "We have to bury them." He stands up and brushes the dust off his pants. "He was my friend."

"Your friend kidnapped us and almost killed us." Yet, I think of Arn drug out for the coyotes. It's no way to go, even for someone as low as Bennett. I scoot to the edge of the Jeep and stand. My legs tremble, but I steady them. "Let's get this over with."

Clay nods, a ghost of a smile on his lips. It fades as he picks up his lifeless friend.

We move Bennett and his father into a little rock crevasse. Clay slides loose rocks over the opening to discourage scavengers and then lingers around the bodies for a while. I head back to the Jeep to see if Ethan's awake. Walking past the man I killed makes my legs go to jelly. The blood pool has seeped into the dirt, but as I walk past, his moccasin gives a twitch. I jump in the Jeep and focus on keeping food in my stomach.

Clay leans against the Jeep tailgate. His face is ashen and slack. When he spots my brother, he frowns. "Why's he still out?" It's his turn to put his hand on Ethan's chest.

I shrug. "His breathing's regular. His pulse is fine. I think he got a heavy dose of those damn tranqs."

"Didn't we all? Goddamn that Bennett."

"Yeah," I say, clutching my knees. "How'd you find us, anyway? Last I saw, you were face down on the rug."

Clay leans against the side of the Jeep. He track a vulture that's already circling. "When I came to and you were gone, I had a pretty good idea of what happened. I followed your tracks for a while. When those disappeared, I took a chance that they'd be trading to the Riders. It's a pretty regular post."

My eyes narrow. "Wait a minute. You've traded with the Riders?"

Clay turns his eyes to the rise of buttes in the north. The pain's written on his face.

Now I remember all the reasons not to trust Clay.

Around us the sounds of dusk start up, the shrill insects, a howl of a predator, filling in the gaps created by our awkward silence.

Clay breaks it. "Your brother looks a lot like mine."

My eyes trace the line of Ethan's mouth as it moves in his sleep. "You left your brother behind?"

"Nope," he says, throwing a rifle over his shoulder and turning toward the ridge. "He died."

CHAPTER TWELVE

Night falls. Ethan won't wake. The worry sits on me like a soaked comforter. I spend the time while Clay's gone checking Ethan's pulse over and over.

When the moon's big and yellow in the sky, Clay returns with a musk hog, dead and dangling over his shoulder. He drops it with a thump into the dirt and sets the rifle in the passenger seat.

"Where'd you get the pig?" I ask, sliding forward on the tailgate, the metal ridges pushing into my knees.

Clay shrugs. "Found him rooting along the ridge. When I've got the bullets, hunting's as easy as picking food off the ground." He flicks out his hunting knife and begins to butcher the hog. He deftly slices the blade up the pig's belly, releasing a mess of blood and guts. I wrinkle my nose at the warm, wet smell of animal innards.

I slip out of the Jeep and stand over him, watching. "That's what I don't get. How come you're such a crack shot and those Riders weren't worth a damn? They didn't stand a chance."

Clay's making quick work of the pig. He strips the skin and sets to work on the haunches.

He keeps his eyes on the hog as he talks. "Road gangs are all the same. Big on guns. Short on one little thing." Clay pauses and squints up at me. "Bullets. These gangs don't got a handful of lead between 'em. Even if they get a shipment, they've never had enough to practice with. Couldn't hit the broad side of a barn."

He saws through more of the musk hog, his hands smeared red. He wipes them on a cloth and squints out at the last strip of light in the west. "My pa kept us eye-deep in lead. Said he rather go short on whiskey than ammo. And my pa loves whiskey." He pauses, wipes his forehead with his shirt sleeve. "Pa used to take me out and we'd shoot all day. Wouldn't let me quit till I could hit a bottle at 300 yards." His face tightens. Then he stands, wipes his hands and pops the kinks out of his back. He digs through his pack and hands me a flint. "Start the fire, will ya? Can't burn her long, but I won't eat raw hog."

I set off to gather scrub brush and branches. It's a good excuse to mull over everything he said. As I pick up the scrub, I think about Clay's father-son target practice sessions. Did the Sheriff smile and pat his son on the back when he blew a bottle into little glass shards, or did he backhand him when he missed? Somehow I can't imagine them smiling, sharing a flask of homemade whiskey and whistling on the way home.

Above the ridge, the moon highlights the rocky peaks against deep valleys of shadow. The coyotes howl mournfully in the distance. It's been a while since I've spent a night in the desert. I've forgotten how cold it gets when the sun goes down. I gather my armload of prickly shrubs and hurry back to where Clay's set up camp. The stars begin to spread out before us, pinpricks of light in the dark blanket of sky.

Once the fire's going, we set to work building a spit and setting the meat over it. Clay and I sit before the budding fire and warm our scraped and numb hands. I shoot a glance at Clay. He's abnormally quiet and fidgety. The flickering glow highlights his cheeks a ruddy orange. His look is distant, his eyes wrinkled at the corners as if he's still pondering all he left behind.

Now's my chance to unravel some of this boy's mystery. I take a deep breath and try to sound causal. "What was town life like?"

Clay eyes follow the dancing tongues of flame. "Easy most days. Hard on others."

"What'd you mean?" I run my hands over my arms and watch the fire burn up my scrub brush. The smaller twigs pop and bend as the flames consume them.

He leans back against a rock, his hands laced behind his head. "Being the Sheriff's brat made life easy as pie. We had fresh meat, books, toys— a lady to housekeep. I had my own bike, a red ten-speed with a bell. I'd pop wheelies and tool around town all day on that puppy." He smiles. Then his face darkens.

"Then I turned thirteen and my pa said it was time to man up. Taught me the trade." He says trade like it's a dirty word.

"What'd you have to do?"

Clay glances at me, his brow creasing. "Pa took me on raids. Had me sit in the car when he did business with the Riders and other gangs. At first I thought it was exciting, you know, fun to travel around, watch my pa do business. People talked to him like he was the Almighty. They'd give me gifts. One man made his boy give me his lunch. I'll never forget the look on that kid's face when he handed over the sack. Looking back, he probably hadn't eaten in days." Clay turns his eyes to the moon, his frown deepening.

"What then?" I ask, picking up a stick to poke the fire.

Clay sighs, big and heavy. "Well, then I turned fourteen, my brother died. After that, my dad didn't just want me to do ride-alongs anymore. He gave my shootin' irons," he says, caressing the silver revolver slung on his hip with the pads of two fingers. "Made me get my hands dirty." He looks down at his palms. Then he clasps them together so tightly the knuckles whiten. I flick my eyes away as he looks over at me.

"What you want to know all this for?" he asks, throwing more scrub on the fire. "You know what they say about the curious cat."

I blush and shrug. "Just wondering what goes on under that ten-gallon hat of yours."

He throws more wood on the fire until the flames soar and the heat cooks my shins. "I know what you're thinking," he says. "I shoulda lit out. It took me too damn long, but I done it, so you don't need to judge."

I look down at the holes in the knees of my jeans and pick at some of the loose strings. "I'm not." There's one more question burning at the back of my brain. Should I ask? I squeeze my hands at my sides. "Who's Kody?"

He shoots me a glance that chills my insides. He opens his mouth as if to speak. Then closes it, stands and stalks off.

I've broken the quiet moment. My eyes flick to the fire that's eaten up most of the scrub and sunk into a few guttering flames. The night air grips me. I hug myself and feel deeply alone again.

Movement. Clay's back, standing at the edge of the circle. He's breathing hard, as if he were running. His eyes are wild. He seems to have trouble getting the next words out. "I'll say this once and then I never want you to ask me again."

I nod.

He takes a deep breath and steels himself. "Last month my pa made me take a twelve-year-old boy to the Riders. The kid …" His jaw tightens. "The kid wet himself when I carried him to their truck." He looks into my face, his eyes shining with unshed tears. "He cried my name as they drove away."

"Kody," I whisper.

Clay sniffs and stares into the dancing blue and orange flames of the fire, the veins tight cords on his neck. "I'll see his face forever. Knowing what I did to him …" He curses and tugs at his hair angrily. Then he lifts his sorrowful face to me. "That day I swore I'd never trade another human being. That I'd get out."

I pull my knees up to my chest and think about Clay handing over the boy to the Riders. It's awful. Then again, if my dad was the Sheriff, would I have done any different? Having Arn's death on my hands is bad enough, but I didn't actually kill him. What must it be like for Clay to carry that kind of guilt around?

The raw emotion hangs over the fire like a cloud. For several moments we sit in silence as the fire dies down. The hog legs emit a delicious aroma, but right now I don't feel like eating.

Finally, Clay walks forward as if unstuck. Some of the wildness has fallen off him. "We need to eat," he says handing me my portion of meat.

I take it from him. My stomach grumbles at the smell. Maybe I can eat.

Clay kicks dirt over the fire until it sizzles. "Come on. We'll eat in the Jeep."

We slide into the Jeep, Clay in the driver's side, me in the passenger seat. Normally, I'd fuss. It's my Jeep. But, surprisingly, I don't mind. Maybe I'm starting to trust Clay. Maybe I'm grateful he's rescued us again. Either way, I'm looking over at Clay and smiling as he's carefully holding the hot meat with the pads of his fingers. I shouldn't trust this much. I'm worth enough for even a good man to lose his scruples. I pull the zipper on my coat all the way up to my throat.

I check on Ethan. He's tucked into the back of the Jeep, the blanket I curled around him still in the exact position I placed it. He better wake up tomorrow or we have real problems.

I'm thinking about Ethan when Clay's voice cuts through my thoughts. "Your turn."

"Huh?"

"You didn't think that back story was free, did ya?" He's smiling for the first time in a while. "Your turn to answer my questions." He takes a bite of his hog leg, the grease shining on his lips and chin.

I concentrate on not burning my fingers on my own leg, unable to meet his gaze.

"Let's see," he says. "Where to start? How about explaining your aunt to me. She seems … interesting."

"Auntie's wonderful," I say, a bit indignant. Then I think of her bashing the cupboard to capture the bat. "She's a bit off, but she loves us. She makes fantastic cornbread." I take a bite of the leg and the savory roasted meat fills my mouth. I don't realize I'm smiling until I wipe the corners of my mouth on the sleeve of my jacket. How long has it been since I've smiled like this?

"How'd you keep your ma a secret for so long?" Clay eyes trace a falling star streaking across the dark blue sky.

The smile drops from my face. This question is not one I want to answer. It touches too close to my secret.

"Oh, you know, traveling around a lot." My next bite is huge, filling my mouth.

"Had to be more than that," Clay says, watching me. "Breeders have spies everywhere. Had to be hard to keep her hid."

I turn my eyes to the stars and note the constellation Andromeda. My mother called her the chained lady. Where is my mother tonight?

"We did everything we could to keep her free. In the end it wasn't enough, was it?" Now it's my turn to slip my eyes away, the emotion welling up, choking me.

Clay's eyes linger somewhere in the stars. "I lost my ma, too."

"What happened to her?" I ask, shifting to face him.

He sighs, still looking up. "I was too young to remember, but my pa said the Breeders just came for her one day. Said if he didn't give her up, they'd kill the whole town. Guess they pack a lot of firepower, weapons we ain't even seen. So," he blows out his breath, "he gave her up. My pa don't get emotional, but sometimes I see him lookin' out and I know he's thinking about her, the only woman he ever cared about."

I nod and let the silence hang around us. We sit and look out at the stars and think of our mothers. Could they be together? The thought gives me a little comfort.

Clay turns to me, his face set in reassurance. "We'll get to your ma." His voice is so kind.

I nod. "Yours, too." There it is again, that warm feeling that floods me when he gives me that look—eyes sparkling, smile comforting. A burn runs up my cheeks.

I miss the first words Clay says as my thoughts spin. "Huh?"

"I said, what's it like being a bender?"

I scan Clay's face for malice, but he's just curious. I'm curious about benders, too, never having met one. I swallow hard. "People don't look at you the same. It's pretty … lonely."

Clay finishes his hog leg. He chucks the bone off in the distance. He scoots down in the driver seat, a revolver over his lap and stares sleepy-eyed over the moonlit landscape. "Good talk, but I'm tuckered. Can you take the first shift?"

He falls asleep within seconds, his hat down over his face, his revolvers hugged tight to his chest.

I let my eyes wander to the crescent moon hung in the sprinkle of stars. Alone with my thoughts again. I expect that they'll turn to Mom or Auntie, but they keep turning to Clay. The way his mouth turns up in his sleep. The moonlight in his brown hair. Before I know it, I'm watching the rise and fall of his chest. I turn my eyes to the road and try desperately not to think of the boy murmuring softly beside me.

CHAPTER THIRTEEN

I wake to a strange sweet smell, distant and musky. I nuzzle closer, my cheek rubbing against the warmth. It smells like home.

My eyes flicker open. My face rests on the soft suede of a worn leather jacket. It rises and falls rhythmically. My eyes fly wide open. My cheek rests on Clay's chest, my body pressed to his across the Jeep seat.

I snap upright, the panic skidding through me. What've I done? I was supposed to keep watch, not cuddle. My jerking wakes him and he blinks at me.

"Mornin'," he mumbles. He rolls over and goes back to gently snoring.

He doesn't know. Relief floods me as I slump back in my seat. I must've just fallen asleep and snuggled into him for warmth. *Yeah, right, warmth.*

With my heart pounding, there's no way I'll fall back to sleep. Looking back, I find Ethan in the same spot. I slip my hand under his nose and feel the soft puffs of breath against the pads of my fingers. Satisfied, my eyes travel over the first lights of dawn stretching out over the rocky landscape. I slide out of the Jeep and take off toward the pink horizon. I hike over the dusty ridges, trying to shake off my unease. I spot a large clump of cactus that will give enough cover as I empty my bladder. Up ahead a roadrunner skitters across the sand, his legs pumping into a blur as he darts over the hard pan. A lizard bolts under a rock as I approach. Dawn is a busy time in the desert. I need to be careful.

I drop my pants and duck down behind the bush. I try to keep my mind on the sounds of the desert, but it keeps turning elsewhere. Mostly back to the Jeep. My brother is still knocked out, and if Bennett weren't already dead, I'd think about killing him. What if Ethan doesn't wake up? I know Clay cares about Ethan, but what lengths would he go to save his life?

Then there's of Clay. God—Clay. I've developed a pretty severe crush on him. It's impossible not to. He's handsome, talented, kind and smart. The reasons not to like him are weighty, but I find myself coming up with excuses for his past. After all, he can't help how he was raised.

The real reason you shouldn't like him, the voice inside pipes up, *is he thinks you're a bender. That if you told him you were a girl, he'd turn you in faster than you can say "horrible scientific experiments."*

I want to tell myself to shut up, that he's not the type, but I can't. I'm worth a lifetime's salary. Even if he doesn't turn me in and actually wants to be with me, he'd have to devote the rest of his life to protecting me from, well, every other person in the world. It's a lot to ask.

I'm still contemplating all this when Clay calls my name. I snap upright and almost pee on my boots. I pull my pants around my waist and spin around, hoping Clay hasn't seen.

He's running to me at a full clip. My heart pounds again. Why is he sprinting? I run. "What?" I say, breathless. "What is it?"

A smile breaks over his face. Out of breath, he points to the Jeep. "Ethan. He's awake."

We run to the Jeep. In the butte's long shadow, the Jeep looks miniature and my brother looks even smaller in the passenger seat. When I scramble to the door, his face breaks into a huge smile. "Riley," he says, groggily. He wraps his arms around my neck.

My hands shake as I clutch him to my chest. "Don't ever scare me like that again," I whisper into this shoulder.

When I let him go, his eyes slide from me to Clay. The delight on his face rivals what he had for me. I'll have to take it. If I'm falling for Clay, I can't deny Ethan his big brother.

"Thanks, Clay." He turns to me. "He got you for me. I was worried you were gone."

"I told you I'd never leave. Are you okay? Hungry? We need to get you something to eat." I sound like my mother. I dig in the back for some food.

He holds up a hunk of bread. "Clay got it for me."

"Oh." I pull out a jug of water from the pack and hold it up. "How about some water?"

Ethan lifts the water jug sitting next to him with the other hand.

I keep smiling, but something's shifted inside of me. I turn away from the boys and busy myself with folding the blanket. It keeps me from snapping at Clay who's only trying to help. Maybe that's one thing not to like about Clay—he's too efficient. But if someone doesn't give me something to do soon, I'll go crazy.

***

By mid-afternoon, I wish I'd never longed for something to do. Clay's driving when the car slows. At first I think he's spotted road trash, but no. He glances at the fuel gauge, then back at me. "We're out of gas."

"Pull over and we'll fill it with the reserve can in the back." I glance back at Ethan who's busy counting abandoned cars. "How many so far?"

"Thirteen. Why are we stopping?" His bright eyes follow mine.

"Just out of gas," I say. "We have more."

"We do?" he asks.

"Yep."

"More than what was in here?" He holds up our reserve gas jug. He turns the red plastic jug toward me. It's empty. The large bullet hole at the bottom right corner took care of our gas. It must've been hit in the shooting. We're screwed. I look back to Clay.

"No gas?" he asks.

"No gas." Panic bells ring in my head. Stranded on the side of the road is bad. Not getting to my mama on time is worse.

Clay glides us to a stop and turns off the Jeep. For a moment we all sit on the side of the road without speaking. Ethan's the first to break the silence.

"What'll we do now, Clay?" he asks.

I'm already worked up about running out of gas and now he's asking Clay, not me, what to do. I can't take it anymore. I swear and I punch the Jeep's dash. All it accomplishes is a loud thud and some throbbing knuckles.

"Hey, relax," Clay says to me.

I want to tell him where he can shove his advice, but he's already turned to Ethan, giving him that reassuring smile. "Listen, bud, we're fine. There's a town about ten miles up. We'll just hike on up and crash in some beds for the night. In the morning, I'll catch a ride back and gas up the Jeep. Easy peasy Japanesey."

Yeah, right. Easy? He doesn't mention to my brother that three kids on the side of the road are open to any number of hazards—coyotes, snakes and road gangs to name a few. He doesn't mention that we're walking on desert blacktop in the heat of the day. That ten miles will feel like a hundred in this weather. Nope. He just keeps smiling at my little brother.

I don't smile. I concentrate on the throbbing in my knuckles and try not to hit anything else.

We throw the most important supplies in our packs. Water, of course. Then food. Then Clay packs bullets, antiseptic, the amber bottles with little white pills he brought to trade for gasoline and shelter for the night. He slings his rifle over his back. He hesitates for a moment and then hands me Bennett's father's rifle.

"Just don't shoot me in the back," he says with a crooked smile. He slips on his pack and helps Ethan with the lightest one. "Okay, bud, let's go. Bet we see some lizards if we keep our eyes pealed. First one to spot a scaly buggers gets this." He holds up a red and white peppermint wrapped in plastic for Ethan to see.

Ethan's eyes grow big. "I'm good at spotting lizards. Aren't I, Ri?"

"Yep, the best," I say, as I pull on my pack. I can't manage the enthusiasm he's looking for, but he doesn't seem to notice. He's beaming up at Clay. "Let's go. Sooner we start, the better."

We walk. The land here is flat, with dirt and scraggly cactus and bushes in either direction. The sun sears the top of my head and heat rolls in waves off the pavement's black surface. This must be what it's like inside a furnace. Even with several water breaks in the shade of some tall cactus, I'm dying. My leather jacket traps so much heat I'm sure to pass out. My breasts are still bound and my long-sleeved cotton shirt would mostly cover me to passersby. Yet, anyone up close might get suspicious. I glance at Clay and then, finally, shrug off Arn's jacket. It's too bulky to fit in our bulging packs. I smell the collar once for his scent. An image of him standing at the kitchen window, his hands in the pockets of his overalls floods me until I'm nearly choking with it. Arn. I fold his jacket and set it on a rock. When I leave it, I feel like I'm burying him all over again.

Clay and Ethan wait for me to catch up. Clay gives me a nod. "I know your pa's jacket meant a lot to ya, but it'll kill ya out here."

I glance back at it once more. It's just a brown lump in the distance now. I could run, pick it up, carry it until I collapse. "I shouldn't just leave it," I say more to myself than to Clay.

Clay looks back. "I'll snag it when I come back for the Jeep."

The grumpiness from the past dissolves. I offer him a look of gratitude. Good, solid Clay. I'd hug him if I weren't worried he'd feel my secret through my shirt.

Ethan and Clay spend the hours spotting lizards or pointing out vultures circling in the sky. Clay gives him a few lessons on the local flora and fauna. He teaches Ethan how to get the fruit from a prickly pear. I keep my eyes on the strip of highway beside us. Any dust cloud and we're running for cover.

After an hour of trekking through the heat of the day, Ethan's asthma kicks in. I try to carry him, but he waves me away, wheezing slightly with his purple lips. At the two-hour mark, he tumbles into the sand. I run up to him and roll him over. The fine sand crystals dot his flushed face. His cheeks blaze bright red on his pale face.

"Ethan, you alright?" I gasp.

He blinks at me. "I feel dizzy." He struggles to sit up.

I put a hand on his chest. "You need to drink. Just hold on." I pull his head onto my knees and use my body to shade his face. I hand him the water jug.

"Sip slowly," I say when he takes it.

Ethan drinks and rests for a moment. Then he sees Clay blocking out more of the sun.

"Sorry, Clay," he says, still wheezing.

"No problem, hoss. One time when I was your age, I got sunstroke, blacked out and pissed my pants. Try explaining that to your pa."

Ethan smiles, but at the mention of his dad, his face falls. He looks up at me. "I wish we were home, Riley," he whispers.

"I know." The emotion chokes in my throat. I push the sticky hair out of his eyes. He would normally bat my hand away if I did this in front of Clay, but not this time.

I lift his pack and mine. It'll be a struggle and my boots have already worn blisters on both big toes and the left heel. I smile at my brother. "Come on," I say. "I bet in town they might have caramels. If you're good, I'll get you one."

His face lifts. "Clay, do they have caramels?"

Clay lends him a hand up. "Any town worth a damn's got caramels."

When Ethan falls the second time, I run over to him again, pick him up and get him the water. I glance up at Clay who's leaning down with concern on his face.

"How much longer?" I ask Clay, trying to keep the desperation out of my voice.

Clay scans up the road. The sun's growing fat and orange in the west which means we're close to dusk. When the sun goes down, we'll be forced to camp without shelter while the nocturnal predators prowl for their suppers. This situation can't get much worse. I fight the panic that's clawing at my throat.

Clay takes off his hat and wipes the sweat off his brow. "Think we got another mile or two."

"Which is it?" I ask, the panic gathering. "One mile we can do. Two, he'll never make it." I grit my teeth and brush the sand off Ethan's cheeks.

"One mile," Clay says. He picks Ethan up and puts him on his back.

I scan up and down the road again. The fact that there's no traffic to this "town" is a bad sign. If there is some bustling city center one mile away, wouldn't trucks be coming and going? Clay probably has no idea what he's talking about. Good thing he's a crack shot. He'll need to be to defend us from the swarms of coyotes.

Only when we begin to spot road trash do I believe there's a chance Clay might be right. The tumbling bits of paper, old mufflers, rusting food cans—all mean people have been here. Clay points to an empty water jug. "See," he says, giving me an I-told-you-so look. Then he picks up the pace. Even with my brother on his back, he's hard to keep up with.

In the distance a decrepit house comes into view on the side of the road. As we approach my stomach sinks. The house looks like a blackened skull in this ruddy light. The warped wooden beams sag and bulge. The house hunkers in a yard of weeds and thorns. Thin, tattered curtains flutters like ghosts in glassless windows that trail us like sunken eyes. Goosebumps break out over my arms.

Stripped of anything useful, the sagging house is likely infested with bats, rodents or a starved vagabond who will kill us for our shoes. As we stride past, our gait quickens. I peer in, wondering what lurks in those shadows. Who's watching us as we walk by? A mile down the road, I still feel eyes on the back of my neck.

When the town wall appears, a brown scar across the face of the horizon, I know something's wrong. The broad stretch of wooden wall has a gaping hole in the center like a mouth widening in a scream. The gate creaks mournfully in the breeze. No town would leave a gate open like that. Clay's eyes lock with mine and we exchange a look. The fear in his eyes is unmistakable.

"Do we keep going?" I look around at the gathering dusk. The first stars peak through the navy canvas above. "It's getting dark."

He shifts Ethan up on his back and wrinkles his brow. "I guess so. Can't bed-down roadside or we'll be coyote food. And our water's 'bout as dry as a dead dog's dingo."

Up until now Ethan's been dozing on Clay's shoulders. He lifts his head, rubs the hair out of his eyes and peers toward the town. "Why's the gate open?"

"Maybe it's busted," Clay offers.

Maybe they're all dead, I think. I nod along with Clay, but I pull the rifle into my arms.

When we reach the gate, Clay puts Ethan down and draws his guns. "You two stay put." He takes a step forward, tightening his jaw.

I shake my head and turn to Ethan. I think about telling him to stay behind, but we can't leave him alone outside the gate.

Ethan shakes his head as if reading my mind. "We stick together."

We turn toward the gate as the twilight thickens around us. The two massive wooden doors on either side of the road give phantom sighs as they sway in the breeze. The slow *screech* sends more goose bumps over my arms. The long stretch of road leading into town is empty. On either side are squat brick structures lining both sides of the street in various states of disrepair. A broken stoplight, drooping on a few fraying wires, jangles in the breeze. A rusted car with a smashed front end sits off to the side as if someone got in an accident as they were trying to leave. And leave they should. The eerie quiet—not even animal sounds breaks the stillness—makes the thudding of my heart too loud. The smell of decay hangs on everything. Warning bells blare in my head. *Turn tail and run.*

"Come on," Clay says, as he takes a step in.

What else can we do? We follow.

CHAPTER FOURTEEN

When I was young, Auntie used to tell me about picture shows they had when she was a kid. Back then there was enough electricity to run a local theater once a week. I'd sit on the warped porch boards and listen as she wove tales of adventure, love, laughter. I learned the plot to *Cinderella* by heart. But on nights when my mama went to bed early, and I could drag them out of Auntie, she'd tell me about horror movies. Horror movies with dark basements, raspy breathing coming from a bedroom closet, ax-murderers running after their victims who screamed into the night. I'd clutch my knees to my chest and listen, barely breathing. Those nights I'd be so scared, any sound would send me flying upstairs to sleep on my parents' floor.

That is how taking our first few steps into this ghost town feels. Like any minute we're going to die. In the twilight, shadows lean from every corner. The dark doorways remind me of rancid open mouths. When the wind whips through, paper rustles and gates squeak, making me sure an ax-murderer will come barreling toward us from an open doorway. Each shadow might hide any number of horrors.

We shuffle through the gate and stop just inside. My legs feel like lead. I can't make myself leave the safety of the open road. What if we get inside town and the gate slams shut? What if this is some horrible trap? What if there are monsters … *Cut it out*, I tell myself. I'm supposed to be brave. I look to Clay. His face locked up tight, his lips a white line, his eyes locked forward. Sweat beads beneath the brim of his cowboy hat. Ethan, to my left, trembles like an eight-year-old should. His bug-eyes flit between doorway, alley, abandoned car. I grab his sweaty hand. I want to feel him next to me.

From here the town looks abandoned. There's no signs of struggle. No dead bodies. No blast holes. There are a few vehicles parked on the side streets, but they look long abandoned. Not beat up, really, just left behind. That raises the hairs on my arms. No one leaves a good vehicle lying around.

To our left is a row of shops, all empty. Trash lies in clumps on the cracked sidewalks. I jump as a rat darts out from a pile of bricks, spots us and then scurries back. If animals can survive here, the water's okay. Probably.

A howl from the road behind us shakes everyone into action. I look to Clay on my right and Ethan on my left. Nodding, we start forward down the desolate street. I grip Ethan's hand in mine and feel Clay's shoulder inches away. It takes all my will to keep my feet moving forward.

We pass a small grocery store and I point it out to Clay. I stare at the faded sign until I can puzzle out *Top Shelf Groceries and Liquor*. Inside it's a mess of clotted paper, wet garbage, crumpled drywall. A bird has built a nest in one of the top shelves where they used to display apples or peaches. From here it looks picked clean, no canned goods, no bottled water. I think of going in, scrounging around, but the light is so scarce it wouldn't do much good. I swallow and turn away. So many shadowed doorways. And it just keeps getting darker.

More empty stores. Old traffic lights with busted glass dangle above our heads. The dryness in my throat seems to doubles as I spot a hydrant with the cap off. I look at the water jug that swings off Clay's pack. Three, maybe four cups left. I turn my thoughts away from water and to each building we pass. We'll have to pick a building soon and bed down. I can't imagine huddling in a dark shop, not knowing what might lurk in the wings. Each building seems darker than the next. A shop that used to be a cafe has a large, brown stain covering most of the tile floor. Blood. It has to be.

Clay stops and stiffens beside me. I swing around and look where he's staring. Between two shops is a dark, trash-strewn alley and something's moving. I tighten my hand over the rifle and Clay raises his guns. The thing moves. It's fury and too small to be human. The animal looks up at us. Four legs, round eyes, a dark muzzle. Coyote? I raise my gun. Then I see the patchy brown fur, the droopy ears and tail. It's a domestic dog. Sensing no real threat, it goes back to whatever it's eating. I think about calling it over until Clay's grips my arm.

"Get Ethan down the road. Now." He pushes me forward as he turns toward the alley. "Wait for me at the corner."

What does he see? I pull Ethan away. Luckily he's got his eyes on some collapsed movie theater down the block. I take him to check it out the busted marquee. Just before I slip past the alley, I glance at the dog. A bright piece of fabric lies on the ground beneath the dog. A t-shirt? Then I see the arm, pale, bloated with crooked fingers. A body. That's what the dog's been eating. I clutch my hand to my mouth and fight the urge to vomit.

Ethan looks up at me as I pull him down the street. "What is it?" His hand squeezes the blood out of mine.

"Nothing." *Oh God,* my head screams. *We're going to die!*

He watches the alley where Clay disappeared with wide eyes.

The dog skitters out of the alley. Clay follows. When he meets us, his face is the color of uncooked dough. He nods at me and keeps walking. I want to ask him about the body. How did it die? Will we end up like it? Yet, Ethan's here and my imagination's supplying enough details on its own. I look up the street at more shops and dark alleys. What do I have to do to get out of here?

"Let's go," Clay says. "We need to get some place safe."

Safe? Nowhere here is safe. We speed-walk down the street. I don't scan the shops. I'm too afraid I'll spot another body.

We find a long driveway at the end of the block. A two-story brick building looms large at the end of it. In the dark I can barely make out the words etched into the concrete sign covered with bird droppings: *Magdalena Christian Academy.* Three graying wood crosses lean on the weed-filled front lawn. At the entrance stands the greening sculpture of a woman, one arm outstretched, palm up. The other arm lays in a few shattered pieces at her feet. Her face, though, turned to the sky as if seeking forgiveness, is the first welcoming thing I've seen.

"Let's sleep in there," I say, pointing to the building.

Clay arches his eyebrows up at me.

I shrug. "Looks less scary than the rest of this God-forsaken place."

Clay nods. "Sure. We need to get inside anyway. Can't see a damn thing."

We stride up the busted blacktop to the front doors. A thick, rusted chain slinks through the handles on the big wooden doors. I yank on them and scowl. Nothing in this town comes easy. I scan either side of the brick building. The glass windows are long gone, but they're high off the ground with nothing to climb but flat, slippery brick.

Clay nods to the first window on the right. "Come on. I'll give you a boost."

A boost? That means Clay putting his hands on me, pushing me upward. At any point his hand could slip and feel something that would solve the mystery of my gender once and for all. I follow him, biting my lip. I could suggest Ethan, but he's too short to reach the ledge and besides, I'd be sending him into a dark creepy building alone.

Clay stands at the base of the window and looks up. He hands Ethan a revolver and tells him to watch the road. Then he laces his fingers together and nods at me. Facing him, I can see the stubble that's grown on his normally smooth chin. His eyes are red rimmed and bloodshot from exhaustion. I remind myself that he could be at home right now, soaking in a tub of warm water while Auntie rubs his feet. Instead he's here in the third circle of hell with us.

I put my hands on his shoulders. His muscles tense as he looks deep into my eyes.

"I got you." His face is calming, reassuring. "On the count of three. Okay?"

I'm so close to him, I can see the flecks of gray in his blue eyes. I grip his shoulders. He stills smells like aftershave.

"Okay," he says. "One. Two. Three."

I put my foot in his hand and push up. As he hoists me, my body brushes past his, but I think I've avoided him noticing anything suspicious. Then I realize my inseam is hovering near his face as he lifts me. Oh God. I wobble.

"Grab. The. Ledge," he grunts. His hand grips around my feet, pushing upward.

My fingers find purchase on the cool stone ledge. Being this close to Clay has tingles going in all the wrong regions of my body. All I can think is his hands on my body. My fingers slip. We rock backwards and almost topple. I gotta focus. *Dark, scary building*, I think. My thoughts fly off Clay's hand cupping my calf. I pull up and tumble into the dark room.

I bash into something hard. It crashes and goes skittering. I lie on the floor, panting in the dark silent room. Please God, don't let there be anything in here to eat me.

I sit with my back against the wall and will my eyes to adjust. The air's musty despite the open window, like no one's stepped foot into this space for a long time. I smell mold, dust, the thick scent of all things man-made crumbling to particles. Soon I can see faint outlines of chairs, tables, the remains of a classroom. The tiny desks and chairs are thrown together in random upturned piles. The one I smashed lies upside-down, its legs in the air like a dead insect. Rotting papers that disintegrate at the touch of a finger lie scattered on the floor. Some of the ceiling lies crumpled by the door. From first glance I don't see anything too frightening. No bodies at least.

"What's going on in there?" Clay calls from below.

I swing over and peer down at him. Both their faces stare up at me. "A classroom."

"Right," he says. "What else?"

"Not much. I think it's okay so far."

Clay nods. "Ethan's coming up. I'll hand him to you."

Clay picks up Ethan and lifts him to the window. I pull.

Ethan tumbles in and looks around. "Cool," he whispers.

I hear Clay trying to scramble up the wall. That kid really thinks there's nothing he can't do. I grab a little desk and carry it to the window. "Watch out," I yell down to Clay. He backs up and I chuck the desk out the window. Luckily it survives the fall. He grabs the desk, places it under the window and stands on it. I pull him up and he almost falls on top of me when I drag him over the window ledge.

The three of us sit in the little classroom, taking it in. Ethan peeks in a few cupboards. I want to stop him, but they're too small to house any real threat other than rodents or insects. He finds a few broken pencils and a coffee mug.

Clay holds it up to the light from the window. "I prayed for hope and God sent you," he reads. "Huh. Don't think hittin' their knees really paid off for these folks, or they'd still be around." He frowns and sets the mug on a tiny desk.

"All clear," Clay says, scanning the room. "But no water. Let's make sure the rest of the place is safe."

I look out the window nestled in the door that leads to the pitch-black hallway. "Can't we just sleep here for the night? There's only one door to defend and we can take turns on watch."

Clay removes his hat and musses his damp hair. "We'll use up the last of our water tonight. I'd feel better if we made sure there's more, but I guess you're right. Wouldn't do any good to go skulking in the dark like a bunch of blind fools. And we're wore out, right, bud?" Clay runs his hand over Ethan's hair. Ethan sags into the Clay.

I pick up a couple plastic orange chairs with rusted metal legs and start stacking them in a pile by the door. It won't stop someone who wants to come in, but it'll slow them down. Then we make camp. In the back corner I find a decaying beanbag and offer it to Ethan. He's the only one tiny enough to curl into it. Yet the thick dust that swirls up every time we move is getting to him. He coughs until his cheeks are crimson, until his eyes bulge. Clay glances at me and then we give him the rest of the water. He gulps it down between coughs.

I sit back against a buckling closet door and dig into my pack. I find a can of Spam, open it and pass it around. Clay cracks a can of peaches and we each take one with our fingers until they're gone. He and I take turns with the juice. My stomach's still seizing with hunger and my mouth feels like the desert floor, but weariness is winning this battle.

"Can you take first watch?" I ask Clay. He nods. I lie on the musty carpet and shuffle around for a comfortable position. On the closet door above me a faded and curling poster pressed in some sort of plastic shows a decorated evergreen tree. It takes me a while but I finally read, "Jesus is the reason." As I drift off I wonder what he's the reason for.

Daylight. I sit upright. Clay should've woken me for my turn at watch. I see that he's fallen asleep sitting up against the warped plaster wall next to the door. His revolver rests in his lap. Ethan's still curled in his dusty beanbag chair. I feel surprisingly well rested except for a kink in my neck. When was the last time I had a good night's sleep that wasn't induced by horse tranquilizers? It's been a while.

My tongue feels thick and sluggish in my mouth. My throat burns for water. I stand up slowly, letting my spine crack into place. Then I tackle removing the chairs as quietly as possible so not to disturb the boys. Twice they bang against each other, but the boys never stir. They must be dead tired. I think about how happy they'll be when I wake them with a big glass of water. If I find it.

Somehow survival seems possible today. The sun looks warm and upbeat coming in the open window, and the classroom is way less creepy in the daylight. It drastically improves my mood. Making sure I've got my hunting knife in my pants just in case, I slip out the classroom door and pull it closed.

On the other side of the door, my mood dims. There are piles of papers strewn about, broken desks and dried-out rodent droppings. Ceiling tiles hang in saggy fragments or lay in bloated piles on the cracked tile. In one corner I see a small rib cage. Some rat, long dead and forgotten. Each doorway could hide any number of horrors. My eyes trace down the long dark halls. I could turn back to my quiet classroom, but my burning throat won't let me.

I slip down the creepy hallways, peeking in each room. The classrooms look just like ours with small differences. One has larger desks for older kids. Our cute posters are replaced with faded charts and graphs pressed in that same plastic covering. One room has no desks, just piles and piles of wet and rotting garbage. Another looks like it had once been a music room. A tilting, three-legged piano grimaces at me with its black and white teeth strewn on the floor. I pass a room with a fallen roof, exposing one corner to the sky. Each room is coated in undisturbed layers of dust or mildew. No one's been in here in some time.

I should go in the classrooms and dig through the cupboards, but I'm a coward. Maybe with Ethan and Clay behind me I could brave pulling open those doors to see what's behind. Animal nest, bugs, spiders, or worse. I think about the body Clay found. I can't face something like that on my own.

I turn the corner and spot a cracked porcelain water fountain. It's a long shot, but I hit the button. Nothing. I push open the door labeled *Ladies' Room*. Inside there's no windows, so it's pitch black, and besides, if there's no plumbing, there's no water in there anyway. I let the door slip shut and turn down another dark, garbage-filled hall.

Near the front of the building, I find what used to be the greeting center. Though it takes me a while, I sound out the word *Office* on the sign. With big windows facing the front, there's enough light to see in. Disheveled chairs, their fabric turning to dust, line the wall leading up to a receiving counter. A dust-encrusted crystal dish still perches delicately on the counter top, but whatever was in it has long since been carted off by mice. Another chair lies wheels up behind a paper-covered desk.

My eyes lock on a black rectangle sitting on a desk in the back. I walk in and touch my finger to the dusty screen. On the table next to it is another black rectangular gadget with rows of lettered keys. I tap a few with the pads of my fingers. Arn said these were called computers. Long ago people used them for communication. I trace my initials in the dust on the screen. Then something catches my eye.

A big blue jug attached to a white base sits in the very back of the office. Liquid was once stored in these. I thumb down the little spigot. In a dispenser, I find a stack of rotting paper cups that fall apart at my touch. Could there be more jugs? A slim door sits next to the water dispenser. The wood is warped so I have to yank on the handle for a while until the thing pops open. I cross my fingers and peer in.

No bodies, just rows of pencils, clips, paper, folders, more paper cups and on the floor ... a big jug of water. Full.

I clap once and the sound startles a mouse. He shoots from a paper nest in the corner to a hole in the floor. I wrap my hands around the lip of the water jug. The boys will be so happy.

It takes me five minutes to carry the jug back to our classroom. I underestimated how heavy the jug was and how weak I am from travel. Still, I half drag, half carry the prize in and plunk it down on the floor in front of Clay. Clay raises the revolver, but then the recognition dawns on his face.

"Riley," he says, "What the hell?"

"Water," I say with a triumphant wave of my hand.

They both blink at me and rub their eyes. I was expecting more fanfare than blank stares.

"Well, I'm thirsty." I start working on the cap. When I finally get it open and figure out how to pour it in one of our jugs without dumping the whole thing over, I take the first drink. Water's never tasted so good. I sigh in relief.

"Nice job, ace," Clay says, stretching and reaching for the jug. I hand it over and he drinks. "Tastes like plastic," he says as he smiles. "Where'd you get it?"

"Down the hall. Sign said *Office*."

Clay takes another drink, a few strings of water dripping down his stubbly chin. "Soon's I can wake up, we'll go exploring."

"It's kind of a mess out there," I say, pouring water for Ethan. "Looks like nobody's been in here in years."

Clay looks at me, puzzled. "I'd heard of people trading here last year. I can't figure what happened."

"Did you see anything when … you know …" I frown and glance at Ethan. "When you saw that *thing* in the alley?" Ethan's eyes are locked on me. I smile as if I've nothing to hide.

"She means the body. Do you know how he died?" Ethan asks matter-of-factly.

Clay and I stare at Ethan with our mouths open.

Ethan scowls. "You guys think I don't notice anything. I'm eight, not four." He's trying to be so big, but when he sticks out his lower lip at the end of his sentence, all I can see is the baby I touted around the yard on my hip.

Clay nods. "Sorry, hoss. We'll do better."

I nod, but I'm lying. He'll be my baby brother whether he's eight or eighty.

Clay shakes his head as his eyes turn toward the open window. "There was nothing on the body to show what killed him. It was in bad shape, decay-wise. And the damn dog didn't help. I didn't see gunshots or stab wounds, so that's something. But it doesn't tell us much."

"At least with no people, we can get what we need and get out," I say. I don't want to hang around here very long. Other than our little classroom, the rest of this town feels like a morgue.

"Fuel and water. Those are our main priorities." Clay holds up two fingers. "Riley already got us water. If we can find fuel, we can jack one of the cars we saw and hit the road."

He makes it sound so easy. I look out the busted classroom window toward the blue sky outside. I hope it is.

We dig through our bags for breakfast. Ethan pulls out a hunk of bread wrapped in paper. We split it and try to chew the hard crust as best we can. My stomach growls, but I quiet it with more water. It'll do for a while.

We work through each room for supplies. This time, with the boys at my back, I lose my fear. I pull open cupboards, frighten mice and spiders out of their homes, dig through moldy wads of paper. Ethan pockets a sheet of gold stars, soggy but miraculously somewhat sticky. Clay finds a heavy-duty pair of scissors with decent blades, an empty aluminum water bottle and a ball of twine. I pick up many things, kid's socks, a mug that says World's Best Teacher, a little pink boot with daisies painted on it. My mind wanders to times when these things were in use. What did these people look like? Were they happy? What happened to them? I leave each item in its dust outline where they'll decay like the rest of this place.

Classrooms pilfered, we find a set of double doors.

"Gymnasium," Clay reads on the sign above the doors. "Come on."

We push through the double doors and find a large echoing room with a wood floor and bleachers on either side. Two hoops with nets stand on each end of the floor. There's a board with faded numbers on the far wall.

"Basketball," Clay says, pointing to the hoops. "Teams of five dribble a ball back and forth. They try to scores as many points by shooting the ball into hoop. The town south of mine had an outdoor court."

Ethan and I walk around and examine everything, the tilting bleachers, the hoop with the fraying net. When this school was in use, the kids got to play games. Their life couldn't have been so bad. Ethan finds a flat orange ball and tries to bounce it. The noise of the ball smacking the floor makes me jumpy. Eventually, I shoot him a look and he sets the ball down.

We push through another set of double doors and find a similar space with rows of tables and benches. Some are turned over. Some are covered in bits of ceiling that have fallen down. Big gray bins are stuffed with ancient food wrappers and paper napkins that flow out and trail across the floor. I walk over and peer in the bins. This trash has been here so long it doesn't even smell. We find nothing but useless garbage, but I know we're getting close.

A doorway at the back leads to a dark kitchen. There's rusty old metal stoves and empty molding refrigerators. We find a few utensils scattered around the floor and in the drawers. In another drawer I find red and yellow packets, some kind of food dressing that still looks edible. I drop them into my pocket. Clay snags a decent looking frying pan and a serrated knife. Then Ethan calls my name.

I run toward the sound of his voice. He's standing in a little pantry stacked with shelves. Most are empty. At the bottom though, I see some large metal cylinders the size of small drums. He hefts one up. The label has fallen off and decayed, but on the top in small writing I see a label. "Green beans," I read slowly. I smile and pat him on the head. "Nice job, Superman."

He hefts the can and smiles so wide I can see all his little, white teeth.

We take two trips to carry all of the cans back to our classroom where we stack them neatly. We've scored three cans of green beans, two cans of what's called fruit cocktail, two cans of baked beans and a can of corn. It's a good haul. I smile as I look at our stack.

"How do we get one open?" I ask.

"I saw a can opener in the kitchen drawer. I'll go grab it," Clay says.

"I'll get it." I have to pee from all the water I drank anyway. It'll give me a good excuse to go alone.

I head out of the classroom and down the hall toward the bathroom. Just before the ladies' room I notice our tracks, three sets of shoe prints in the dust on the floor. We've been all over this school and it shows. Then something draws my attention: the large boot prints running along the far wall, fresh in the layer of dust. They're too big to be any of ours and they weren't there a few hours ago.

We aren't alone.

CHAPTER FIFTEEN

I run back to our classroom and slam the door. I stand against it, panting, wide-eyed. Clay and Ethan were sorting through a deck of cards they found in the kitchen. They stare up at me.

"What's going on?" Clay asks, standing up.

Ethan stands, too, still holding a six of clubs in his hand.

"Footprints," I pant. "Not ours. In the hall."

Clay glances out the little window in our classroom door. "Maybe they're old."

I shake my head. "They're fresh."

Clay pulls out one of his revolvers. His eyes get that look they always do when that silver revolver is cupped in his palm. "I'll check it out. You stay with Ethan."

I don't protest. Something about stalking through the quiet halls to meet some unknown predator doesn't seem fun to me. As he's opening the door, I put my hand on the door jam. "Be careful," I say as I look into his blue eyes, the color of a summer sky.

He lets a little smile dance across his face. "Sounds like you're getting used to having me around."

And he ruined it. "Never mind," I say, waving him out the door. "Go be as reckless as you want. We're totally fine without you."

"Liar," he says, his smile growing. "You need me."

I cross my arms over my chest and glare at him.

He chuckles and then disappears out the door.

I sit with Ethan against the far wall with a revolver in my hand. The minutes tick by slowly. I listen, but hear little else but a few birdcalls from the window and my heart beat in my ears. Footsteps sound, heavy and coming this way. I rise, the gun leveled. It's Clay. He bursts back in our room.

"Anything?" I ask.

He shakes his head, holsters his gun and picks up the jug of water. He lifts it to his lips. I watch his Adam's apple rise and fall as he swallows. Then he drops the jug, panting. "Ahh," he sighs.

"What?" I say, impatient. "What did you find?"

He smiles wryly. "Thought you said you didn't need me." He takes another long pull from the jug. I cross my arms over my chest and tap my foot. He can be so infuriating.

One more devious smile and then he sets the jug down. "No sign of anyone except the footprints. Must've heard us come in, checked us out and took off. His trail leads out a lower window. Just curious 'bout visitors."

"Why didn't he want to talk?" I ask, the hairs on my arms still standing up.

Clay shrugs and wipes his mouth with his sleeve. "Probably as scared of us as we are of him."

I shake my head. "I wanna get out of here."

Clay pulls the can opener out of his pocket and hands it to Ethan. "We have to get gas and that's going to mean digging through this hell hole. We do that after we eat. We're safer in here than out there if there's something to fuss about."

I say nothing, but can't shake the feeling of dread.

We open the canned corn and eat until our bellies are stuffed. Then we fill our packs with water jugs and a hose and bucket Clay found in the janitor's closet. Clay scrambles over the window ledge and jumps down. I pass Ethan to him and then lower myself down.

The bright daylight lances my eyes. I cover them and squint into the distance. The scene outside is just as creepy. The street is deadly silent. The buildings sit as lifeless and desolate as ever. A few birds call and a squeaky hinge squeals from somewhere downtown. Penetrating tragedy is the only thing that would leave a town this empty. Yet, someone survived. Who is this stranger slinking around in the night? Then a gruesome thought grips me. Maybe he killed all these people. I scan the dark windows and alleys as we walk.

We head down the abandoned street to the big yellow sea shell billboard that Clay says marks a gas station. When we find it, the roof covering has collapsed and has mangled at least half of the pumps. Clay fiddles with a remaining pump, pushing buttons, looking into the metal nozzle, but even if the tanks still had gas, with no power, they won't pump. I watch as he scans the busted concrete until his eyes light on a metal disk nestled in the pavement. He heads into the little shop attached to the gas station.

"What're you doing?" I call.

He returns with a long metal rod, rusted, but still sturdy. Then he sets to digging out the cover. When he dislodges the cap, we all gather around the hole. It's an underground tank. Clay picks up a pebble and drops it in the dark hole. It clanks against metal. This gas station is tapped out. Of course it is.

We wander into the little store behind the pumps. The store named *Tom and Jerry's* is little help, either. It's lined with toppled shelves and more trash. We spread out, looking for any usable items. Ethan pulls out a little packet of pills that must be medicine. Clay holds up an empty gas can triumphantly. I want to be excited, but empty cans will get us nowhere. My hands reach under toppled metal shelves and fallen light casings, until I find something plastic and crinkly. I pull out the wrapper sure it's trash, but this one has weight. A candy bar—*Baby Ruth*, according to the label. Both boys stare at it like I've just found gold.

"We'll split it three ways," I say, opening it.

It's been smashed and melted and hardened several times, but when I put it the chocolate my mouth, the sugary flavor explodes over my tongue. It's so sweet it puckers my lips. A grin spreads over Ethan's mouth as he chews. Clay licks his fingers when his portion is gone.

"Find another one of those," he says.

But I can't. We dig through the piles for a while until our fingers are grimy and I've scraped the skin off two knuckles. The best I can do is a bag of chips that has been pulverized to crumbs. We take turns sliding the tiny salty crumbs into our mouths until the bag is gone. Then Clay nods to the door.

"Let's go get some gas before it gets dark."

We head back toward the front gate. We pass several abandoned buildings with nothing but rodents, debris and more trash. Then we come up to a dumpy brown building with a flaking sign. Clay reads: "*Urgent Care Medical Clinic*. Hang here. I want to see if there's any drugs in there. We can trade 'em in the next town over for what we need."

I know how expensive medicine can be. Arn would trade months worth of pelts for a few pills or salve or even iodine. The three of us file in through the frosted glass doors.

Something's very wrong. The putrid stench sends everyone's hands over their mouths. Flies buzz in the hundreds and their carcasses line the front windowsill and the floor. Broken needles, dirty bandaging and a dried mess that looks like old vomit cover the floor. I stagger back toward the door. I don't care what's salvageable in here. My brain is telling me to run. Then I see dark mounds blocking the hallway.

Corpses. The pile of bodies is three feet high and stretches down the hallway. The stained sheets cover many, but to my left a clawed hand dangles over a soiled table. Lank, blond hair sprouts from under a sheet near the front. Another is slumped in a chair, his legs purple, his face a bloat mask of decay.

We gotta get out. I grab Ethan and pull him with me as I run out of the building.

As soon as I hit fresh air, I vomit on the sidewalk, my corn lunch splattering against the wall. I close my eyes, but I can't see anything except rows of bodies. The flies swarming around them. The smell. I spit and swipe at my nose trying to get the smell out. I hear Ethan gagging beside me. Then Clay follows. He pulls at my wrist.

His face is green and slack. "Come on. Gotta get away."

We jog and then run up the road. My stomach lurches again and I stop and throw up what's left of my lunch. Then we find a three-foot high brick wall surrounding a parking lot and sit with our backs to it. I can't stop my hands from shaking as I drink from the water bottle and pass it along. Visions of the bodies swim in my mind.

"What happened to them?" I ask.

Clay shakes his head and sips from the bottle. "Disease. All those needles, the sick beds. Probably some flu epidemic. God."

Ethan looks up at him, the whites of his eyes large in his terror. "Are we going to die?"

Clay shakes his head and pulls Ethan closer to him. "No. We're fine." But when he glances at me over Ethan's head, I can tell that answer is hollow.

I grip my water bottle between my shaking hands. "We can't go back there. I don't care what kind of meds we find. We can't catch whatever killed those people."

Clay rests his head on Ethan's for a moment. "You get no protest from me."

I clutch my arms, trying to hold myself together. Up the road, the desolate buildings stretch on endlessly. A broken streetlight sways in the wind. Dark, empty shops, their windows smashed, their contents spilling into the street, wait for us. Now more than ever I want to leave and there's only one way I can. I stand up and grab the empty gas jug and hose.

"Let's get that gas and get the hell out of dodge."

The first car we find is empty. And the second. With the third I manage to get a mouth full of gasoline, but after I get the gas flowing into the hose, we get about a gallon before that tank runs dry. We walk several more streets and find one more car. This time Clay gets a mouth full of gasoline and another gallon and a half. The sun is sinking low and we only have enough gas to get us a few miles down the road.

"This sucks!" I scream, hurling the hose against the car and then kicking the tires. I want to dump the gas on something and set fire to it. A little of my common sense kicks in and I just kick a hunk of broken sidewalk into the road.

Clay puts a hand on my shoulder. "It's okay, Riley. We'll try again tomorrow."

I whirl around. "I don't want to sleep here again! It's a graveyard! If we get stuck here much longer, we're going to die just like them!" I flap my arms in the direction of the medical clinic. I'm behaving so badly, but I can't stop. I pick up a chunk of brick and hurl it through one of the only intact windows in town. The glass explodes with a satisfying smash. I watch the shards rain onto the ground.

Ethan's grown stiff and pale beside me. I see his lip starting to tremble. I've scared him. What have I done?

Clay takes Ethan by the hand. "Well, if our neighbor didn't know where we are, he sure does now. We're going back." He pauses and looks at me. "You done or you need to break something else?"

Exhausted and embarrassed, my shoulders slump. I'm done being mad. Now I feel like cowpie on a boot sole. I lower my head and follow behind, back to the school, trying hard not to cry.

When we get back to the classroom, I can barely pull Ethan into the room when Clay pushes him up. They settle down and start digging into the can of corn, but my stomach churns from the gasoline and the scene at the medical clinic. I curl into the little beanbag, grateful that I can escape for a little while. Sleep comes hard and fast.

When I wake, the room is dark. Ethan breathes evenly beside me. Clay leans against the window ledge, lit by a little square of moonlight. A pair of wire-rimmed glasses perches on his nose. I've never seen him wear those. To top it off, he's holding a crinkled book up to the light. It the moonlight he looks entirely transformed from the rugged gunslinger of the day.

"You know how to read?" I ask, sitting up.

He startles and looks up. His hand strays to the glasses and yanks them off, a blush so red rising up his cheeks that I can see it in the dark. He tucks the frames in his breast pocket and slips the book behind his back.

"I was just … looking for something." He rubs a hand over his neck and gives me a sheepish grin.

He's embarrassed. God, how adorable. I point to the book. "What is it?"

He blushes again and shrugs.

"It's okay," I say. "I really want to learn to read. I've tried, but …" I shake my head.

Clay walks over and sits on the floor next to me. He slips the book in my hand.

"Ro ... me ... o and—What's this?" I ask, pointing to the last word.

"Romeo and Juliet. It's a love story. It's a dang tough one, too. It's written in this funky English. Been working on it for six months."

I run my fingers over the worn paper binding. The picture on the front is a man and woman enfolded in an embrace. With Clay sitting this close to me, the image brings a blush up to my own cheeks.

"Why'd you get embarrassed?" I lift my eyes to his face. There are two red ovals on the bridge of his nose where the glasses were perched.

He shrugs. "My pa's got no love for book learnin'. Used to tease the hell outta me if he found me reading. Don't know why I like it so much. It's just ..." He pauses, thinking. "It takes me somewhere else for a while, you know?"

I hand him the book. "Anywhere but here," I say quietly.

For a moment we sit in silence. I can feel his body next to me purring like an engine, thrumming, giving off heat. He leans over, picks up a can and slides it to me. "Ethan said you'd like fruit cocktail, so we opened that one." Clay hands me a spoon. The fruit tastes deliciously sweet in my mouth. I roll the little chunks of peach or pear around on my tongue. For a while it helps take my mind off Clay's even breathing, his increasingly familiar scent. I must smell like gasoline and body odor. What I wouldn't give to smell like meadow flowers just once when he's around.

"Must be hard for you," he says quietly.

I turn to him, trying to read his expression in the dark. "What do you mean?"

He nods toward my little brother. "I know how much I care about the little bugger and he's not even mine. Must be hard to worry about him every minute of every day. Bet it wears on you." He turns and gives me that reassuring smile I've come to depend on.

God, how can he be so good when I'm so awful? My eyes fall over the soft curves of his cheeks, the hard line of his jaw, the dark lashes around his comforting eyes.

He smiles at Ethan's sleeping form, the curled dark shadow in the corner. "Hell of a kid to go through what he did and still want to play cards with me."

I swallow the lump that's forming in my throat with a little of the fruit cocktail. My eyes watch Ethan's chest rise and fall. His bottom lip twitches. "He's about the only thing worth a damn in this world." Tears prick at my eyes. Oh God, am I choking up? I swallow some water and force the tears back.

Clay leans against the wall beside me and stretches his legs out on the moldy carpet. His eyes trail up to the beam of moonlight trickling in from the window above. "You don't give yourself enough credit. You're as brave as he is, as kindhearted." He shifts and a beam of moonlight trickles over his face. Through all this grime, dirt and sweat, he's one of the most beautiful people I've ever seen. I turn my eyes to the carpet. A tear escapes and slips down the bridge of my nose.

I don't know if it's the frustration from earlier or the exhaustion from the travel or Clay's nice comment or all of them combined, but I can't stop the tears that begin sliding down my face. They trace my cheeks and drip off my chin. I pretend to itch my nose and to wipe some away. They just keep coming.

Clay looks over at me. "Hey, are you crying? Don't do that." He digs in his pocket and pulls out a weathered cloth. "Here."

I shake my head. More tears fall and now sobs threaten to shake out of my chest. I can't control myself. I put my head in my hands and hunch over, letting the tears fall between my legs and onto the floor.

I feel his arms around me. Tentative at first, then stronger, circling me in an embrace. His body is so warm next to mine. And my heart is pounding. I can smell remnants of his aftershave. I don't even think. I lean into him. Smell his musky scent. Feel his chest against my shoulder. Then I'm tilting my head, leaning toward him. My cheek brushes against the stubble of his chin. The sweet smell of his mouth intoxicates me. I lift my mouth up to meet his.

He drops the embrace and pulls away. "I don't ..." he stutters. "I didn't mean ..."

Oh heavenly Lord, what have I done?

I jump up, the fruit cocktail clattering from my lap. I run to the door, yank it open and vault into the hallway. I race blindly down the corridor. How could I?

I skid to a stop at the front office. I scramble in and curl myself into a little ball under the desk. In the dark, maybe he won't be able to find me.

I'm the biggest idiot on the planet. I just tried to kiss Clay. Clay—who's supposed to think I'm a bender. It's not unheard of for two guys to do that sort of thing, but judging by his reaction he was definitely not into that. Not into me. How will I ever face him again? I tuck my knees under my chin and bury my face in them. Stupid. I'm so incredibly stupid. I'll just hide here for the rest of my life. Sure, there's dusty bunnies the size of, well, bunnies under here and I think I just spotted a fresh rat's nest, but anything's better than facing Clay. I don't think I can do it. Ever.

I replay that moment in my head, but all I come up with is the desperate overwhelming feeling of longing. Longing for Clay. For his body next to mine. To feel his arms around me. I've ruined it. Now any time he looks at me he'll think I'm trying to make a pass at him. I destroyed the comfortable friendship we had when I leaned in, mouth puckered.

I hear someone walking down the hall. Heavy footsteps. Not Ethan's.

"Riley?" Clay calls. "Come back."

I clutch my knees to my chest. I can't face him now.

"Riley, come on. It's not safe out here."

He's right. I have no weapon and we know for sure that someone was prowling around this morning, but I don't care. My embarrassment is bigger than my fear.

"Riley, look, I'm sorry. Can you just come back so we can talk?"

His voice is close. He must be outside the office door. Then I hear him wander away, calling my name. I uncurl and peak over the desk. He's scanning the classrooms for me. He'll be at my door soon. Then I have the task of deciding to sleep with the dust bunnies or slink in there and pretend nothing happened. He wanders down the hall and calls my name one more time.

That's when I see the dark shadow emerge from the boy's bathroom.

Silent, statuesque. I wouldn't have spotted him except for the twinkle of moonlight on a metal object in his hands. A man. He's watching Clay from the darkness of the bathroom. My heart hammers dangerously in my ears.

He steps out of the bathroom and into the hallway. I see his rifle when he raises it and aims at Clay's back.

"No!" I scream.

I jump over the desk and run toward the man. The shot explodes through the hallway. The bullet misses Clay by inches and blows a huge hole in the wall near his head. Drywall rains down everywhere. Clay dives to the floor.

But my eyes aren't on Clay anymore. They're on the stranger as he swings his rifle toward me.

Just before I zag left, I take my opponent in. Skinny, sickly, his hair hangs in limp strands down his back. He's wearing a dark trench coat and holey boots. When he turns his eyes on me, their strangely vacant, the whites gone yellow, the skin below purple. He slides the bolt on the gun and aims the rifle. I throw myself to the ground.

The gun explodes and a window shatters behind me. Glass and debris pelt my head and arms. My ears ring, blotting out most of the sound. I sit up and shake my head. Then I realize he's reloading. I'm not prepared to dodge it. The silver barrel centers on my chest. I can see the sheen of sweat on the man's upper lip as he pulls the gun to his shoulder. This is the last thing I'll see before I die.

Clay flies in and tackles the stranger. They both go sprawling into the wall with a loud thud. A drooping ceiling tile dislodges and crumbles on their heads, covering them in soggy white clumps. The stranger lets out a strangled cry as Clay's arms circle around his throat. His fingers claw at Clay's arm as the stranger gags and digs his boots into the tile. Clay pulls tighter, his jaw locked, the veins in his neck bulging. The stranger jabs elbows into Clay's ribs. Clay *oomphs* and his grip loosens. The stranger wiggles out of Clay's arms, turns and grabs Clay by the throat. I watch as Clay's eye pop and his face purples. I've got to do something. I run over.

Clay cocks an arm back and slams his knuckles into the stranger's nose. There's a loud crunch and a muffled cry. Two rivers of blood gush from the stranger's nostrils. Stunned, he touches his upper lip with the pads of two fingers. His yellow eyes go wild. He finds his rifle as Clay's catching his breath, pulls it back and bashes it into Clay's forehead. The sickening crack as the gun smashes Clay's skull makes me cringe.

Clay goes limp, eyes dropping closed, mouth open. The stranger lifts a sick, bloody smile up over his rotting teeth. He claws up the wall, leaving a red handprint. Slowly he turns his grin toward me. With his long, stringy hair; popped, yellowed eyes; and blood-covered face, I have one thought: this is what crazy looks like.

He lifts his rusty rifle up to his shoulder and points it at Clay's chest.

Clay. I don't think. I move.

I jump on the stranger's back and I throw my arms around his skinny neck. He smells like death in a moldy trench coat as I try to tighten my arms around his throat. He claws at my arms, tripping over Clay in the process and we fall. My body hits the floor and pain snaps up my spine. A second later his weight lands on top of me. All the air slams out of my chest. As I gasp for air, his scent of urine, sweat and decay gag me. My arms go limp. He squirms out of my grip, his elbow digging into my chest. The stranger rolls away and staggers up.

"You came to take the castle." His hands shake as he pulls the bolt on his rifle to reload. "But I'm not going give it ye. No, no. No, siree. You brought the bugs and the blood and thought it'd do me, but no. I survived." He strikes his fist against his skull once, leaving a red smudge there like a third eye. "Now you come to drag me down to hell." He swipes blood from his lip before he lifts his rifle. "You're going along first."

I need to run, but I can't get my breath. I scramble on my hands backwards in a strange crab crawl. The gun fits into the grove of his shoulder. He squeezes one eye shut as he aims for me.

Please don't let the end hurt.

"Riley?"

Ethan. I whirl around. He's standing in the hallway, staring in horror at the scene before him. The man swivels the rifle away from me. He points it at my baby brother.

"No!" I croak. I lurch upward. The gun goes off with a sickening crack. A massive force punches my stomach. Any air I had is knocked away. I crash to the floor, a gun blast ringing in my ears.

Time slows. The world dulls until everything has soft edges. I want to move, but the world's far away. I close my eyes, and when I open them, the stranger leans over me. I see the sweat mixed with blood on his upper lip. Deep in my brain something tells me I should be concerned, but all I feel is a warm, tingling ache.

When I open my eyes again, the stranger's gone. I manage to slide my head over and there's Clay. He pounds his fists into the stranger, who's lying in a bloody mess on the ground. At least that. At least he can't hurt anyone else.

I'm having trouble focusing. There's a dull ache just below my ribs. I touch my stomach and lift my hand to my eyes. It's slick with blood. I've been shot. This thought dawns on me slowly like a cresting wave. But Ethan's okay. Clay's okay. The man with the gun isn't moving. Darkness creeps around the edges of my vision.

Ethan's crying behind me. I want to comfort him, but I can't move. Then Clay's above me. He reaches down and touches my stomach. It's the first time I feel pain, but it's fuzzy and far away. He's ripping off my shirt. I want to tell him to stop. My secret will be revealed, but I'm being pulled backward into the blackness. The night air on my skin tells me my chest is bare. The shocked look on Clay's face tells me my secret's out.

Then it's dark.

CHAPTER SIXTEEN

Pain. Pain like being gutted.

I open my eyes. Clay's carrying me in his arms. I try to speak, but my throat's a dry cave. Pain sears my stomach. Hot coals burn me from the inside out. I writhe in Clay's arms. He looks down to me, his face awash in worry. "Shh," he murmurs sweetly. "We'll get you help, Riley. Just hold on."

I lean into his chest and inhale his musky, male scent. Then the pain rips through my abdomen. When I lose consciousness, it's a sweet release.

***

Pain. Bouncing. I blink in the darkness. I'm in a dark box. Oh God, a coffin? Then I hear a car engine. We're driving. I'm in the back of a car. We hit a bump and the pain blazes white-hot. I moan and pass out.

***

Light.

Then darkness.

Then light again. Light seeps through my eyelids and pokes at my brain. Ethan's probably left the curtains open again. I try to throw a hand over my eyes, but my arm doesn't want to move. I open my eyes.

Blinding white is all that registers. Then blurry black shapes form into furniture, a door, a bed. This isn't my room. A dull pain twinges at my stomach as I move. Then it all comes flooding back—the gunshot, Ethan crying, Clay clutching me tight to his chest, telling me to hold on. I should be dead. No one survives a gunshot wound to the stomach. You bleed out in a messy puddle and if you're lucky someone will bury you so the coyotes don't eat your insides. Yet when I look down, there's the outline of my legs under a thick beige blanket. My hands are curled on my lap, the nails clean and trimmed. Where am I?

I scan the room. The clean, cushy bed smells like meadow flowers. The sheets are so white they hurt my eyes. The white walls have no cracking plaster, no clumps of black mold growing in the corners. Behind me something's beeping. There's a black screen with scrolling squiggly green and red lines that appears to be a working computer. My eyes shift up to the overhead lights, blazing bright with electricity.

A quiet panic grows in my chest. I rip the sheet down and search my abdomen for the gunshot wound. Last I saw, a bright red pool was spreading through my shirt. Now I'm wearing a clean white gown. I probe my stomach with my fingers and feel the dull soreness. I hike up the gown and find a clean white bandage. I've had medical attention. Good medical attention. There's only one place I could've had medical attention like this.

With my breath hitching in my chest, I roll my palm up to reveal the skin of my forearm. Three inches from my wrist I find the brand, a cross with a head on it. The ankh. The Breeder's mark.

My head buzzes. Oh god, no.

Before the terror can grip me, the door slides open and in waddles a girl. A girl? She's got blonde curly hair done up in a pink bow at the top of her head. Her white hospital gown billows around her plump body and her red cheeks throw off a heated glow. She waddles over with a dimpled smile on her chubby cheeks. When she turns to lower herself into the chair by my bed, I see why she waddles. She's eight months pregnant.

This is all wrong.

"Well, it's about time you woke up, puddinhead. I've been waiting for days." The girl smiles at me like we're long lost friends. "They had you on some whopper drugs while they fixed you up. How did you get shot, by the way?" She cocks her head and blinks at me in a way that reminds me of a curious pup.

I sit up, ignoring the flare of pain from my wound. "Where are we?"

"Oh dear. Got the brain wipe, eh? Too bad. Well, at least you won't know what you're missing." She leans over and snags the bread roll on the tray by my bed. "You gonna eat this?" She stuffs it in her mouth.

The electric lights. The pregnant girl. The Breeder's mark. Terror floods my brain until I'm choking on it. I yank off the sticky pads connected to wires on my chest. The monitors next to my bed go wild.

"You shouldn't do that!" the girl says. "Dr. Rayburn's not going to like that!"

I yank out the tube that's snaking into the vein in my arm. When I stand, I wobble a bit, but then I'm out of bed. The girl wraps her arm over her belly as if some wild animal has just been unleashed. I ignore her and turn for the door.

Three men rush in. Two guards in matching white uniforms spread out, arms outstretched to block my exit. A short, pudgy teen in long white coat peers at me behind the wall of guards.

"I told you," the girl says from behind me. "I told her, Dr. Rayburn."

My eyes flick to the teen in the lab coat. He's the doctor? He doesn't look older than fifteen. His pimpled cheeks and soft chin quiver as he gives me that wild-cat-out-of-its-cage look. His nasal voice warbles when he speaks. "Miss, uh, please get back in bed. You will re-injure yourself," He waves the guards toward me.

I dive under the guards as they reach for me. My hands scramble on the hard tile as I make it under the first guard, but the second grabs my legs. He pins me beneath him.

"Stop!" I scream. There's a sharp pinch as the guard jabs a needle into my butt.

"I told her," the girl says.

It all goes dark.

***

Light. I slide my eyes open and see the same hospital room. I try to sit up, but straps tie my arms to the bed rails. When I tug against the bonds, the same plump girl turns her attention from the flickering TV to me.

"You'd better knock that off," she says with a yawn. "They've got cameras. If they see you trying to bust out again, they'll just slip the tranquilizers in your I.V." She scratches under her round belly and then blinks at me.

"I have to get out of here!" I turn and yell at the camera. "Let me out!" I pull back and forth on the bonds.

The girl shakes her head at me and glances towards the door. "Geez, will you cut that out? You're gonna get me in trouble."

"Get me out of here! Undo my wrists!"

The girl looks at my wrists and then shrugs. "Sorry, Charlie. Doctor's orders. You stay tied up until you stop acting like a loon."

"What does that mean?" I say through my teeth. Instead of thrashing, I work my wrists back and forth testing these straps. They're solid. It's going to take a miracle to get free.

The girl points a plump finger at me. "You, young lady, need to learn the rules. And that's what I'm here for." She smiles and cocks her head, letting her curls bounce from side to side. "I'm your friendly neighborhood tour guide. I'll show you around. Teach you the ropes. All that jazz." She holds out her hand to me as if to shake, but then remembers mine are strapped to the bed. She drops her hand back in her lap. "I'm Elizabeth, but you can call me Betsy."

"I'm Agatha," I lie. I take in Betsy's face. Small, dark eyes blink in her round head. She keeps smiling widely, making her fat cheeks dimple. I'm not used to seeing anyone who isn't starving, so she's off-putting. The fact that she's so chipper about being a prisoner in the Breeders' hospital makes think she's gone over the high side.

I narrow my eyes. "Where are we?"

"Albuquerque General. I'm told it's the best hospital in the country, if not the world." She spreads her hands across her face with a flourish. When I don't smile, hers droops, but she continues. "We've got all the latest and greatest here: TV, all the best food, *a pool.*" She leans in, smiling to take in my excitement at the mention of a pool. I shake my head.

"Are you a prisoner here, too?"

She blinks at me.

"Are they holding you against your will? Making you have that baby?" I ask, nodding towards her stomach.

Her brow wrinkles. "I live here."

I narrow my eyes. "You mean you *want* to live here?"

She nods happily, patting her watermelon-sized belly. "It's the best. Of course when little dumplin' comes, I'll move into the nursery with her for a year. Then she'll go live with the nannies and I'll go back into the prenatal rooms."

"So, you're a prisoner here? You've never left this hospital." My heart thumps in my chest. The monitors above beep in agitation.

She shakes her head. "Why would I want to leave? It's awful out there. War. Disease. Look at you. You came from out there and you got shot. When that boy turned you in, you were basically dead."

That boy. Clay. Clay who sold me to the hospital. He saved my life. It probably helped to justify making me a prisoner. How much money did he make off my enslavement? I lower my eyes and clench my hands open and closed. If I could move, I'd chuck something at that beeping monitor.

Betsy leans toward me. "They told me if I get a guard, I can give you a tour. Wanna see the place?"

She's so innocent and sweet that I try a smile. My face won't allow it. The only way I want to see this hospital is in my rearview. Then I remember that my mother was supposed to be here.

"Yeah, show me around. I'm dying to see it."

She pulls out a small rectangular device that looks like a miniature computer. With a swipe of her finger the screen flares to life. She waggles it in front of me. The screen shows a map of the hospital. She points at a green dot on the screen. "This is you."

When I look up puzzled, she tries again, slowly like I'm a baby. "They're tracking you. Here, let me show you." She heaves herself out of the chair, waddles over and presses a finger to the back of my neck. The skin there aches.

"They implant a tracking device in here," she says, pressing just below my hairline. "It embeds itself into the skin and runs off the thermal and kinesthetic energy of your body." She notes my confused look and tries again. "They know where you are. All the time. So don't mess around. If you dig that one out, they'll just put a new one in. So don't."

Satisfied, she waddles to the little box on the wall. She pushes a button and the speaker crackles to life.

"Yes?" that nasal male voice asks. The chubby doc is listening to our conversation.

Betsy leans toward the speaker, her cheeks flushing red. "Dr. Rayburn, she agreed to take the tour. Can you send in a guard?"

In a few minutes, one of the guards walks in. He releases my restraints and replaces them with metal handcuffs. When he's done, Betsy heads for the door. It buzzes and slides open.

Betsy claps her hands. "This is so exciting. Your first tour. Let's start at the lounge." She waddles out of the room and down the hall. I follow, feeling as though I'm walking into someone's sick dream.

The halls are white, bare and sterile. They smell powerfully clean. A doctor in a white lab coat brushes past us without a second glance. Then a guard in his white jumpsuit. Apparently the three of us on our tour aren't as much of a spectacle as I thought. I count the steps down the hall, memorize every metal door with the little window similar to mine. When I make my escape, I'll need to know every detail.

Betsy takes a right and the floor plan opens into a large common room. Puffy couches, their tan fabric as plush and velvety as newborn kittens, line the walls. Groups of plastic tables and chairs are clustered here and there. The chair legs are so shiny and rust-free, glimmering in the electric light, that the glare hurts my eyes. A large shelving area with rows of books and brightly colored game boxes lines one wall. My mouth drops open. I've never seen more than a ratty box of checkers or a mildewed Connect Four in a closet of a house we moved into. I want to run over and investigate the colored spines, flip the pages, smell the new ink, but the guard's at my back and Betsy's droning on and on about the huge TV screen mounted to one wall. The video, a black-and-white picture show with a man and woman riding in a car, is playing with the sound off. Everything in this room is newer and cleaner than any item I've ever seen in my life. It takes my breath away. Two pregnant girls sit at a checkers board.

Another is asleep on the couch in front of the flickering TV. All these forms of entertainment Ethan and I would have died for back at home, and yet the girls seem more bored than we've ever been.

Betsy shuffles over to the girls playing checkers. The girls glance up at me with sour expressions. Then they go back to staring at the black and red board.

Betsy stops before them and waves me over. "Latisha, Sammy, this is Agatha. Agatha, meet Latisha and Sammy."

Both girls glance up. Latisha is a dark-skinned girl with a slim body and round belly, like a basketball stuffed under her white hospital gown. Her brown eyes scan me and then dismiss me in the span of a few seconds. Sammy is petite with dirty-blond hair thrown up in a messy ponytail. She looks up at me unhappily, but I can't tell if she's displeased or if her sour expression is her typical one. She rubs a hand over the small bump on her belly. They both wear the shapeless hospital gowns, matching pants and bright yellow socks with grippy souls just like mine. Apparently patients got no need for shoes.

Latisha leans into Betsy and pokes a finger in her flabby chest. "You took my breakfast again, tubby. Do it again and I'll break your fingers."

The smile falls off Betsy's face. "Tish, I didn't. I swear." She clutches her hands in front of her chest and her lower limp trembles.

Latisha shakes her head and her black springy curls follow. "Don't lie, lard butt. I can see my sausage links on your hips." Tish pinches her and Betsy winces. "Don't mess with a pregnant lady's food, girl. I know they got you on calorie restriction."

Betsy gives a low moan, her shoulders slumping. "It's awful. They have me down to two meals a day."

"And whose fault is that?" Sammy adds. Her voice is high pitched and nasal. She picks up a checker and taps it on her thin lower lip. "You keep gaining and they'll drop you down to liquid diet. They did it to Vandra."

I haven't eaten more than some mouthfuls of corn and dry cracked toast in days and these girls are whining over two square meals a day? I look down at my skin-and-bones frame. I'm all angles compared to their rounding bodies. For a moment I wonder if Clay would prefer a rounder woman. Then I remember he sold me to this hospital and I chase thoughts of him out of my head.

Sammy notices my confused expression. "Don't worry, beanpole. They'll fatten you up soon enough. Can't knock you up until you put on a little weight."

It feels like someone's punched me in the stomach. I can't be pregnant. I'm only sixteen.

Betsy—smile faded, hands worrying the front of her gown—plods away and leads me out of the lounge. My mind's still clogged with the horrors of pregnancy. Being a woman is terrible. If you aren't being used for one purpose, someone find another use for you. And what choice is there? The hard, painful fight for freedom. The fight I've lost. I look down at the silver cuffs on my hands. I'm so tired. Tired of running, tired of worrying and fighting. It would be so easy to give up, become cow-eyed like Betsy and be a walking incubator. I'd get three meals a day, I'd watch picture shows on that plush couch and then fall asleep to the sound of Betsy's snoring. Easy.

A vision of Ethan swims up before me. Is Clay taking care of him right now? Is he eating, staying out of the sun? And my mother. Is she here right now behind one of these sealed doors? No, life here would not be easy. I'd be haunted by all the people I'd let down. I go back to counting tile squares as Betsy leads me out of the lounge and down another sterile white hallway.

We stop at four gigantic glass windows that overlook a large room. In the center is a rectangular concrete pond, sparkling with clear blue water. My nose crinkles at the strong chemical smell. That must be how they keep that water so clear. In it, half a dozen slack-faced pregnant girls bob up and down in large shapeless bathing suits, while one elderly woman in a blue swim cap directs their movements. The women spin and move to the beat of music that echoes from above.

Betsy peers down, her heavy breathing fogging up the glass. "Water aerobics. We're required forty-five minutes of exercise everyday." Then she glances at me. "Not you. You're still healing." She taps a pudgy finger to the glass, pointing at an older woman who lifts blue floatation devices shaped like dumbbells over her head. The other pregnant girls follow. "That's one of the nannies. They help run the place. Them and the doctors." Then she leans toward me, her eyes big in the doughy flesh of her face. "Don't mess with the nannies. They may look like sweet old ladies, but they can be real cranks."

I scan the women bobbing like seals in the water. None are my mother.

We shuffle down the hall into a cafeteria. The brightly lit eatery has a tile floor that's been freshly scrubbed. The rectangular benches and seats line up in neat rows. In the back, a few nannies scour pots over a large steel sink. The cooked meat smell makes my mouth water.

I look around the empty cafeteria and remember the one we found in that haunted school. A pang of loss washes over me. I think of Ethan, this dark hair falling over his eyes. Then my last image of Clay floods up before I can stop it. Him holding me to his chest, telling me to hold on. That everything's going to be okay.

Betsy waves a hand in front of my face. "Did you hear what I said?"

I blink and shake my head. I scan the faces of the women in the kitchen. None are familiar.

"I said," she huffs, "meals are served at eight, noon and five. Unless you're on room restriction, which you are. See why you have to behave. You don't get to use any of the facilities until Dr. Rayburn says so."

"Whatever will I do?" I mumble.

Betsy's face darkens. Behind her chipper exterior, she might have a nasty side.

As she walks us down the cafeteria aisles, I realize I've made no headway in finding my mother. I need another plan. As we pass a door marked with a stick figure of a woman on it, I get an idea.

"I have to pee," I say. Both Betsy and the guard who's been following us stop.

"I could go, too." Betsy turns to the guard. "I'll take her in."

The guard leans casually against the wall. "Just hurry up. Rayburn said to be back in twenty minutes."

I offer him my shackled wrists. "Can you help a girl out?" I ask. "Hard to wipe with the cuffs."

The guard shrugs. "Figure it out."

I scowl, but drop my hands. I don't need them for what I'm about to do.

Betsy pushes open the ladies' room door and waddles into a stall. The pristine sinks and mirrors, hell, just the indoor plumbing and running water are enough to make me gawk, but my mind's on my plan. I scan the room. No video cameras tucked in the corners. No intercom boxes on the wall to call for help. I walk into the stall next to hers and pretend to get to business. She settles her weight on the toilet.

"So, you see why you need to follow the rules. It's so much nicer when we all get along. Don't you think?"

I don't answer. Instead, I flush the toilet for the water noise. I run out of my stall and slam into Betsy's door. The simple lock gives way and the door flies open.

"What the—?" Betsy yells. She tries to heave her weight off the toilet. I jump in and straddle her. She lets out a little shriek before I get my hands on her mouth, but the flush drowns it out.

"Listen to me," I whisper vehemently in her ear. "If you scream, I'll strangle you with the handcuffs. I can crush your windpipe with my hands." I lean into her until she winces. "I have nothing to lose. Do you understand?"

She nods, fat tears welling in her eyes.

I back off her a little, but keep my hand clamped over her mouth.

"You're going to tell me about a patient that's staying here. I'll know if you're telling the truth, too. There's no easier book to read than your face."

Betsy furrows her brow, but gives a curt nod.

"Her name's Janine Meemick." Just talking about my mother brings a tremble to my voice, but I grit my teeth and keep going. "She has a huge burn over the left half of her face and head."

Betsy's eyes widen. She nods.

My mother is here. I can't catch my breath. I look Betsy right in her wet cow eyes. "I need to know where she is."

Betsy shakes her head. My hand's still clamped over her mouth. Slowly, I peal my fingers back.

I worry she'll scream, but instead she speaks. "She's gone."

I clench my fists. "Don't lie. I'm not afraid to hurt you."

Betsy scowls at me. "Shut up and listen. She was here a week ago. I even gave her the tour. I remember her from the burns." She runs her hand over the left side of her head. "But, she's gone. I don't know what happened, but I think …" She pauses and scans the metal stall walls like she's checking if the coast is clear. Then she leans in and whispers, "I think she escaped."

"Escaped?"

Betsy nods. "The day she disappeared, I was in the lounge, watching my shows, and the alarm sounded for a lock down. When we were escorted into our rooms, I saw the guards running to the emergency stairs like they were after someone. The next day she was gone. Normally, if someone escapes, they drag them back and put them …" She pauses and looks up at me. "Put them on restriction." There's something she's not telling me, but she moves on without missing a beat. "But that woman, she never came back." I try to process this, but Betsy keeps talking. "Either she ran away, or she's *dead*."

Betsy's giving me a steely glare I never would have thought her capable of when she says the word dead. She's trying to hurt me. And it works. The thought of those guards shooting my mother in the back cuts me deep. Betsy can see it on my face because she smiles and pushes up on me. I stagger back, bang through the bathroom door and stumble into the stainless steel sink. She heaves herself off the toilet, walks over and casually washes her hands. When she turns to run her hands under the electric drier, she glares at me. "Next time, just ask. If you threaten me again, I'll find a way to make restriction look like a dang tea party." Then Betsy flops out of the bathroom, pushes open the door and hollers back to me. "Come on in there. Quit pooping around."

I follow her out the door and back to my room. My eyes count each step back because now that I know my mother's gone, I have one job. Escape.

CHAPTER SEVENTEEN

The next week is one of the most frustrating of my life.

I spend all day strapped to my bed. The skin on my wrists burns and chafes from pulling on my restraints for hours on end. The only activity I'm allowed is the horrible TV in the corner. Betsy says it's to give me something to do, but I know it's their way of driving me crazy. They play constant loops of black-and-white shows with titles of *I Love Lucy*, *Lassie* and *Leave it to Beaver*. These shows are so sickeningly sweet. These folk's biggest problems are getting a bad mark in school, or two friends wear the same dress to a party. It's maddening, slow torture watching people long dead live out their life while I can't do a damn thing to live my own. If I could move my arms, I'd throw something at the TV.

Betsy eats these shows up like hot bread rolls. It helps me understand her a little better, knowing she's been bred on this stuff. Each shows has women in their place: cooking, cleaning and raising babies. The men make the tough decisions and every episode ends in a family hug. She sits in front of my TV everyday with her mouth open, repeating every word Lucy says to Ricky.

"Isn't it magical?" she says, turning to me. Her hands cup her plump chin.

"What?" I've been going over escape plans in my head. The guards never leave their posts, the bars are fastened tight, the restraints are annoyingly affective. I have nothing.

"You know," she says pointing to the TV. "The way that Lucy and Ricky *love* each other."

She says love like its a verb, something you chose to do. In my experience you either love someone or you don't. Love boils under your skin like fire. Even when you don't want it to.

I shrug and turn my eyes back to the ceiling. The black camera watches from the corner. I want to smash it. Smash them all.

Betsy pushes up, comes over and sits on the edge of my bed, which creaks and slumps down under her weight. She keeps inserting herself into my life like this, trying to get me to follow the rules so I can get off restriction. And I tried at first. I ate the food they set before me, just not enough. I listened to Betsy drone on without strangling her. I even took their damn pills. Of course, I kept them under my tongue and pretended to swallow. When a guard found my stash of gloppy pills under my mattress, they put me back to square one. The look on Betsy's face when that happened mirrored my mother's when I set the kitchen drapes on fire while playing matches.

Betsy leans in my face and waves a hand to get my attention. One of her yellow curls bobs inches from my nose. I blow it away and roll over.

"Can't I just go to sleep?" I moan.

Betsy shakes her head and the bed jiggles. "Part of your restriction is that you have to listen to me. If I say you're doing better, Dr. Rayburn will believe me. So listen, or you'll be peeing in a tube for the rest of your life."

"Fine." I stare exaggeratedly at Betsy.

She scowls, but talks anyway. "Lucy and Ricky. Their love is *amazing*. I wonder what it would be like to be in *love*."

She hangs on *love* like it's a cliff's edge. I look down at my hands, tied to a bed frame and think of Clay. Someone I could have loved did this to me. I bet behind the cameras, Ricky shakes Lucy until her teeth rattle. I glare out my barred window. The sun is a hazy cataract in the sky. "Forget it, Betsy. You're stuck here forever. You won't find love, and neither will I."

Betsy's mouth drops like I just slapped her face. She pulls away, her arms crossing her swollen breasts. She stares angrily at the TV for a while. "My babies love me," she mumbles. "That's something."

I've been mean. Even though Betsy's so irritating, I can't be mean to her. It's like kicking a puppy. I clench my fists and try being nice. "How many babies have you had?"

"This is my third," she says, patting her stomach.

My mouth drops. She looks no older than me, just a kid. Three babies?

"How old are you?" I ask.

"Fifteen," she mumbles. She pulls a hospital pillow up to her chest and rests her chin on it. "I hope they let me stay with Esmeralda longer than Susanna. They pulled me at nine months with her. Said I was getting too attached."

"Esmeralda?"

"It's what I'm going to name her," she says, rubbing her belly. "Isn't it pretty?"

"Yeah," I sit up as much as my wrist restraints will allow. "But, why can't you keep your kids with you? Are they sick?"

She shakes her head, her curls bouncing around her head like springs. "No, they just want the mothers to focus on staying healthy for the next child. We can't be running around after toddlers all day and be ready for the next baby."

Her words are something they've fed her. Her eyes tell me she doesn't believe it.

"Who raises them?"

She looks down and picks at a string on the pillowcase. "The nannies. When I'm too old to breed anymore, I'll be a nanny and then I'll raise other girls' babies for them. It'll be my time to see them grow up." She throws on a fake smile.

I frown. "But they won't be yours."

Her smile falls. "In a way they will."

I shake my head. "In what way? They take your kids away and they make your take other people's kids later? That's not right."

Betsy jumps up from the bed, fresh tears wetting her eyes. "You don't know anything! You're cruel and cranky and your boyfriend left you, so you can't talk about what I do!" She huffs to the door and pushes the call button. Then she turns to me. Her eyes are darker and harder than I've ever seen them. "No wonder they're going to plan B with you."

A chill falls over me. "What's plan B?"

She says nothing and clomps out the door.

When the door slides shut, I curl into a ball on my bed as best I can. I've hurt Betsy and that's not okay. But my mind traces back over what she said. Plan B? Whatever it is, it can't be good.

***

When the door to my room slides open the next morning, I have my apology ready for Betsy, but it isn't her. It's the short, pudgy doctor in the long white coat, the one who stabbed me with a needle my first day—Dr. Rayburn. He slips in the door, his eyes tracing my every move like I'm a rabid raccoon.

"Ahem. Good, uh, morning, Miss …" He looks down at my chart, realize there's no name there and then blinks up at me. "Good morning. How are you, uh, feeling?"

I stare at him, this strange little man. His oversized lab coat trails down to the knees of his faded black pants. His hair is sticking up like he just woke. There's a yellow stain on his sleeve. I remember the images I had in my head of what Breeders looked like—cloaked monsters with yellow eyes and sharp teeth. He doesn't even look like an adult, let alone a monster.

He scratches at the pimply skin on his cheeks and then takes a wary step toward my bed. He squints up at the camera and then fumbles keys from his pocket. When he unlocks one cuff, his fingers tremble. Then he hands me the glass of juice from my bed tray.

I take the juice and grip it in my fist. "You're not a doctor."

He blinks at me bug-eyed. One of the burst pimples under his chin has dotted blood onto the color of his lab coat. "Yes, uh, I am. I'm Dr. Rayburn."

I shake my head. "Where's Betsy?"

Rayburn glances at his clipboard and then to the black dome of a camera in the corner. "Betsy chose, uh, not to see you this morning. It seems you've, uh, had a disagreement."

I narrow my eyes. "I want to see her."

He cringes at my tone, but continues. "You see, Miss … We never got your name."

"No, you didn't."

He clears his throat and starts again. "Betsy is a …" He clears his throat again like there's some phlegm lodged there. "A delicate girl. She's never left this, uh, hospital." He looks up at the camera. "Her choice, of course."

"Of course, my ass," I mumble.

Rayburn clears his throat and looks up at the camera. I wonder who's watching this. "What you don't understand, uh, is how safe it is here. Once you've proven you aren't …" he pauses and looks at me, "a danger to yourself and others, you can begin to enjoy all the, uh, the benefits this hospital has to offer."

I meet his squinty brown eyes. "This isn't a hospital," I say deliberately. "It's a prison."

He rubs his hand nervously under his pimpled chin. His fingers graze over the popped pimple and knock away the clot that had formed there. A slow dribble of blood slides down his neck. He doesn't seem to notice. "For you, uh, yes, it is. For now. To Betsy, it's her, uh, her home. Every time you, uh, you insult it, you stomp on everything Betsy loves." His speech hiccups. His eyes keep flicking up to that black lens in the corner. "I'm sure you, uh, you never saw it that way until I just, uh, clarified it for you." The doctor straightens his shoulders, but his face is the color of tile grout. He gulps, his Adam's apple bobbing like a cork, and speeds through the rest of his speech. "Now that you know, it is your job to, uh, do better for her."

I wonder who prepped him on what to say. I wonder what they think of his performance.

"And then they'll impregnate me?" I can't keep the disdain out of my voice.

"It's our duty," the doctor spreads his clammy hands, "to, uh, do all we can to build up the population."

I clench my jaw. "So, that includes imprisoning women and experimenting on them without their permission?" I can feel my hands trembling as my anger builds.

The doctor clears his throat again, a sound I'm beginning to loath. "Have you heard, uh, the story of what caused our current, um, predicament?"

My curiosity gets the best of me. I want to know. "I heard the government poisoned the water and then no more girl babies were born."

The doctor shakes his head, his jowls jiggling back and forth. The next words come out in a flat tone of rote rehearsal.

"Several decades ago our predecessors made a, um, a mistake. The petroleum we were using as fuel was perilously low. The public panicked. Then Dr. Borgen and the Hansen Center for Developmental Research created a, uh, a synthetic fuel. It was cheep, clean, efficient. Everyone in the, uh, modern world made the switch. The air was cleaner. There was less, uh, fighting in oil rich countries. It was a wonderful time for the world." He stops and looks up at the camera. Is he making them proud?

"What we didn't, uh, know then was that this fuel was poison. Over the years our bodies became exposed to more of the synthetic compounds. It built up in our systems while we were, um, unaware. Only when the government census began did we, uh, find the birth irregularities. At first only a few more males than females were born, uh, each year. That doubled and quadrupled. Even hormone treatments for, uh, for fetuses stopped working. While the experts researched and tested, the countries warred. Human trafficking abounded. Civilized life as we, uh, knew it ground to a halt. By the time we had the answer, uh, well …" He gestures out the window. "Well, you see what's left."

He pauses and takes a few loud breaths. "With the advancements we've made here, we can, uh, fix it. Our bodies and our environment are still full of these dangerous compounds. With, uh, new hormone therapies to the fetus produced in an environment free of, uh, the compounds that mutate the fetus, we can produce as many girls as we have, uh, women to bear them. That's why we need Betsy." He pauses and meets my eyes for the first time in several minutes. "That's why we need you. What you, uh, will do this generation may save the next."

"How noble," I murmur.

But his eyes say it is. Even with the scripted answer, I can tell Dr. Rayburn believes in what he's saying. He thinks he's part of mankind's salvation. But the look in his brown eyes somehow doesn't put a fire in my belly. Instead it leaves me cold. Who do these people think they are?

I try to cross my arms over my chest, but forget one's still strapped to the bed. I settle for clasping my hands around the bed rails. "I don't care how much humanity needs us; it isn't right to use people like cattle."

"I'm sorry you feel that way." The doctor takes a step backwards. It's clear he's done his duty and wants to get the heck out of here. "We must think of the, uh, greater good. If you can't learn to comply, we move to ... Well, we move to plan B."

"What's plan B?" I ask, as he trundles to the door. He doesn't look at me. "What's plan B?!" I tug at my one restrained arm.

He turns and glances at me once, and then slides out the door without a word.

***

This time when the door slides open, it's Betsy. Her face is puffy and sunken. She doesn't smile at me. She shuffles in and slumps in the chair next to my bed. She nearly folds in on herself, as if her bones could no longer support her frame.

"Are you ready to stop being such a witch?" Her face glows feverishly and her breath is ragged.

I study her face. "Are you okay?"

"Yes. Shut up. I'm nine months pregnant and very uncomfortable. I've come to take you down to dinner. Dr. Rayburn okayed it."

"What's plan B?" I ask, trying to hide the panic in my voice.

Betsy looks over at me for a moment and then shrugs. "Nobody tells me nothing."

"Betsy, I know that's not true. If you'd just ..."

"Let's go." It's a three-step process for her to get up out of the chair. "Guard, uncuff her please."

The guard releases my restraints. I hold my hands up for the handcuffs, but none are offered.

"Doc says you don't need cuffs as long as you behave." Betsy shrugs and lumbers to the door.

I follow after the waddling Betsy. She holds her belly with both arms as if she has to support it to keep it attached. I rub my hands together, watching her waddle and gasp for breath. I can't help but worry. She's sucking back raspy breaths when we find our cafeteria table with the two girls from before, Latisha and Sammy and another girl I've never met. They look up at me from their fish filets, some cooked plant material and brown bread. I can see Betsy eying everyone's bread roll as she pants.

"Getting ready to pop, huh, Betsy Wetsy," Latisha says, grinning. Her black eyes flash wickedly.

"She'll be Betsy Wetsy when her water breaks," Sammy laughs.

Betsy only moans and accepts her tray from the nanny who brings it over. Mine has two rolls. Betsy has none. Forget calorie restriction. If I can get the rolls into my gown, they're going to Betsy.

Latisha leans in toward me, a sick smile spreading on her brown face. "What about you, newb? They plant it in you yet?"

"Tish, don't be gross," Betsy says between bites.

Tish laughs again and twirls a finger in her kinky splay of hair. "Well, did they? You one of us sorry suckers now?"

I shake my head. Is that plan B? God, I have to get out of here. I glance around. The guards are posted at the doors, and the nannies shuffle about in their shapeless slippers, making sure each girl is eating their allotted portion. The black cameras track around the room, watching our every move, but I don't think they can hear us—not at this distance. My heart says I can't trust these girls enough to ask about escape, but I'm running out of options.

I lean toward Tish and Sammy. "Betsy told me some story about a woman busting out of here a few weeks ago."

The girls look at me warily and then at Betsy. She doesn't seem to notice. She stares at her weird vegetable and circles her belly with her hands.

Tish taps her fork on her straight, white teeth. "Why you asking, newb? You got an itch?" She pushes even closer. "Wanna bust out?" That wicked smile is back.

I drop back, quickly shaking my head. "Nope. Just saying it would be exciting to see someone try. Pretty tough to get out of here, I figure. Must've been one hell of an escape plan."

Tish is watching me carefully. She sets down her fork, glances around and leans in. "I know what you thinking, newb." Her voice pulses hot against my ear. "Don't know why you'd want to get out of here. Out there you'll be dead or somebody's love slave in the outside of a week. But, you ain't the first to itch. There are ways, but you gotta pay."

Betsy moans and rocks back on the bench. I find myself rubbing her back lightly. She swats my hand away.

I turn back to Tish. "I don't have anything to trade, but I could get something."

Tish smirks and skewers her fish fillet. "You ain't paying me and you ain't trading goods. You trading *services*." She hisses the services like a dirty word. Her plump upper lip curls nastily.

I furrow my brow. "What're you hinting at?"

She glances sideways. "See that guard over there?"

I turn. She grabs my hand and yanks. "Don't look. Just *glance*."

I reach around and pat Betsy on the back. A tall guard with curly orange hair and a thick red mustache like a fuzzy carrot stands with his back to the cafeteria door. I'm trying to be stealthy, but he catches me looking and winks at me. I whip back around, my cheeks burning.

"Rusty's such a perv," Tish mutters. Then she leans in and lowers her voice to a pale whisper. "Here's how it works. You give Rusty what he wants and if he can, he gets your ass out. Simple as that."

I blink for a moment. Then the full force of her words rolls over me like a boulder. The thought of Rusty coming anywhere near me makes me want to throw up. And if that's the only way out, what does this mean about my mama? I squint my eyes and try to push that thought out of my head. I try to forget the look on Rusty's face, his little disgusting mustache.

Betsy moans beside me and then rocks hard, making the table quake and forks rattle to the floor. I look up to see her trying to rise. She's clutching her belly. Her face has gone white with two large pink circles on her cheeks. Her mouth is a shocked O. The bottom of her gown darkens, liquid tinkles to the floor beneath her and splashes on my ankles.

Sam shakes her head. "Betsy Wetsy."

I stand up and take Betsy's arm. "Doctor!" I call. "Help!"

"Calm down, newb," Tish says. "Happens all the time around here. Her water just broke."

CHAPTER EIGHTEEN

By the time the nannies usher us down the hall and into an exam room, I'm nearly hysterical, but Betsy's already there. Her eyes roll into the back of her head. Her forehead glistens with sweat. She reaches out and grabs my hand, crushing my fingers.

"You come," she mutters into my face. "Come with me."

I follow, too shocked to do anything else. The nannies get Betsy on the bed, and Betsy pulls me along, the tips of my fingers turning white.

I am not good in these kinds of situations. Give me a burn, a cut, a coyote bite and I can handle it. But a little iodine and a bandage won't help Betsy. She's got her legs in some weird metal stirrups and she's making sounds like the piglets did before Arn cut their heads off. I've never seen a baby being born. When my mama was having Ethan, Auntie shooed me and Arn into the barn. We stayed there for the twenty hours it took for my pink, squirming baby brother to be born. But my mama never screamed like Betsy.

Before the ache of missing my family can grip me, a doctor blows in, a white sail with black-rimmed glasses. He notes me and gives me a questioning look, but Betsy grips his arm. Her fingers make indents in his flesh. "Doctor, the drugs! Please, the drugs! I need them."

There is too much white showing around the irises in Betsy's eyes. She grits her teeth and squeals again. I wish to God he'll give her the drugs. The doc checks her, putting his hand were no strange man outta. Then he shakes his head, removes his glove with a snap and drops it in the trash. "Sorry, Elizabeth. You're too far along. I told you this one was going to go fast."

Betsy moans and clutches my fingers, as more pain rocks her.

I shoot the straight-faced doc a frustrated look. "Why can't you give her the drugs? She needs them!"

The doc stares at me over the rims of his glasses. "The drugs will only slow things down. She's already at eight centimeters." He pats Betsy's trembling knee.

"Almost there." He slides off his white coat and nurses bring him a blue gown and a mask.

Betsy screams and writhes on the bed like someone's gutting her. "Help me, Agatha," she says, drawing me close.

I look into her pinched, sweaty face. "I'm here. It's going to be okay." God, what a lie.

Betsy looks as if she's about to nod, but then her face scrunches up as pain rolls through her. I scan the room for these drugs they're talking about. I'll give them to her myself.

There's no time. Between Betsy's moaning and writhing, all I can do is pat her hand and wipe sweat off her brow. The doctor gears up, and they remove the lower half of the bed. I'm thankful Betsy keeps pulling me closer to her head. I do not want to see what's happening down at the other end.

The doc says push, and Betsy screams. Though I'll be deaf as well as fingerless by the end, I just keep murmuring sweetness like Auntie would. There's a grunt and a scream, and suddenly there's a new noise in the delivery room. A mewing cry. The doctor holds up a gooey, purple baby.

"Oh God," Betsy cries. Fat tears trace her puffy cheeks. "I did it," she whispers. "I really did it."

I watch the baby wriggle and cry in the nurse's gloved hands. It's amazing, really, how we're brought into this world. Red and squalling, but so, so beautiful. I feel the corners of my eyes dampen as I watch a fresh life take her first breaths. A real-life miracle.

"You did it," I whisper. "You were amazing. I couldn't have done that."

Betsy smiles up at me. "When it's your time, you will." Then she turns her smile toward her baby.

The room chills suddenly. I can't do what Betsy just did. The pain, the torture. Not to mention the nine months of agony beforehand. And Betsy's already done this three times. I step back, shaking my head. I'm not thinking about Betsy or the baby. I'm thinking about escape. I glance around the room and realize no one's paying any attention to me. The doctor tends to Betsy. Two nurses clean off the mewing baby in a heat tray. Two steps and I slip unnoticed into the quiet hallway.

Then I take off running.

Time has slipped away while Betsy was pushing. The hallways are dark and empty. As I creep down the hall, I hear the murmur of someone's TV set, the steady hum of the air ventilators. Other than that, it seems everyone's asleep. If I can find the stairs, maybe I'll have a chance at getting out. I pull up to a corner and peek around.

There's a guard at a desk twenty feet away. His half-lidded eyes watch the flickering surveillance screens in front of him. I watch, barely breathing, as his heavy lids slide down. I can't believe this is the best security the government can offer. They must think that their patients are as easy to tend as mindless sheep. Well, tonight I'm more wolf than sheep. I slink past his desk and into the stairwell. I fly down the stairs at an amazing clip. The only sounds are my footsteps and the beating of my heart.

At level G and the bottom of the stairs, I pause, panting. A solid metal door separates me from whatever lurks beyond. Nannies, Doctors, Guards—all three could wait on the other side. Or it could be the fresh air under the twinkling midnight sky. There's only one way to find out. My hands slowly push open the door.

It's another dimly lit hallway. My heart sinks. There has to be a way out of here. My panic building, I head left and run past a number of closed doors with key-card swipe locks. The distant hum from behind a set of double doors gets my attention. It has a key swipe box, but someone's propped the door open a crack with a wooden wedge. Maybe it's an electrical room that has a passageway to the outside. I take a deep breath and open the door.

I stumble in the dark room and let the door click behind me. It's pitch black, but there's an odor I don't like. My eyes find a shape here or there, but little else. I clutch the door handle and will my pupils to adjust. Soon soft silhouettes appear. The quiet echoes inside let me know it's much larger than a patient's room. At first I think cafeteria, but then I see blinking monitors every six feet or so. Some sort of computer facility?

Something shifts in a dark corner. I freeze, barely breathing. Is someone there? After several seconds, I hear nothing but the beat, beat, beat of my heart. There's no time. Across the echoing expanse, a fan hums and a puff of air dances on my face. On the far wall, I can just make out a large rectangular metal plate. It's the first dirty surface I've seen, stained with dried smears of what looks like garbage. A garbage chute? Does it lead out to a dumpster or down to an incinerator? I shuffle toward it.

I bump into something at thigh height. A table? I reach down until I feel the spongy material at my fingertips. Blankets. A mattress. It's a hospital bed like my own upstairs. My fingers trace up the sheet until I touch something firm beneath. My hand slides around the shape under the blanket. I stagger back. A foot. It's a human foot.

The room seems to slide sideways. There's a pounding in my ears. Is this the morgue? But why the monitors at every bed? I can't breathe. I spin to leave and bump into another bed.

Trembling, I peer down, my hand over my mouth to cover the gasp.

It's a girl, though I can hardly call her that. Her lank hair has fallen out in clumps and lies in piles beside her head. Her pasty sore-pocked skin is nearly see-through on her skeletal face. Cords and wires jut out of her arms, chest and head like she's some kind of machine. Long, thin fingernails curl from her lifeless hands. An odor like rotten meat wafts from the bed, gagging me.

She's the living dead. And she's eight months pregnant.

Icy waves of fear wash over me, weakening my knees. I scan the dark beds. There must be dozens of girls in similar states. They're human incubators. A fate worse than death. On a bed next to me a legless creature lies nine months pregnant, her face covered by paper-thin skin. The stumps of her legs still oozing. Oozing.

I gag and stumble back. Have to get out.

"Dear God," I whisper with trembling lips, "What is this?"

"Plan B," the husky male voice behind me says.

I whirl around, but it's too late. He slams me to the ground. My knees bang into the tile, then my wrists, and finally the ground hits my cheek like a punch. I shove up and scamper forward, but he's got my ankle. He pulls. My fingers find a bed sheet. I claw up the bed. The sheet slips back and the unconscious woman's head lolls towards me. It's then I see the burns.

My mother's burned face lies before me. She's unconscious, a tube taped over her mouth like a transparent snake burrowing into her throat. Tubes coil out of blue veins in her arms. One hand lies cupped on the bed as if she were reaching out to me. But she's not. She's unconscious. One of their plan B experiments.

"No!" I scream. The guard yanks on my arms, pulls me across the tile floor. I lock my eyes on my mother until it's too dark to see, until she's a ghostly blur in my tear-filled eyes. "Mama!"

God, no. Please no. Not her. Not like this.

I used to think the Breeders were monsters. Now I know they are.

The guard drags me back upstairs to my room. I'm glad he grips my arms because my legs are jelly. When he pushes me on my bed and straps me down, I barely have the strength to fight back. All I can see in the darkness is my mother's lifeless face. The tube in her throat. Her hand clutching, finding nothing in the dark.

Dr. Rayburn stands at the side of my bed. He waves the guard away.

"You're a monster," I manage to croak.

"You … uh, you are not authorized to roam the hallways." His eyes flick to my face and then away again. "Full restriction is back in place."

"What did you do to her?" I blink back tears. I won't cry. Not in front of him.

The doctor's voice is thick and full of phlegm when he speaks. "It's, uh, it's not your concern." His eyes flick to the camera. Then he leans in and lowers his voice. "This is what I've been warning you about."

"How could you?"

"Those girls could not comply. The hospital feels," he pauses and looks up at the camera again. "We feel it's for the, um, greater good. No fertile female can be wasted."

"That's my mother, you bastard!" I say through my teeth. "She has children! You turned her into a living *corpse!*" I bang my fists on the railings. "How can you sleep at night?!"

"Uh, yes, well, listen," he says, running a hand over his greasy mop of hair. He steps closer to my bed than he's ever dared and lowers his voice to a whisper. "You've got to comply. If not, you'll end up down there. There won't be much I can do to help—"

The intercom on the wall squawks to life. "Dr. Rayburn, please report to your supervisor immediately." The voice is cold, calculating and surprisingly female.

Rayburn stiffens. His eyes grow as wide as a child's caught in some unspeakable act. He's been kind, and now he's in trouble. I swivel my head away as he turns to leave, feeling the tears starting to well. Even the smallest kindnesses are banished here. I can't stand it. I look out the dark window. Dawn's graying the sky. I wonder if it will be one of my last sunrises. What does it matter? My mother can't see sunrises anymore.

"Forty-eight hours," the doctor mumbles as he stands at my door. "You have that long to prove to them that you'll, uh, you'll go along with the program. After that, well," he looks at me with sympathy, "you know."

When the door clicks closed, I let the sobs break free. Crying is one of the only things I'm still free to do.

***

I'm in my room, staring at the clock. The TV is on. Some show with two men fighting. I can't focus. I watch the second hand tour the clock face and think of my mama. What did it feel like when they put her under? Could she hear me when I screamed her name? If I could get to her, could I somehow wake her up?

I roll over and stare out my bedroom window. Even if I could get it open, there are the heavy metal bars. Even if I could pry the bars off, we're seven stories up. I roll over and look at the door. It's monitored day and night. It doesn't open without a guard pressing a button from the control room. Yet there has to be a way to get my mama out. I refuse to give up and let her live out her last awful moments in that room.

The only possible option is what Tish suggested earlier. Rusty. Rusty with his filthy smile and ugly mustache. Thinking about him makes my stomach churn. I can't imagine letting him touch me. But if he could free my mama, wouldn't it be worth it?

Would he get her out and me out, too? Images of Betsy writhing in pain flash through my head. I don't want to bring a baby into this world, be a part of this twisted system that manufactures girls like canned soup. Then my daughters would be faced with the same horrific decision I'm forced to make. I shutter at the thought of having a baby, just to lose her to plan B.

I've wound my bed sheets into knots. I lean my head back on my pillow and look up at the clock. Forty-four hours, fifty-five minutes. Soon, by not acting, my decision will be made for me.

***

When my door slides open, Rusty struts in with my breakfast tray. The sight of him smirking, rubbing a finger over his carrot-colored mustache, is revolting. He's tall and rail thin, with a head of red, curly hair. He's wearing the white guard's uniform and black loafers. But it's his eyes, slipping over my body like filthy hands, that make me want to gag.

He sets the tray on the table, takes a napkin and drapes it over the surveillance camera lens. His voice oozes like rancid oil. "Hey there, sweet thing. Heard you called for a little side of Rusty with your breakfast this morning." He reaches out and tugs on the sheet covering me.

I pull my knees to my chest and wrap my arms around them. "What're you doing here?" I ask, trying to stall. I hate the way he's looking at me.

Rusty's smiles, a smile that reminds me of a snake-oil salesman on one of these shows Betsy watches—wide, white and entirely false.

"Tish said you wanted to trade. A one-way ticket out of this joint. Well, Rusty's all about helping little ladies." He leans over the bed and presses his palms onto either side of the mattress where I sit. His face hovers less than a foot from mine. I can see the dandruff around his collar, the chunk of something green between his teeth.

I lean away from him. "I've changed my mind. If I'm going to trade," even discussing this makes me feel ill, but I press on. "If I'm going to trade, I want my mama out of plan B."

He leans down. His body nearly on top of mine. I feel his hand on my thigh above the blanket. "No can do, sweat thang. Nobody comes out of plan B. But I can get you out. You'd like that, right? Out to see your boyfriend?"

He puts his weight on me now. His heaving chest presses into mine until I can't breathe. The smell of raw desire and cheap cologne is suffocating. One rough hand's running down my thigh and pulling up the fabric of my gown. The other hand grips my neck like a vice. His mustache brushes the skin of my neck as he runs his tongue along my jaw.

If he can't get my mama out, I want him off me. Now.

I slam my palms against his polyester uniform and shove and kick until he tumbles off and onto the floor. He pulls up on the side of my bed, the greasy smile sliding off his face.

"What gives?" He swipes one hand over his mess of red hair.

I scrunch back farther into the bed, as if the pillows could hide me. "Get out! You aren't touching me!"

He gives me a shocked look. "Tish said you wanted a *trade*." He says trade like he's already undressed me.

"She was wrong."

Rusty frowns. "You're slotted for insemination tomorrow. Don't you want to get out before they put a bun in that oven?" He points towards my stomach.

"Not bad enough to let you touch me," I hiss.

He tucks his shirt back into his pants and stalks to the door. He turns back angrily. "You'll regret this, *sweetheart*."

"No, I don't think I will."

Rusty and his proposition are out.

Forty-two hours.

***

When dinner arrives, Rayburn lets me eat in the cafeteria as long as I'm under guard. When I walk through the doors, a slap of cooked fish smell welcomes me. My guard leads me to a table with Tish and Sammy. I don't want to hang with these two, especially since Tish will ask about Rusty, but the guard won't leave until I sit. Tish and Sammy stop their talk, glance at me, and then continue complaining about the food. I pick at the clumpy fish that's already cold on my plate.

When the guard's out of earshot, Tish leans into me. "Heard you screaming at Rusty this morning." The smirk on Tish's caramel-colored face is unmistakable. She loves other people's misery. It gives her something to do. "Thought you wanted out so bad you'd do *anything*."

"Not bad enough to let that slimy bastard touch me." I push the fish around my plate. I've lost my appetite.

Tish nudges Sammy. "It's not so bad, right, Sammy?"

Sammy doesn't look up, but stabs angrily at her lettuce.

I raise an eyebrow.

"That little bun in the oven," Tish says, pointing to Sammy's stomach, "didn't come from no Petri dish, if you know what I mean."

I do, though it makes me sick. Sammy's cheeks flush bright red. She shoots Tish a searing glare, grabs her tray and tromps over to another table. I catch Rusty's eyes following Sammy as she goes.

"I'm just saying," Tish says with a smirk, "might not matter if you've turned him down. He might find a way to get what he wants."

I grip my fork until my knuckles are white. Rusty's everything that's wrong with this place. I think of my mama in the dark, a tube snaked down her throat. Hurting Rusty won't make that right, but it might make me feel better.

I turn to Tish, letting all caution fall to the wayside. "Does anyone ever get out of plan B?"

She turns to me, her eyes wide, her mouth open. "How do you know about—"

"I just do. Tell me. Is there a way out?"

She slowly shakes her head from side to side, her black curls jiggling. "Once you're in, you're in. I never seen anybody come out."

The look on her face makes me believe her. My mama. What can I do? I can't give up and let her rot in that basement hooked up to monitors. The thought of that would drive me insane. There has to be a way.

Then the cafeteria doors fly open. Betsy barrels in, white hospital gown billowing around her like a sail. She's sobbing and shaking. She spots me and makes a beeline over. When she reaches us, she wraps her hands around my arm and hangs on for dear life. "Oh, Agatha, they've taken her!" The tears darken the fabric under her pudgy neck. "They won't give her back."

I take her hands. "What'd you mean? Your baby?"

"Esmeralda. Only those witchy nannies say that name is gaudy. They put Jane on her bassinet card. Jane. What kind of name is Jane? Plain Jane. Jane goes down the drain. Jane insane in the brain."

Betsy's eyes roll wildly in her head. Behind her, the guards stride up. I stroke her arm to sooth her. "Betsy, what're you talking about?"

"They won't even let me nurse her. They say I'm too *hysterical*." Her voice rivals howling coyotes. She wipes her nose on the sleeve of her gown and emits big barking sobs that shake her whole body and me with it.

"There has to be a mistake," I murmur, patting her arm.

A mistake—or the cruelty this place masks as kindness. After all she went through and they take away her baby? The rage I've been feeding shakes its cage, wanting release. A shadow falls on us. Two guards stand on either side. The slash of red hair tells me all I need to know. Rusty, to my left, winks before reaching down and grabbing one of Betsy's arms. The second guard grabs the other. They begin to drag her to the door.

"Agatha!" she wails. "Help!"

My face flushes. My breathing deepens. This cannot stand.

"Let her go!" I say through clenched teeth.

One corner of Rusty's mustache rises as his eyes meet mine. He turns to the other guards. "If this one causes any disturbance," he says, nodding to me, "feel free to use appropriate force."

He sounds so professional when he's not trying to seduce a child. He won't sound so professional in a second. I clench fists and bare my teeth. He drops Betsy and faces me, his arm out, fingers splayed as if readying for a fight. "Let's do this," he says, grinning.

In my head that little voice is screaming, *Don't! Think of Mama and plan B!* I look down at Betsy, the hot, crumpled, sobbing mess on the polished linoleum. The voice of reason goes silent as I run toward Rusty.

I slam my shoulder into his chest. Tensed though he was, he underestimated the force of my blow. He crumples backward, his back slamming into a cafeteria table. Trays go flying. Girls scatter. My eyes track a clump of half-eaten fish as it arcs through the air and smacks, wet, onto the linoleum.

Rusty pulls up and shakes his head like a punch-drunk fighter. When his eyes meet mine, the gaze is anticipatory, almost gleeful. He wants to fight. Well, bring it on.

He runs, head down, arms out. I clamber over a table, pushing past two very surprised girls who wrap their arms around their pregnant bellies. "Move!" I shout. They scatter like frightened birds.

Halfway over the tabletop, there's a hand around my ankle. Rusty's fingers grip vice-like at my foot and pull backwards. I'm dragged backward on my belly, arms clawing at the tabletop for something to hang on to. My shin hits the bench and pain jolts up my leg. My fingers curl over the table's far edge and stop my decent into Rusty's awaiting arms.

"Come on," he grunts, his mustache twitching. His hand claws up my bleeding shin, drawing me closer. "Come to papa."

My fight with Rusty can't end like this. I search madly for some kind of weapon. My eyes run over plastic trays, plates of fish, plastic glasses. Rusty grunts and tugs harder. My fingers slide to the very edge of the table. One by one, they'll peel off and it'll be over. That's when my eyes lock on the smooth metal curve of the utensil to my right.

I grab the fork and release the table in one swift motion. As I tumble into Rusty's waiting arms, I rotate until I'm facing him, the fork ready. My body slams into Rusty's. There's a pain in my jaw as it smacks into his shoulder. As we tumble to the ground, I jab the fork.

When it connects, the sound of the fork sinking into Rusty's eye sounds a lot like slipping a knife into a jackrabbit's belly.

We lay in a pile on the ground. I scramble off and stare at what I've done. Slowly, Rusty sits up, the metal fork sticking out of his eye. Then he starts screaming.

I meant to hurt Rusty, but this, this is something else entirely. As I'm watching in rapt horror, something stings the skin of my forearm. What the—? Barbs attached to long wires arch from my arm to a strange gun in a guard's hand. Then he pulls the trigger. It's a moment before the current hits me.

Pain. Raw, snapping, agonizing pain. I crumple to the floor and shake on the tile. My teeth slam against each other in series of loud cracks. The tang of blood spikes my tongue. I seize. I choke. I'm dying. I'll die fried by coursing electricity.

When the current stops, I can't move. I lay on the ground twitching. My skull's exploded. My mouth tastes like bile and blood. I think I've bitten through my tongue. That little voice in my head comes back. *What have you done?*

As two sets of hands grab my body, I get one more glimpse of Rusty clutching his useless eye.

At least he won't be winking anymore.

CHAPTER NINETEEN

They drag me out of the cafeteria and toss me on a gurney. Cuffs snap around my wrists. My body still trembles with the current, and I can't turn my head. Had I eaten, I'd be throwing it up. Behind me, uproar ignites the cafeteria, but Betsy's wild moans blanket the frightened murmurs as she's dragged past me. I hear Rusty's screams as they escort him away.

The gurney rattles forward before I can hear more. I stare straight upward. The florescent lights blink overhead like the faded lines on a long stretch of bad highway.

"Where are we going?" I croak. My mind fights off images of the girls in the basement. "Take me back to my room."

I look up. It's Dr. Rayburn. His lab coat's buttoned crookedly and his shirt's poking out the zipper of his fly. He doesn't answer. My belly fills up with liquid lead.

The gurney squeaks to a stop. When I'm able to lift my head, I see we're parked in front of the elevator. The glowing red triangle on the control panel sends shivers down my spine. We're going down. Down toward plan B.

"Don't!" I scream, hoarsely. "You can't do this!"

Dr. Rayburn pushes me into the elevator. When the door closes, I lean up, trying to catch his attention. His normally pale face is flushed. One corner of his mouth twitches nervously. He does not look like someone bent on destroying me. "You can't do this," I plead. "You're not a monster."

He swallows hard and shifts his gaze back to the changing numbers on the control panel. "It's best if you, uh, don't talk."

"No," I say, shaking my head, leaning forward until my wrists ache against the metal cuffs. "You can't take me to plan B. Let me go! Please!"

He won't meet my gaze. "Best if you don't talk."

With Rayburn I thought I had hope. Now hope has flown and what I'm left with is the stunning realization that my life is over. I'll be turned into a living corpse, left to sleep out my days to the rhythm of a heart monitor, my only friends the ghosts of girls who could have been so much. And my mama. I'll never save her. We'll rot together in some basement lab while the rest of the world goes on.

"Janine Meemick," I choke, sobbing. "Can you put me next to her?" At least we could be together. It's the only thought that gives me a speck of comfort.

Dr. Rayburn looks at me and then flicks his eyes back to the numbers as they light up on the control panel.

Tears slide down my face, into my collar. I think of Auntie, Ethan, and Arn. I think of Bounty, who was someone's dinner long ago. I think of Clay, whose fault this is. I'll never see any of them again. Their faces swirl around. I try to remember every facet of their being, what they smelled like, what it felt like to touch them, how much they loved me. Maybe I can bring some of that with me into the darkness. Oh, God, this can't be it, can it? I'm sobbing uncontrollably when the elevator doors slide open.

We exit the elevator and swing around a corner to a set of double doors. When he pushes me through, I wait for that rotten meat smell, but we enter an echoing warehouse instead. What's going on?

High industrial shelves line walls stocked with paper products, cardboard boxes and linens. Food cans are stacked in neat pyramids. Every supply must be stored in here. It's a looter's dream, which also explains the huge, metal blast doors and the giant control panel next to it. There's a few machine guns mounted above the panel, grenades, bullet-proof vests. They're taking no chances in defending their stock.

Two vans are parked just inside the doors. The first is a polished supply van, but the second is dusty and battered. Through the darkened windows people move inside.

My sobs subside. "What's this?" Rayburn's already shuffling toward the van, muttering.

The passenger door opens and Rayburn leans in. I crane my neck, but the windows are black. Rayburn talks to someone inside. Then he stumbles out, closes the door and shuffles back to me, raking a nervous hand through his greasy hair.

I strain forward wildly. "Who's in the van, Rayburn?"

He gives me a sidelong glance, as if he's forgotten me. Then he starts undoing my handcuffs, a slight tremor back in his hands. "Don't run," he says, as he leads me to the van. "You've got nowhere to go."

I struggle against Rayburn as he pushes me up to the back doors. "Who's in there?" I scream. "Tell me!"

The doors pop open. A giant, bare-chested man in overalls stares blankly at me, his mouth open, his eyes slipping over my body. His giant hand cinches around my bicep.

"No!" I scream as the thug pulls me into the van. His hands are the size of baseball mitts. They clamp me to his large sweaty body. The van doors shut. The engine starts up.

Pressed against some strange man's chest, his hot breath in my ear, the reality of my situation sinks in. First plan B. Now this. What is happening?

Huge biceps block my view. I can't see over the frayed backseat. I struggle against the beast holding me. We pull out of the hospital warehouse and bounce onto the road. We're leaving Mama. I open my mouth to protest. Then several things happen at once.

A head pops over the bench seat. "Riley!"

It's Ethan.

My fear recedes at the joy of seeing my brother. Ethan. What's he doing here?

There's another voice from the front. "Let her go, Hatch."

That voice. I turn toward the front of the van and there he is. Clay's climbing over the bench seat toward me. His dimpled smile washes over his face as he drops into the back and pulls me from Hatch's grip.

"I thought I'd never see you again." His fingers delicately cup the skin of my wrists. He kneels, his face expectant, astonished, relieved.

Clay. Clay's here. I meet his eyes.

Then I lean back and punch him in the face.

"God!" Clay yells as he cups his jaw and shoots me a wounded glare.

Before I can process anything, giant hands grip grab me back in a thick, muscled embrace. I bat out with hands that must seem infantile to this giant. He squeezes me to his chest, the metal buttons of his overalls digging into my cheek. His chest is sleek with sweat.

I hear Clay behind me. "I said get your hands off!"

The giant releases me just as the driver swerves. The van rocks and I crash into the wall with a *thunk*. My elbow throbs where it dented the van wall. When I sit up, Hatch squats beside me, staring wide-eyed. My hospital gown has slipped off revealing my bare shoulder. As I snatch at the gown, his eyes watch my hand and then trace down other parts of my body. I don't like the hungry look on his face. He leans forward. Clay grabs the straps of his overalls and hauls him backward.

"I told you to keep your goddamn hands off her!" Clay's tone is dangerous, considering this monster, with his tree trunk arms and barrel chest, has eight inches and seventy-five pounds on him.

The giant brushes Clay's hands off with a flick of his wrist. "Boss said keep her still." Even his voice is meaty and slow. His sausage fingers curl into fists.

Clay pokes a finger into the denim bib on Hatch's chest. "I'm boss's son and I say get the hell away before I make you!" His hand claws toward the revolver at his hip.

"Boys," says a familiar voice from the front, "knock if off, gawddammit."

I see the crescent-shaped scar first. Then the crooked smile. The Sheriff grins at me from the driver seat.

"Been a while, little lady." He nods and tips an invisible hat. "Welcome to the family."

CHAPTER TWENTY

The tension in the van sits thick and heavy.

They let me ride in the middle bench with Ethan. Clay sits up front with his father. Hatch rides behind us. No one talks. Every now and then, Hatch farts or the Sheriff whistles a little tune through his teeth. The only other sounds are the road and the thoughts blaring in my head. How did this happen? Where are we going? Is Ethan okay? Looking at him, curled into me, his hair's too long (he keeps blowing it out of his eyes) and he's got what looks like his lunch smeared at the corners of his mouth, but he's all there. Clay's been taking care of him after all. I slink one arm around his shoulders.

My eyes flick to Clay up front. There's a puffy, red lump where my knuckles mashed his jaw. He sits ramrod straight, tightened fist in his lap. He's worked up, though I'm not sure if it's Hatch or his dad or me. He deserved the punch. He put me in that hospital where I was almost raped and used for birthing experiments. And now he's here with his father. They saved me from plan B, but whatever the Sheriff's got in mind can't be much better.

I watch Albuquerque, or what's left of it, zoom past as we drive by. Ethan stares up at the angling buildings, their windowless sides tracking up higher into the sky than any he's ever seen. "Did people live way up there?" he asks, his eyes on a battered skyscraper.

I nod. Ethan stares upward, his mouth open. My eyes are on the dark doorways, the abandoned cars, the empty parking lots with garbage skittering like crumpled animals. Every now and then we see vagabonds with dark vacant eyes and tattered clothes living in abandoned buildings. Occasionally we see people with matching shoes, full sets of teeth. There's one benefit to the Breeder's hospital. They've created jobs, income and a sustainable place to cluster around. Some of the buildings show signs of repair: boarded-up windows instead of gaping holes, swept sidewalks, cars that might actually run. We drive past what must've been a park, with decrepit benches, tall branching trees and a large grassy field. Vendors have set up booths made of recycled material. Ethan points at a vendor selling both scavenged office furniture and handmade items, chairs pieced together with plywood and two-by-fours, tables molded out of street signs and rusted rebar. The delicious smell of cooked meat wafts in the open window. A man ladles stew out of a large vat, spewing steam into the air. It makes me think about all we've lost as a civilization. How so much seemed to fall away when the population tanked and we were reduced to basic survival. As Auntie always said, "Leave men to their own devices and this is what you get." Maybe the Breeders will bring some civilization to our uncivilized world after all. Too bad they're willing to sacrifice human life for progress.

A little further out of town, we drive into what used to be a housing area: cozy lanes that now hold abandoned houses falling into decay. We drive past a row of houses burnt to a crisp, their blackened walls standing alone like charred tombstones, marking the demise of the American dream. I spot a square adobe house. The garage door is long gone and piles of fallen plaster litter the garage floor. Next is a sagging two-story where the walls have shifted and the roof bowed. The trees and shrubs someone carefully planted and outlined with stones have withered and died to yellow stalks.

The Sheriff turns down a particularly long driveway and stops in front of another adobe house. I stare at the matching white garage doors, both bent, rusty and cracked open like sleepy eyes. To the left, up a little walkway, the front door stands open. I peer inside to a dark hallway, my heart spurring up in my chest.

"Boys," the Sheriff says, drawing his gun, "search the premises. No dinner guests. You got me?"

"Stay here," Clay says to us as he slides open the door.

The men jump out. Ethan and I scoot to the edge of the battered bench seat and watch out the front windshield as the men slink up the sidewalk and through the door, guns drawn, faces tense.

After five minutes, Clay strides up to the van and pulls the side door open. "All clear. Come on in." Ethan jumps out. Clay offers me his hand to help me.

I glare at his hand like it's a viper and push past him.

The fresh dusk air is clean and cool after the smog in the van. I inhale deep. It's the first free air I've breathed in a week. Then my eyes meet Sheriff Tate's as he saunters back to the van for supplies. Not so free after all.

I take a step toward the house when Clay blocks my path. "Hold up," he says. He's got a pocket knife in one hand and pair of tweezers in the other. I gape at him. He points to my neck. "We need to get that damn transmitter out or they can track you. I can do it." He looks down at his utensils. "Gonna hurt a little."

I shrug. "Won't be any worse than what I've already been through."

His face tightens. Then he twirls his fingers in a turn-around gesture.

I face the van. He steps behind me. I feel the heat of his body as he leans in. "Close your eyes and count to ten," he says in my ear. I try not to focus on his breath pulsing on my neck, the pressure of his fingers cupping my shoulder.

One, two, three … There's the small jolt of pain as the knife pierces my skin. *Four, five, six* … A deeper pain as the tweezers go in. *Seven, eight* … I feel something detach. *Nine* … The trickle of blood down my neck. *Ten* … His hand pressing a cloth to the wound.

"Done," he says, sounding relieved.

I turn around slowly. His hand's still on the cloth on my neck. My eyes travel up his outstretched arm to his face. If he weren't so handsome with his steel blue eyes and easy smile, it might be easier to stay mad.

"Here," he says holding the tweezers out. He drops the bloody chip into my palm. It's so small, about the size of a button, yet so complex with its tiny wires. A green light fades in the center, like a firefly winking out. "You can keep it," he says. "A memento if you want one."

I place the chip carefully in my pocket. I have to remember the hospital. My mama's there.

"Come on," he says, waving me into the house.

The smell of mildew and decay hits me as we walk in the front door. The air's thick, swirling with dust we churn up with our boots. The foyer opens into what used to be a kitchen and living room. The part of the kitchen ceiling has fallen onto the buckling cabinets. Everything of value has been stripped, so all that remains is warped linoleum, dirty carpet and piles of trash. My hand brushes over a flaking newspaper on the kitchen counter that crumbles to pieces before I can read the headlines. Cobwebs drape from the corners. I spy a trail of brown animal droppings near the splintered sliding glass door. It'll be an interesting night's sleep.

The barren backyard doesn't look much better with the tilted swing set rusting in the dust. Other dilapidated houses dot the landscape as far as the eye can see. I grab Ethan by the hand and pull him toward the yard. I need to get him alone to ask all the questions thudding around in my brain.

Clay looks up from the armload of wood he's carrying—a broken kitchen chair, piece of a picture frame, what looks like a dusty jewelry box. "Where you two going?"

I narrow my eyes at him. "To pee. Do you mind?"

He frowns and shakes his head. "I don't think you should wander around alone." His eyes flick across the yard to where Hatch drags a fallen tree trunk like a twig to the woodpile.

I hold up Ethan's hand that I'm clutching. "I've got Ethan, okay? We'll be back in a few minutes. Feel free to hold your breath till we return."

I turn on my heel and drag Ethan along. We trudge past Hatch and into the neighboring yard. Before us stands the remains of a three-bedroom ranch, but the back half has been eaten by fire. I pull Ethan in, stepping over what looks like a dead animal, but I don't stop. When we get to the middle of what used to be the living room, now blackened and missing the roof, he pulls back. "Riley," he says, crossing his arms over his narrow chest, "I *do not* want to watch you pee."

"You're not. Listen, I need to ask you some questions. No fooling around, okay. We only got a few minutes."

He squishes up his face, but nods.

I brush the hair out of his eyes. "What happened after I got shot?"

Ethan frowns. "You were bad, crying and bleeding all over. I thought you were gonna die. Clay said we had to take you to the hospital. I didn't want to, but we had to."

I nod rapidly. "How'd we get outta town?"

"Clay found gas and we took a car and drove to that big hospital, the one with all the shiny lights."

My eyes flick out the open front door. Out there are men. "What else?"

Ethan scratches his head and looks across the room. His eyes lock on a splash of red in the corner—a plastic toy car, melted and half-buried under a pile fallen plaster. I lean over until my head blocks his view. "What. Else."

His eyes flick back to me. "After we dropped you off, Clay got us a room. We sat on our butts for days, trying to figure how to get you out once you was better. One day, Clay's daddy just shows up at the door. Riley, I thought you and Dad were bad, but you should hear Clay and his daddy fight."

Arn. A mention of him still hurts like a finger dug into a raw wound. I twirl my hand in a hurry-up gesture. "How did they get me out of the hospital?"

Ethan shrugs. "Clay just said, 'We're gonna get Riley.' That was yesterday. We got in the van and drove to that big hospital. What's it like in there?"

"Later." I stare up at the charred ceiling as I try to piece it all together. A cloud slips over the setting sun, plunging us into shadow. The birdcalls stop for a moment. I shiver. What does the Sheriff have to gain from getting me out?

Clay's voice calls from the front door. "Hey, you two in there?"

"Yeah, Clay," Ethan yells back.

"It's getting dark." Clay's voice sounds strained.

My time is up. I grab Ethan's shoulders and turn him around. "Look away if you don't want to see me pee."

As we step over the broken concrete steps and into the open, Clay's there. His hat's tucked into the crook of his arm and his damp hair clings to his forehead. His shirts stuck to his body with sweat. His normally clean-shaven face sprouts a stubbly beard. His eyes flick to mine for a second and then swing uncomfortably away. He throws his arm around my brother's neck. "Come on, little bro. Pa brought us some chicken."

Little bro? Pa? A flash of anger burns through me. He knows how to pile it on. I clench my hands and follow.

Clay leads us back to the campfire the boys have constructed in our house's backyard. They've even pulled out some seating: a log, a kitchen chair with three legs, a nightstand, a fraying armchair. Hatch sets pink hunks of raw chicken on a cast iron skillet near the fire. The Sheriff sits in the armchair and tips a jar of brown liquid up to his mouth. Clay gestures to the log for Ethan and I. Then he sits down next to his father and takes a pull from the jar when it's passed to him. The tart smell of homemade liquor fills the air.

My eyes flick to the Sheriff. He lounges in his ratty jeans, the stains around his pits a dark yellow. His little paunch belly sags over his belt buckle. His jagged C-shaped scar crinkles when he lets out one of his big belly laughs. The little hairs on the back of my neck stand up.

"So, missus," he says, leaning toward me, his thick hand on his knee. "Tell me what's so special 'bout you that made my son run out on his ol' man." His smile is wide, but in the flickering firelight, his eyes look calculating.

Clay fingers tighten around the jar he's holding. "Pa, don't."

The Sheriff emits a dark laugh. "I'm just introducin' m'self since you wouldn't do me the pleasure."

Clay glowers at his father. "Riley doesn't want to talk." Then he takes a big drink from the jar, swallows and winces.

The Sheriff snatches the jar out of Clay's hands, takes a long pull and wipes his mouth across the back on his arm. "See, here's the thing. I paid for this filly—"

Clay stiffens. "She has a name."

The Sheriff cackles and slaps his knee. He tilts his head toward me slightly. "Beg yer pardon, missus. Force a habit." His smile widens to let us all know he's not one bit sorry.

"All's I want to know, *Riley*," he says exaggeratedly, looking at Clay. "Exactly what feminine wiles you worked on C-boy here," he slaps Clay on the shoulder roughly, "to make 'im pick a cooz over his own pa."

My cheeks burn red at what he's insinuating. Clay's jaw is a rock.

"'Cause, see, I'm not sure she's worth what we paid, but you're the one who got a taste, not me." He elbows Clay in the ribs and cackles. "Might have to have a taste m'self, just to see."

Clay stands, his arms ramrod straight at his sides, fists clenched. "I swear to God, Sheriff, if you don't shut up—"

The Sheriff barrels upward, both elbows plowing into Clay's chest. Clay topples back, landing hard in the dust beside the campfire.

Everyone goes silent. The Sheriff hovers over Clay, fists clenched. Clay lays on his back, shock spreading over his face. Then his hands curl into balls. He pops up and stands a foot from his old man.

The Sheriff points a thick finger in Clay's face. "Lest you forgit who you speakin' to, boy."

Clay holds his father's gaze, venom blazing in his eyes. "I didn't forget."

Their hands stretch toward their hips like they'll draw guns, but the Sheriff lets out another dark laugh, thumping his thigh with his hand. He turns to Hatch and points to Clay. "Boys, this stallion needs to stud or he'll buck his rider. Let's give the love birds some privacy." He turns to me with a disgusting smile. "You call me Daddy from now on. Make me a proud grandpa and we won't have no trouble."

Hatch lumbers up and follows the Sheriff out of the circle. Even Ethan gets up. I want to protest and grab his arm, but he's gone. The Sheriff hollers as he's turns the corner. "You kids behave." I hear him cackling long after I can see him.

I feel like a tornado has just torn through the campsite. My hands shake as I curl them over my knees. I glance up at Clay. He's still standing between the fire and me. In the wake of his father, he looks as shaken as I am.

He stares at the flames a long time, his hands squeezed into fists. Finally, he turns to me. "Sorry."

"What did he mean by *make me a proud grandpa?*" My voice trembles more than I'd like.

The log I'm sitting on rocks as Clay settles beside me. He keeps his eyes to the fire, his face slack, his hands still in fists. "My goddamn father." He rubs his hands over his face. "That S.O.B. doesn't understand why I wanted you back so bad. Why I couldn't just take one of the infertile girls the Breeders ship us. He thinks ..." his eyes flick to my face and then away. "He thinks I'm in love with you."

"Oh." I clutch my hands together at my knees and stare at them.

Clay shifts on the log beside me. "Anyway, I just thought it'd be easier to let him think that."

"Right." My ears burn red. "So when we get home," I say slowly, "you and I would be what, exactly?" It feels as though the fire's burning hotter each second.

Clay flicks at a bug crawling up the log. "According to my pa," he pauses and swallows, "you'd belong to me."

I look to his face. "I'd *belong* to you?"

He shakes his head, holding up his palms in an it's-not-what-you-think gesture. "Only according to my pa. It wouldn't mean you'd be mine, I mean, to, you know ... We'd just be the same. As before." He clutches at the log as if he might fall off.

I stare at the cooking chicken on the skillet, once pink, now singed. I can't meet Clay's eyes.

Clay stands abruptly, rocking the log back. "Just don't worry about it, okay? Everything will be fine. I, uh, I gotta go help ... I'll get Ethan to show you to your room."

When he leaves, I wrap my arms around myself and stare at the flickering fire. Even in its glow, I feel chilled to the bone.

CHAPTER TWENTY-ONE

"Clay says this is your room," Ethan says, pointing to the nine-by-nine square of musty carpet, cobwebs and spiders. The walls in here are a faded pink. On the floor I see a wallpaper border that used to circle the wall, yellow ducks. A long time ago this was a baby nursery.

"What about you?" I ask, batting away a cobweb that's tickling my cheek.

Ethan frowns and looks back down the hallway to where Clay's voice floats toward us. Oh, I see. They've been bunking together. I pretend to be very interested in the pile of bedding they've left me as I swallow back the pain.

"I'll get my stuff." Ethan scampers off.

I tread carefully toward the bedding set in the corner so as to not disturb the dust. Three threadbare blankets each smell of body odor and mildew. At least fresh air blows in from the shattered window facing the dying campfire. The firelight will soon be gone and I'll lie awake on the hard floor, listening to the rats scurry through the crawl space.

"Eh hem."

Clay's lean shadow darkens my open doorway. He's clutching a two-foot tall metal barrel to his chest. He hefts it up slightly. "Found this. Thought you could have a fire in here if you wanted. Make it a little more cozy."

I could reject his gift, but a little warmth might make this night bearable. I point to the corner. "You can put it there."

He nods and drops the barrel with a metallic clang. He goes out and returns with an armload of wood and lights the fire. I stand off to the side, arms wrapped around my body. Being alone with him sends goose flesh over my arms.

"I got it from here." I stride to the woodpile and pick up a splintered chair leg. When I raise it to toss it in the barrel, Clay flinches.

A tight laugh bursts from my throat. "Did you just think I was going to hit you?"

Clay shrugs and lets his fingers stray to his jaw where I punched him. "You got a hell of a right cross. Hate to see what you can do with that."

I smile, but remember how angry I am. I toss the chair leg in the barrel with a clunk. Clay tosses in his log and dusts his hands on his jeans.

"I only hit people who deserve it." I study his face in the orange flickering glow. His expression is hard to read in the weak light.

"I'll be on my best behavior," he says, "but if you punch me again, I don't care if you're a girl, I'll have to defend myself." He leans in to warm his hands over the blaze and there's a smirk on his face. He's trying to be playful. And he's just called me a girl. It's been a long time since anyone in the real world acknowledged that fact. Chills run over my arms. I'm still wearing a hospital gown and pants. Suddenly I feel naked. I cross my arms protectively over my chest.

Clay points to the pile of clothes next to my bedding. "They're some of my old duds. Probably be too big on you, but it's better than that flimsy thing." His eyes flick to my gown and back to the fire. Is that blush on his face or heat from the fire? We fall silent. The crackling fire and the hushed voices of Hatch and the Sheriff supply some background noise. The air feels charged. I keep my eyes on the flames that waver in the barrel.

When Clay speaks his voice is low and tremulous. "You'd have died if I didn't take you to that hospital. I've spent every second since trying to get you back."

I bite my lip and watch the flames lick up a speckled log. "I thought you sold me for the money."

He shakes his head, his mouth a tight line. "I don't care about money."

I squeeze my hands around my arms, holding myself together. "Most people care about *that* much money."

Clay shrugs. "I tried getting in without my pa. That place is locked up tighter than a bender's twat." He blushes. "Sorry. Didn't mean to swear in front of a lady."

I rock back on my heels. "Don't do that. I'm not any different than I was."

Clay runs a hand down his chest and then tucks it into his jeans pocket. His eyes stay on the firelight. "But, it is different," he says quietly. "Everything's different now."

And it's broken, the friendship we had. The room feels hotter, my head lighter.

I grab a stick from the pile and use it to shift some logs that haven't caught. "How'd your dad get me out of that damn hospital?"

"He's in pretty tight with 'em. He's always making trips there, trading with 'em. Sheriff said they were eager to get rid of you. Guess you were giving 'em some trouble." He smirks at me. "Can't imagine you giving trouble."

I can't smile. "Yeah, I was giving them trouble. When that guard wanted to rape me, I gave them some trouble."

He holds his hands up defensively. "Riley, I didn't have a choice."

I turn on him, my hands tightening into fists. "That's bullshit, Clay. You had a choice. You had a choice when you took me to the hospital—and a choice when you gave that boy to the Riders. There's always a choice. You just don't want to believe you've made the wrong ones."

Clay gives me a wounded look. "Yeah, I've made wrong choices. Tons." He crosses his arms over his chest, a barrier between us. "But everything's not as easy as you make it seem."

"I don't want to hear it." I push past him to get to the door.

He grabs my arm and whirls me around, his face wild. "You were bleeding out from a gunshot wound," he says angrily, pointing to my stomach. "When you were conscious, you were screaming and begging me to kill you." He stops, looks at the hand that's gripping my arm and releases me. "I couldn't let Ethan watch you die." He stares morosely out the window. "I ..." He lifts his eyes to mine. "I couldn't watch you die."

My hands drop to my sides. "I don't remember any of that."

"I do." He turns his sorrowful face up to mine.

We're standing so close. Electricity jumps from his skin to mine. My heart starts to pound. Clay reaches out and traces the brand on the flesh of my forearm. The touch sends shock waves through my flushed skin.

"I'm glad you're back." He locks eyes with me. He wets his lips with the tip of his tongue. I smell the sweetness of liquor on his breath. "I went crazy the whole time you were gone."

A wellspring of desire washes over me. My fingers tingle, my lips. He's so close now I can smell the aftershave on his neck. I take a step closer. My eyes lock on the curve of his lower lip. He steps toward me.

Hatch appears in the doorway. "Boss want you."

Clay takes a step back. The gap feels like miles. He drops his eyes from mine and gives Hatch a nod. "Tell him I'll be there."

Hatch lumbers off. My eyes trail after him. "Not sure I like that he's sleeping one room over," I whisper.

Clay's face creases with anger and he bares his teeth. "If I had my way, he'd be taking thumb rides back home. He's a motherless bastard." He glances at me when after he swears, but continues. "My pa says he's worth his weight in muscle. I say he's taken one too many kicks in that boulder he calls a head." The veins pulse down Clay's forearms as he squeezes his fists. "I don't like the way he looks at you."

Clay takes a step to the door, but I grab his arm. My fingertips trace over the skin of his wrist before I let go. My hand's on fire.

"Wait," I say, breathless. "What happens now?"

His eyes track from my face toward where his pa waits for him. "We got an errand and then we're going home."

"Home?"

"When my pa found us, he tried to sweet talk me first. Guess he knew force wouldn't do no good. I'm a better shot than both him and his man put together and he didn't want it to get to that. So …" He pauses and blows out his breath. "We struck a deal."

I narrow my eyes.

Clay curls his fingers over the hem of his shirt. "My pa said I won't have to go on raids or trade with the road gangs. Just keep order in town. I told him he'd have to take you and Ethan in." He lets his eyes wander back to the fire before they flicked up to my face. "Everything's worked out okay, though. You're free and Ethan's got a place to grow up. And all I have to do is agree never to run away again." Clay's eyes are distant, looking out my window onto the moonlit landscape.

I shake my head. "We can't go home. My mama's at the Breeder's hospital. They have her knocked out in this room with all these half-alive girls." How can I describe the horror? I think of her in the pitch-black room, wires hooked to her chest, the tube taped to her mouth. I wince and shake the image away. "We gotta get her out." I look up, pleadingly into his eyes. "We gotta."

He blinks, processing. He reaches for my hand. "Riley, I'm sorry—"

The Sheriff's voice cuts through the room. "Clay!" his father bellows. "Get your ass in here!"

He shoots a look down the hall. His hand, hovering inches from mine, drops to his side. "I'll be back," he says, turning.

"Clay, wait."

He glances back with a look I don't quite understand. His heavy footsteps echo down the hall as he walks away from me.

I crumple into my mound of bedding and stare up at sagging plaster ceiling. I replay the last few moments. Clay so close. His fingers on my arm. The change in atmosphere when his father called him, like a switch flipped inside his head. One minute he was mine, the next he belonged to the Sheriff. I curl into the musty blankets and close my eyes. I may have Ethan and Clay back, but we're no better off than I was before.

***

I wake stiff and groggy. Orange firelight flickers dimly from the metal barrel. A lump beside me shifts. It's Ethan, curled in the sheets, one smooth pale cheek peeks from beneath a flowered blanket. I curl toward him.

Something stirs in the hallway. Someone's there. I look, but at first in the dark all I catch is a giant, lurking shadow. Hatch. I stare, barely breathing. His raspy breath and the creak of the floorboards under his weight seem deafening in the silence. I wrap my arms around myself and watch his shadow increase until it's massive, a thundercloud blotting out the moon. If he comes in, I'll scream.

Moments pass with nothing but breath and the fear creeping up my shoulders. Don't let him come in.

The floor boards creak. Heavy footsteps thud away. I pull the blankets up to my chin and scoot closer to Ethan. It takes me hours to fall back asleep.

***

"Riley, wake up."

I open my eyes to my room bathed in day. Sunlight dances through a battered cobweb across the window. Birds chirp somewhere in the distance. I've overslept.

I stretch the kinks out of my back as Ethan plops down a plate of breakfast—a lumpy mound of yellow eggs and a thick slice of brown bread. I want to gobble it all the minute he sets it beside me. Instead I take the fork and try to eat like a lady. Two bites and I'm shoveling the eggs into my mouth. It's so much better than hospital food.

My brother watches me eat, poking his fingers through holes in a moth-eaten blankets. The rose pattern of large pink flowers and cascading green leaves reminds me of the one stretched across my bed at home. Will I ever see it again? I turn my attention to Ethan. I've seen that wrinkled forehead before. He's stewing about something. I put down my fork. "What's cookin', bacon?" It's an old Auntie phrase. Just saying it makes me homesick.

"What does that mean?" He cocks his head to the side. His chin-length hair hangs off the side of his head like a brown curtain. He doesn't remember.

"What's going on in that noggin' of your'n?" I rap on his head lightly with my knuckles.

His face tightens. He looks to the door and then leans in close. "I heard something, but I—"

"Spill it," I say, feeling my pulse quicken.

He works his little fingers back and forth in the blanket holes. I know he's pretending their worms poking out of the dirt. If I were feeling more playful, I'd pretend to pluck them out for some hungry baby birds. But playtime's done.

He sighs heavily. "Last night I went to get my stuff from the van and I heard Clay talking to his daddy. I didn't really mean to easedrop."

"Eavesdrop. What were they saying?"

"I wasn't listening good until I heard them say something about Mama."

I haven't told Ethan about Mama yet. I just couldn't. Now, the hairs on my neck stand up. "What'd they say?"

"They were talking about how Mama is stuck in the same hospital you were in. Is that true, Riley?"

I bite my lip. "Yeah, bud. She was there."

"She was?" He leans in closer, his eyes widening. "Did you talk to her?"

God, help me get through this without crying. I tighten my jaw. "She was in another part of the hospital, but she's okay." I shift my eyes from his. Lies. All lies.

He sinks back into the mound of blankets, his eyes distant as his mind works this over. "I'm glad she's okay," he says quietly. He goes back to working his fingers into the blanket.

I lay my hands over his. "She is. Now what did Clay and his daddy say?"

Ethan frowns. "Clay told his daddy that you wanted to get Mama outta the hospital. He asked if we could go get her. Clay's daddy said no. A deal's a deal, or something like that." He shakes his head, trying to get it right. "Clay said we need to go, but then Clay's daddy said if he kept bugging him, he'd leave you and me here and drag Clay's ass back to town hisself. Then when Clay left, his daddy said something to Hatch about they're getting rid of the plan B patients in two days anyways. Something about *it ain't working*? I don't know." He frowns, then looks up at me. "What're we going to do, Riley? We have to get Mama." His wide eyes search mine.

When I pull my hands off my knees, I've left white indents where my fingers dug into the skin.

Ethan asks again. "What're we going to do?"

I dig through the pile of clothes next to me, looking for shoes. "What'd you think? We're going after her."

CHAPTER TWENTY-TWO

When I was little I'd sit by my mama's feet and unwind yarn while she knitted. I used to spend hours unknotting those course colored threads. My little fingers would pick at the knots until the tangles gave way. Despite the boredom, despite my sore fingers, I'd give anything to be back there again.

Alone in the mildewed room, I track down the shifting threads of my thoughts and unknot slowly. The facts are these. My mother has been sedated and is being used as a human incubator. Something bad is going to happen to her in two days. The Sheriff refuses to help because if he angers the Breeders, he might lose his kingdom. Plus, he probably couldn't care less. Clay gave in to this father when he said to drop it. Without Clay, our chances are slim.

Fact, says my petulant brain, *you won't want to leave Clay behind if that's what it takes.*

A pain shoots up my chest at this thought. I replay that moment with Clay again and again. The sweetness of the liquor on his breath as he stepped towards me. The touch of his hand on my wrist, hot like the fire that burned in the barrel behind us. I catch myself listening for his voice down the hall, for the tread of his feet on the gravel outside. But, he's the Sheriff's right hand man. Will he help?

I curl my knees under me and stare out the window where I can just see the top of a neighboring roof. Many of the semi-circular terracotta tiles have cracked and fallen away. A small, brown bird lands there for a moment and then ducks down into a hole in the tile where he's made his nest. I watch him settle in, feeling a wave of homesickness so raw I have to fight back tears. I wanna fly home, tuck myself in a warm snug place and fold my head under my wing. Then I think of Mama in that awful room. Whatever "get rid of" means, I can't let that happen.

I take a deep breath and tick off the plan. We'll have to get away from the Sheriff and get back to the hospital somehow. Once there, we'll need a way in. And we need Clay. I'll have to get him alone to find out his plan for Mama. And if he won't help? I wrap my hands around myself. Let's hope it won't come to that.

He shows up at my door for lunch in dusty jeans and boots. His sweaty t-shirt clings to the muscles of his arms and chest. He wipes a hankie across the back of his neck. "You up then?"

I gesture toward the noon sunshine streaming in my open window. "It's the middle of the day. I'll go bananas if somebody doesn't give me something to do."

He smiles faintly. "Thought you could use the rest." His eyes trace down my body. I'm dressed in his simple faded jeans, a cotton t-shirt. "You look … well rested," he says, a blush running up his cheeks.

His blush sends a fire to my cheeks. I shake my head and focus on the question I have to ask. "Clay about last night. There's something I—"

"Lunch is on," he says loudly, his eyes tracing down the hallway as if someone's listening. "Figured you'd like to join us."

"Okay," I say slowly. So it's not safe to talk. He leads me down the warped hallway, stepping past a hole where the floor has sunken in. Just before we come into full view of the others, Clay's hand seeks out mine. The soft pads of his fingers trace the skin of my palm. My heart pounds, but as quick as it came, the touch is gone. He strides toward the fire pit, calling to Ethan. I cup my tingling hand to my chest and step into the sunshine.

Ethan's perched on a log, his cheeks stuffed like a squirrel's, a half-eaten chicken leg clutched in his hand. Hatch sits on the dry grass with a hunk of chicken in his hands. Grease runs from the corners of his mouth, down his thick neck. He wipes an oily hand on the bib of his dirt-streaked overalls. As I sit next to Ethan, Hatch's eyes track me.

Clay crouches over the skillet and plucks off hunks of crispy chicken meat—a little burnt, but smelling delicious. He makes a plate with the chicken, a fat brown roll and a jug of milk. When I take a drink, the milk is warm and fresh. I stare up at him in wonder.

He smiles. "Pa got it in town. We like to eat good even on the road."

I look around for the Sheriff, but he's missing from our circle. I nod toward the ruts in the driveway where the van was parked. "Where'd he go?"

Clay looks at me and then slips a glance at Hatch. Hatch keeps his eyes on the chicken skin he's peeling and eating in big greasy bites.

"He's getting supplies for the ride home," Clay says.

"Oh," I say, feeling stung. "Are we going home?" My voice wavers like I can't seem to figure out what it should sound like.

He takes a bite of his bread roll, chews carefully. "Soon's you feel up to it."

My eyes slip to Hatch. "I feel fine."

My mama, on the other hand, does not feel fine. She doesn't get to eat chicken. She'll take the rest of her meals, however many she has left, through a tube in her arm. I picture her sunken face and a cold shiver passes over me.

Clay's brow furrows. "You cold?" He stands. "I'll get you a jacket."

I reach up, grab his sleeve and pull him back down. I throw on a smile. "Sit down. Just someone walking over my grave."

Hatch belches, stands and lumbers off, undoing his overalls. I watch his hair speckled back recede in the distance. This is my chance. Once he's gone, I lean toward Clay. "What about my mama? We can't just leave her there. Who knows how long she'll hold out?"

Clay locks eyes on the chicken in his hands. "Riley, I know you're worried, but we can't just rush into the Breeder's hospital guns blazing. There ain't nothing we can do till we get home. After that, we'll …" He finally looks up at me. "We'll come up with a plan."

I pull back sharply. "What're you saying? Leave her there? We can't leave her there. That," I say, pointing somewhere in the distance, "is my *mother*!"

"Riley, listen." He turns to me. "I know you love your ma, but it can't work. I just don't see—"

"Of course you don't see," I say, standing up. Fire burns through my brain. There's no stopping what comes out, no matter how ugly it is. "You're the one who let his pa sell his own mother to the Breeders. Did you help pack her bags?"

Anger rushes into his face. "That's not fair," he says, his voice controlled only barely. "I was just a little kid. I don't even remember her."

"What's not fair," I say, my voice trembling, "is my mama turned into a living corpse left to rot in a basement." I clench my fists. "That is NOT fair."

Clay shoulders tighten as he glowers into the fire. "You're ready to fight the Breeders?" He turns to me, eyes blazing. "The most heavily armed, well-guarded place in the whole goddamn world!?" He stands and points a finger in my face. "You're recklessness will get you killed! And him, too!" He points at Ethan.

I stand. "Don't bring him into it." I shoot a glance to Ethan. He's staring at us wide-eyed, a chicken leg dangling forgotten in his hand.

"Yes, I'll bring him into it!" Clay shouts. "You want to know how my brother died? Probably not, because you don't give a damn, but I'm gonna tell ya anyway. Cole was ten. Him and me, we was like you and Ethan. We went everywhere together. One day I was driving us home and I spotted a shiny sports car parked on the side of the road. I pulled over and thought we'd have a look-see. I shoulda known better, but I was stupid and fourteen. When we walked up to the car, they was waiting for us. Two men jumped us. Took everything we had. The bastard cut me here," he pulls down his shirt revealing a jagged three-inch scar above his heart. "Cole—" He grimaces. "He bled out in my arms." He looks down at his empty hands.

He lifts his head, anger replacing the pain. "That's what's going to happen to him," he points wildly to Ethan, "if you rush into that hospital."

I shake my head. "I'm not asking to go on some joy ride in a sports car. I'm asking you to save my mama's life."

"Doesn't matter," he says, stepping away. He looks up at Ethan. "When he dies in your arms, it won't matter why you went."

"Clay—" I reach for his arm.

He pulls away and stalks off into the distance. There's a pain in my chest, like an iron fist squeezing my heart into pieces. When I fit it back together, my heart will be a sharp jagged thing, ready to slash at anyone who gets near me.

Ethan's at my arm, tugging. "Riley, go after him."

I shake my head wildly. "No. And you're not, either."

Ethan cringes at the tone of my voice. "What d'you mean?"

"We leave him behind."

"Why?" he whines.

I stare into Ethan's wet eyes. "Because he's still on the wrong side."

The tears start to well in Ethan's eyes, but I grip his forearm. "No crying. Not for him."

Ethan snatches his arm away and runs off without a word.

I stand alone, batting at the hot tears that prick at the corners of my eyes. Alone is better. The only person that can cut you when you're alone is yourself.

***

It's late afternoon when I finally peak out of my room. The house is quiet. I haven't seen or heard anyone since the incident at the fire. I've been hunkered down, too, licking my wounds, but I gotta pee something fierce. I slip through the dank hallway, out the door and out into the fresh air. The birds twitter in the eaves of the houses around us. The brittle weeds crunch beneath my feet as I walk into the back yard of the abandoned neighboring house.

I slide behind a faded plastic play climber and take care of business. The plastic's hot on my bare skin, but being out of that dust-clogged room lets me breathe again. When I'm finishing up, I hear something moving in the shadows of the house behind me. An image of the deranged stranger who shot me flashes through my head. I step back until I'm pressed against a chain-link fence, my pulse in my throat. Metal digs into my back as I eye the dark entryway. Who's in there? Forget it. I don't wanna know. I grip the rusted fence, ready to boost myself up, I see the shine off an egg-shaped head in the house. Hatch, following me again.

Hatch appears at the doorway and clomps down the rotting back steps into the yard. His bare feet, blackened at the soles, make slapping sounds on the ancient wooden boards. His mouth hangs open as his eyes run up my body again.

"What do you want?" One hand searches my pocket. No weapons. My eyes flit around the yard for something to brain him with and come up with nothing.

He scratches a bug bite on his bald nugget of a head and hunches up his shoulders.

"Clay said you weren't supposed to be around me." I lean into the fence, the metal diamonds pressing into my back. I can be over it and gone in seconds.

Hatch takes another step toward me. The stairs moan under his weight. "Clay's not the boss. Boss don't care where I go, he said." His eyes linger at the swell of my chest beneath my t-shirt.

It might be reckless, but recklessness is all I have left to save my mother's life. I take a step toward the giant blocking my path. "Hatch, were you following me?"

He blinks at me for a moment as if the gears in his head turn real slow. He's missing at least a half-dozen teeth. He points to my hair. "You smell like flowers."

I shiver a little, but try not to show my disgust. "You like how I smell?"

He nods. "Like honeysuckle."

I smell like honeysuckle? I remember the sweet-smelling soaps Betsy used to slide to me in the shower at the hospital. I smile a little at Hatch. "Do you want to smell my hair?" My brain screams, *What are you doing?*

Hatch nods and shuffles through the dry grass. As he closes the gap between us, his massive shadow blocks out the sun. Now he's just a giant dark blob with a halo of blinding light at his crown. Warning bells go off. It's hard to draw breath. I tense and close both eyes. I feel the shift of his weight, hear the crunch of the weed stalks under his feet, smell his body odor and chicken grease. My scalp tingles as his nose brushes against my crown. His hand reaches in and tugs my hair to his nose. Each follicle tingles, sending goose bumps over my arms. I tell myself not to bolt. That it'll be over soon.

He pulls back, a childish grin slathered on his big face. He's looking at me like that piece of meat again. I draw back and cross my arms over my chest. "I have to go now." As I walk away, my legs are jelly. When I'm through the empty house, I run.

Ethan's sitting on the floor of our room when I fly in. He looks up at me as I grip the wall and pant.

He sits up. "What's going on?"

"I don't know." I run a hand over my face. A plan is spinning out in my brain. But would it work?

I lean toward my brother, my hands still trembling. "I need you to be ready. As soon as I can I figure a few things out, we're gone."

He knits his eyebrows together. "What do you mean? Back to the hospital?"

I look out the door toward were I left Hatch. "Just be ready."

***

Late that afternoon the Sheriff returns in a foul mood. Something about the prices of fuel. Sheriff and Clay strap on guns and take off again. The Sheriff tells Hatch they won't be back before morning. Clay stares at me out the passenger window of the van as they drive away, but I can't meet his eyes. Not when I'm leaving him behind.

I find Hatch sitting on a log by the dying fire. In the twilight he looks like a boulder, giant and immovable.

I stop when I'm five feet away. I squeeze my hands together and start before I can think too much about what I'm gonna do. "Hatch, I need a favor."

Hatch's eyes slip from my hair to my cotton t-shirt. He sucks in a loud breath.

"Clay and the Sheriff are going to take me back to town. I have to go back to the hospital. I need you to let me and Ethan go."

Hatch's face darkens in the gathering twilight. He digs slowly at the bug bite above his ear. "Boss said we go home. Didn't say nothing 'bout letting you go."

"I know boss didn't say, but I need to go back."

Hatch shakes his rock-shaped head.

I take a deep breath and smile coyly. I take another step forward. "You like me, right?"

He nods big and slow.

"If you let me and Ethan go, you can, uh, smell my hair all you want." I have no intention of honoring this promise.

He leans his giant elbows on his giant knees. The log rocks beneath him. "Boss'll be mad."

I walk in front of him and lean down until we're face to face. "You're bigger than boss. You don't need to listen to him."

He eyes lock onto the expanse of flesh below my neck.

"Come on, Hatch." I say with honeyed voice. "I need you." I swallow hard and think of Mama.

He's up and grabbing my arms. He hoists me to my feet until my toes scrape the ground. I struggle, but it's no good. He holds me up to eye level and peers in my face.

"You messin' with me?" he growls. "You messin' with ol' Hatchy?" His fingers dig into the flesh of my arms.

"N—no," I stammer. The pain pulses where his big fingers cut into me.

He pulls me closer until his face is inches from mine. I can see every hair in his stubbly beard. A jagged line runs from his nose to the top of his lip, what Auntie called a harelip. Something green lurks in the cracks between his teeth.

"Kiss me."

I shoot him a terrified look. "What?"

He tightens his grip on my arm. I wince in pain. "If you mean it, you kiss me."

Kiss him? Kiss this man ten years older than me with dim eyes, oily skin and chunks of his dinner between his teeth? This cannot be my first kiss. Please no.

I look pleadingly into his eyes. "Hatch, no."

His grip tightens on my arms until a cry of pain escapes my lips. I can see in his eyes if I don't give him what he wants, he'll take it.

"If I kiss you, will you let us go?"

He nods once.

Tears wet the corners of my eyes. What've I done? "Okay." I nod once and choke back a sob.

The big grin creeps over his face as he enfolds me in his giant arms. When his rough lips meet mine, I can't help myself. I pretend it's Clay.

The kiss is rough and wet. His tongue probes at my lips, but I clamp them shut. The stubble grates on the skin around my mouth. I pull back. "Okay," I say. "Let me go."

Hatch shakes his big head, still smiling, though his face has lost its innocence.

"Nope. I keep you."

CHAPTER TWENTY-THREE

The rough twine around my wrists burns, but not as much as knowing I've brought this all on myself.

Ethan sits beside me, bound hands in his lap, chin to his chest. His hair hangs limp over his eyes. It's better that way. I couldn't stand him looking at me right now.

Hatch first bound my hands and feet. Then he sought out Ethan, dragged him out kicking and screaming and tied him up, too. Now, as twilight crouches around the campfire, we watch as Hatch throws more boards onto the blaze. The firelight dances on his face. His eyes look like round black beads in the fleshy dough of his head. He scratches at the bug bite, red and raw above his ear and throws a cabinet door onto the fire. It crackles, throwing coils of black smoke into the air.

My insides smolder and bubble like wood that fuels our fire. I brought this on us, so I need to get us out. I stare into Hatch's blank face. There has to be something I can do.

"Hey, Hatch," I say, smiling at him. He lifts his eyes to mine as he tosses another cabinet door onto the blaze. "Untie us, please. We're not going anywhere."

Hatch scratches his head and smears a line of soot above his ear. "I know."

"We can help you get the fire on. Maybe cook a little something. You hungry?"

"Don't need help." He pulls a can of food from his overalls pocket.

I set my mouth in a firm line even though I'm trembling inside. "Hatch, boss is going to be *so* mad at you for what you're doing. You better let us go or I'm gonna tell him what you did."

Hatch's eyes hungrily trace my body. "I'm boss now."

I drop my head and stare at my threadbare knees. Why did I think this would work? Why didn't we just run while we had the chance?

Hatch lumbers up and thuds into the house for more wood. I search the shadows for escape. There's nothing for miles but dusty back yards, decaying houses, dead trees. Even if we could get free, any attempt to run and he'd be after us in seconds. My eyes trace over our yard: just logs, dry grass, long and matted down from all the walking we've been doing.

While my eyes are sweeping the campsite, movement under the armchair draws my eye. Something's underneath the chair's fraying fabric.

Then I hear a sound that strikes fear deep into my heart. *Sssshhh-thck-thck-thck.* A rattler.

Ethan and I have been raised to avoid rattlesnakes at all costs. Arn taught us they can strike from two-thirds their body length. He said climbing trees can sometimes save you, but diving into water will not. When we were younger, our mutt Bitsy took a diamondback bite on her cheek. The dog languished for a day, writhing and yelping until Arn put a merciful bullet in her brain. Since then, I've had a healthy fear of rattlers. Now one is curled snugly around itself about six feet from me. And it looks big.

The best plan would be to quietly pick up and move away. I'm about to tell Hatch when the image of our writhing dog flashes through my head. Hmm. I revise my plan.

Hatch returns with another armload of scrap wood and drops it next to the fire. He produces a can opener and cracks open a can of what looks like minced chicken. I watch the armchair with rapt interest and hope that Hatch's huge presence will be enough to send the snake out, fangs bared.

Hatch turns to me, a big dumb smile creeping up his face. "When supper's done, you and me go in the house."

I shake my head. "Ethan and I stay together."

Hatch points a chicken-coated finger at me. "You and me." He thumbs to the house. He runs his hands over his bare belly beneath his stained overalls. A sick, anxious feeling climbs over me. I absolutely cannot go in the house with Hatch. The next few minutes seem to stretch into infinity as I try to piece out an escape.

Hatch spoons hot heaping portions of the minced chicken into his mouth with the same dirty fingers he uses to scratch his crotch. I keep my eyes on the rattler who hasn't moved an inch. Then I see the long curved stick Hatch used to stoke the fire. If I could get my hands on it—

Hatch burps and pats his round belly. The dirty overalls swell around his flabby midsection. He holds the last can up and motions to us. He scoops some food out with his fingers and lumbers toward me, his hand outstretched. He wants me to eat out of his hand. Despite the urge to smack the globs of chicken away, I smile and stand up. "I'll come sit by you and you can feed me." I hate the sugary tone in my voice, the smile I plaster on. Then I nod to my feet. "That is, if you undo my feet."

He eyes me, but finally flicks out a little pocketknife and slices through the bonds at my feet. "If you run," he says, hulking over me, "I kill him." He points to Ethan. His face hangs emotionless. He means it. I no longer feel bad about trying to hurt Hatch.

As I step past the chair, my insides crawl. I walk over and stand to one side of the chair, clutching my bound hands together nervously. I do not want to get bitten by a rattler. In the flickering firelight, Ethan watches my every move.

Hatch leans toward me, his fingers slathered in minced chicken that at one time smelled so good to my growling stomach. Now, from the curling ends of his dirty fingers, it looks like chicken brains. I open my mouth and let him jam in the chicken. His thick fingers scrape the roof of my mouth. There's the taste of chicken, but also a tang of ash and dirt. I swallow as quickly as I can. He nods and digs in the can for more.

I turn toward the fire. "Looks like the fire's dying down. Let me stoke it for you." I reach with both bound hands for the branch he's been using.

He watches me warily as I grab the branch. It's about three feet long and springy, harmless. His brain slowly registers this and he bobs his head as I stir the logs around.

"You can feed Ethan while I take care of this," I say, batting my eyelashes.

Hatch shuffles over to hand-feed my brother. I scoot back up on my rock, clutch the stick to my chest and wait.

Ethan looks just as disgusted as I was, but he eats hungrily off Hatch's dirty fingers. I watch, barely able to regulate my breathing. Hatch lumbers back over to me.

"Why don't you have a seat? This chair's nice and comfy," I say, putting a trembling hand on the armchair.

He looks at the chair. "This is boss's chair."

I smile at him. "You're the boss now, right?" He stares at me, his harelip twitching. I can almost hear the gears in his head turning as he considers. Then he smiles and lowers himself into the chair. I hold my breath, but no snake. I grip the stick. I think it's long enough, but my hands are bound and I'm not even sure I can get a good angle.

Hatch stands suddenly. He leans down until his greasy face hovers right in front of mine. "You and me time." He runs a dirty finger over my exposed collarbone. His breath is hot and heavy in my face. He presses his giant form on me until I'm enveloped. I choke on the smell of sweat and animal fat. His big paws grope for my tender regions. He tugs at my shirt, trying to pull it up. Every inch of me prickles.

I close my eyes and jab the stick under the armchair.

My stick grazes off something, but is it chair or snake? I try to swirl it around, but Hatch snatches the stick from my hands so fast a splinter bites into my palm. "What you doing?" he asks, his brow wrinkling.

He raises the stick to strike me. Then we hear it.

Sssshhh-thck-thck-thck.

Hatch stumbles back, searching. I see her, the brown blur slithering across the dry grass. Hatch takes a step back and his foot lands on the rattler's tail. The rattlesnake turns and springs. Her jaw unhinges. I see the flash of white fangs. Her brown, arrowed head latches onto Hatch's exposed ankle.

"Yeeeaawww!" Hatch kicks his foot, trying to detach the snake. Her body thrashes like a long brown streamer on a windy day. She won't let go. Hatch tumbles over the chair and lands hard on his back, his legs dangling in the air. He's still screaming.

I watch with my hands over my mouth.

The snake slithers away, shaking a warning song as she slices an S through the dry grass. My eyes flick to Hatch. He's moaning and yelping. Was it enough to stop him?

He rolls back and forth on his back in the dust, clutching his ankle in both hands. He tugs his foot toward his mouth in an attempt to suck the poison out, his lips curling in an anguished sneer. When he can't get his foot to his mouth, he rolls over and pulls himself up on the tumbled armchair. A string of frothy saliva runs down the corner of his mouth. His body's covered in a scrim of dust. His blood-shot eyes fall on me.

"*You.*" He points a shaking finger. He limps toward me, his face twisted in rage.

If he catches me, he will kill me.

I turn and sprint toward the house. His heavy footsteps thud after me. With my heart flying into my throat, I tear through the yard as fast as my legs will go. I catch my foot on a prickly shrub and take a hard fall. My elbow slams into the dust and pain spikes my mouth as I bite my tongue. I look over my shoulder. Hatch is right behind me. White froth decorates the corners of his mouth as he reaches out with a clawed hand. I scramble up and sprint across the yard. I gotta make it to the house.

I tumble through the sliding glass door, my shoulder rocking into the frame. I thud down the hall. Where to go? Kitchen! I stumble in and yank out drawers. My bound hands scramble over rusty tongs, place mats, crumpled paper napkins. Where's a goddamn knife?

Hatch clomps up the back steps. He blows and snorts like a colt run into the ground. "You!" His face pinches with pain and rage. His arms are out, fingers hooked. He'll tear me to pieces. I don't wanna die at the hands of Hatch.

I sprint out of the kitchen, down the hall. I pull open the first door. A linen closet. Damn! My heart slams against my chest. I yank open the next door. The garage. I stumble down two concrete steps. The air's thick here, the floor strewn with garbage. I slosh through it at a run. My foot *thunks* into something solid and pain shoots up my leg. I crash hard into a pile of oily rags. I think I've broken my toe. I push up and hear him behind me.

Hatch stands at the garage stairs, gurgling, frothing. He looks like one of the brain-eating zombies from Auntie's horror stories. He'll crack me open and scoop out my insides, but not before using me up first. *Go!* I think. I claw my way up.

He growls and tumbles down the steps.

I sprint through the open garage door and into the dark toward the fire. When I reach Ethan, he's standing stock-still.

"Riley, is he—"

"Give me your feet!" I shout, stooping to dig at the twine around my brother's ankles. As I'm prying off the twine, I keep shooting glances back toward the garage. I keep expecting to see Hatch running toward us, his knife raised, but nothing. I pry off Ethan's bonds and I pull him toward the street. We skirt around the house. When we hit the pavement, I can see into the garage where I left Hatch. The dark, moaning shadow on the garage floor lets me know he won't be coming after us. The venom is working its magic. It's the only time I'll thank a rattler.

"Come on," I say, jogging next to Ethan down the moonlit street. "The hospital's this way."

CHAPTER TWENTY-FOUR

The hospital looms in the distance, all nine stories of concrete and glass glowing like an electric beacon. From here you can't tell the horrors going on inside. When we can see each individual window, my palms glisten with sweat. We've jogged on and off for two hours. My shirt is soaked, I have blisters on both heels and I want a drink of water so bad I'd kill for it. Ethan stops in the shadow of a leaning streetlamp, puts his palms to his thighs and sucks in rattling breaths. When he looks up, his eyes follow mine to the building illuminated before us.

"There it is," he whispers.

I nod and pull him into one of the vacant buildings that dot the block. We step over the pile of bricks that block the entryway. Something skitters into the darkness as we walk in, but judging by the sound, it's too small to be a threat. This place must've been a restaurant based on the faded sandwich posters curling off the wall. Booths with faded yellow seats line one wall. The cracked remains of a soda fountain stands next to the cash register. Ethan walks over and pushes the lever but nothing happens. *Subway*, the sign reads in big yellow letters. I thought subways were transportation.

My eyes flick through the dark shadows, examining every doorway. My skin crawls and my heart can't stop pumping way too fast. Part of me expects Hatch to come barreling out, hands hooked to tear me apart. We left him behind hours ago, but the look on his face as he tore through the house haunts me.

We lean against a debris-littered counter and stare at the glittering hospital.

"What's the plan?" Ethan asks.

I gotta get him out of here. He's sucking in far too much plaster dust and mold. He rests a hand on the counter and leaves a palm print in the dust.

"The plan is I get in somehow and you stay here."

"No way." He shakes his head back in forth. "I'm going."

"Ethan, it's not safe. I can't take you in there."

"I can't stay out here," he whines as he looks around the dark, cobwebbed space.

I think of what Clay said at the fire. Before I can stop it, an image on Ethan swims up before me. His face is slack and white. Blood splatters his chest. I shake it away. "You stay here."

"If you don't take me," he says, his fists tightening, his face screwing up into that look of defiance he rarely uses, "then I'll … I'll go knock on the front door. They'll let me in." He juts out his chin.

"Ethan!" I scowl. "You're being impossible." I slump in a booth, streaking the dust on the tabletop. He frowns at me from across the room. The stubborn set of his mouth matches mine. And I don't wanna leave him out here alone and unarmed. He could get in as much trouble here as inside with me.

"Fine," I say, staring out at the glowing hospital. "But you do absolutely everything I say, when I say it." I point my finger at him. "No questions."

He nods, his fists loosening.

"And if I say run, you run and don't stop. Not for me. Not for anyone. You got me?"

He nods.

I sigh, and a puff of dusts swirls off the counter and dances in the moonlight. I rub my fingers over the bridge of my nose. My legs ache from the long walk here. My shoulders are in knots. We have no food or water, no weapons of any kind. I rub my hand over my face. What the hell am I gonna do?

"How we gonna get in?" The garbage crinkles under his feet as Ethan takes a few steps toward the door and peers up.

I shake my head and rub my hand over my stiff neck. There's a tender stab of pain at my hairline where Clay dug out my tracker. Then it hits me.

I reach into my pocket. There, at the bottom, is the little metal disk the size of a button. Carefully I draw out the microchip and hold it up to the light. But will it work?

Ethan peers at the little disk. "What is it?"

"A locator," I say, tilting it ever so slightly in the light. "Betsy said the energy from my body activated it." I peer into the dark cave that used to be a sandwich shop. "We need to find a knife, something sharp. Then I'm going to need your help."

***

I press a strip torn from my shirt to the back of my neck and wince at the pain. Ethan re-implanted the transmitter. He said it started glowing a few minutes after we pressed it in the fold of my skin. Now he crouches beside me next to some smelly dumpsters at the back of the hospital. Black garbage bags peak over the lips of the metal bins. Some of the bags are torn open and garbage litters the ground. I push away a soiled cloth with my boot. Garbage pickers have been here. If we get spotted, it'll be a good cover story—that we're scavenging. I keep telling myself this as I sit with my back pressed to the stinky metal bin, my knees to my chest, my fists clenched at my sides. At least one part of my plan makes sense.

Yeah, but the rest of it's a mess, that nasty voice in my head says. *Even if the receiver still works, which is unlikely, and Betsy sees it, which will never happen, will she even care enough to creep downstairs and let you in? Then you'll have to skirt the guards, find Mama, get her unhooked and get the hell out, all with Ethan at your side.*

I pinch the bridge of my nose. Nothing is more impossible.

In five hours it'll be morning. And if the Sheriff's right, it'll be my mama's last day alive. I take a deep breath and silence the voice in my head. There's no time for plans, only action.

Ethan picks up a crumpled paper wrapper and starts folding it into little squares. His voice is so quiet I barely hear him. "Ri, do you think Mama will be happy to see me?"

His hair hangs over his eyes, so I can't read his expression, but I watch the way his fingers tremble as they fold the paper into neat squares. I put my arm around his slim shoulders and pull him to me. "Course," I whisper. "She'll grab you up and squeeze your guts out. Only ..." I haven't told him. How can I explain this to a little boy? "There's something I gotta tell you."

He looks up at me, his face tightening. His eyes are round saucers in the moonlight. "She's hurt, ain't she?"

I pick up a ceramic shard lying next to my boot and rub my thumb along the smooth surface. "Not exactly."

"What then?"

I take a deep breath. "They've knocked her unconscious." I meet his gaze now and plow through the rest. "She'll look like she's sleeping, but she's not. She may be hard to wake up."

Ethan stares into my eyes for a few tense seconds. I wonder if he'll cry, but his eyes are dry, his face solemn. I keep forgetting all he's been through.

"Okay," he says turning toward the hospital. "Let's go get her."

An old soul, my little brother.

"There's no way I can keep you outside," I say, more of a statement than a question.

He shakes his head.

"Fine," I say, sighing. "I wish for once I could keep you outta trouble."

"You need me," he says, puffing up his narrow chest. I tussle his hair. He's not even nine. God, what a life for a kid.

A hinge creaks behind us. Our heads snap toward the sound. Across the dirty lot, a door opens. The rectangle of dim light widens as we watch. Ethan's hand claws for mine. I grab it and drag him closer. Someone's coming.

"Come on, you silly heads," the shadow whispers. "Get your tushies in here."

Betsy. Oh, thank God. I stand, pulling Ethan up. We jog toward the round shadow. I send Ethan up the five metal steps and I follow. When the door shuts, Betsy throws her arms around me.

"Agatha," she says, her cheek pressed to my ear. "I'm so glad to see you."

I hug her once, pull back and take her in. Her belly has deflated, leaving a saggy middle that pouches beneath her gown. Her hair blond curls are down, bounding onto her shoulders. I grip her hand. "You came. I had no idea if you'd see my signal."

She smiles and nods. "I did. Weirdest thing, I'd put that tracker away when you left, but today I found it on my nightstand. And turned on, too. But here you are. And who is this?" She asks turning to Ethan. "What a *cutie*," she says, pinching his cheek.

I blink, processing. "Wait a minute, someone set the tracker on your nightstand?" The hairs on my arms rise.

Betsy nods. "Anyway, you're here. What're you doing back? Couldn't take it out there, right? Awful, I heard." She turns to Ethan and sticks her bottom lip out in a mock pouty face. "Awful, *wight*?"

"Betsy," I say, grabbing her arm, "we got no time. We need to get my mom and get the hell out."

"That's, uh, that's going to be exceedingly difficult," says a voice behind us.

Stepping through the shadows, a masculine form emerges in dark slacks and too-large lab coat. His smudgy glasses reflect a ray of light.

"Rayburn," I say, grabbing onto Ethan. "What're you doing here?"

"Well, how'd you think I got down here, silly?" Betsy says, putting her hands on her hips.

Rayburn and Betsy. They're both here, willing to stick their necks out for me. Yet something about this whole thing seems off. If I had time, I could puzzle it out. I don't. I turn to Rayburn. "I don't care how tough it is. What we gotta do to get her out?"

Rayburn shrugs and peers at me behind the film of his glasses. "I can get you into the plan B room. Unplugging your mother—well, uh, that's another story."

I reach out and put my hand on his arm. He stiffens at the touch. "You'll figure it out. I know you can do it."

He clears his throat and blinks at me.

"Come on," I say. "We don't have time."

We slip through the shadowed storage room that smells of old garbage, past the shelves of cleaning supplies, the yellow mop buckets, the industrial sink. Then we gather in front of the door that leads into the hospital.

I give Rayburn a little nudge to make sure he's listening. "We go quiet and fast to plan B. Rayburn, can you take us on a route to avoid the guards? If we see someone, we'll have to try to hide, which could be—"

"I can get you past the guards," Rayburn says with more conviction than I've ever heard him.

"Okay," I say. I look around at the faces before me in the dim light: Betsy's round, expectant one; Ethan's slim, worried one; Rayburn's jowly nervous one. "Everyone ready?" They nod. "Okay," I say again. "Let's go."

Rayburn swipes his badge and the door swings open. The hallway outside is dark and quiet. Little nightlights throw triangles of light on the tile floor. Rayburn scuttles out and motions for us to follow. I take Ethan's hand, my heart in my throat.

We skulk down the hallway. Rayburn takes a quick left, then right. He stops at a set of double doors, takes out his swipe card. The automatic doors slide open with a smooth hiss. The room before us is pitch black.

Rayburn disappears into the inky darkness. My heart thuds as I will myself forward. I know what horrors await me, but there's no time for fear. I tug Ethan along. Betsy shuffles so close behind, heavy breathing pulses at my ear. Together we walk into the darkness.

The door clicks shut behind us. A thick nothingness descends. The only thing anchoring me is Ethan's hand in mine and Betsy's breath at my back.

"Rayburn, the lights," I whisper.

They snap on with blinding brightness. We wince and blink into the light. When I look up, I take a step back. "Rayburn, what the hell—"

We're not in plan B. This room is smaller, about the size of a classroom, with echoing tile floors and low ceilings, and there are no beds, no unconscious pregnant girls. Most of the room is empty except one occupied bed in the corner.

Ethan stiffens. "Riley!" He points to the bed ten feet away. "Is it—" He starts to tremble.

It's our mother. I run over and put my hand on her skeletal arm. I mark every blue vein in her semi-transparent skin. She looks worse than when I last saw her. Her belly bulges round and grotesque. She looks far too along to be only impregnated a few weeks ago. But she's alive. The wires run from under her gown to the computer monitor above. The jagged green lines show her breathing, pulse and heart rate all steady.

Why is she here alone?

"Rayburn, what's going on?" I ask, turning on him.

He freezes, giving me a sheepish half smile. He's backing quietly to the door. "You, uh, you wanted, uh your mother. There she is." Beads of sweat have popped up on his hairline. His flabby chin trembles. Warning bells clang in my head.

"Rayburn, what've you done?"

The door opens with a hiss. We've been found.

The Sheriff strides in. My mouth drops open. I tuck Ethan behind me. Betsy's hands tighten around my arm.

"What is this?" I ask Rayburn again. He says nothing.

The Sheriff gives me his dangerous grin and then steps aside. A woman strides in and the door slides shut behind her.

"Oh no," Betsy whispers, sliding close until her gown swishes against my arm.

The woman is dressed like those business ladies I've seen in magazines. She wears slacks with pressed creases and a matching jacket. Her smooth brown hair is clasped at the back of her head. She's about Mama's age, but with none of the wear and tear that comes from life on the outside. Her chin and nose are sharp, her lips thin, unwelcoming, but there's something familiar about her sky blue eyes. They fall on me now as I'm staring, speechless.

The woman lifts her lips in a smile that's supposed to be welcoming but borders on nasty. She takes a step toward me, her shoulders back, her chin held high. "You must be Riley. I've wanted to meet you for a while now."

There's something familiar about her voice. It takes a moment before it hits me. It's the voice I heard over the intercom reprimanding Rayburn when he tried to be kind. She's one of the head Breeders.

We're screwed.

I swallow and raise my own chin. "Who're you?"

She takes another step. "I'm Dr. Nessa Vandewater. I'm one of the people in charge here." She gestures toward the hospital. "It's nice to finally meet you, Riley. I've heard a lot about you." She clasps her hands in front of her and I note her manicured fingernails, long and red.

The Sheriff snorts and she shoots him a pointed look. He grumbles but quiets. He rests his palms on the set of revolvers on his wide hips and glares at me.

Her shiny black shoes click on the tile as she takes another step forward. She's close enough I can smell her perfume, something like wilting roses. I focus on her eyes, piercing blue with flecks of gray around the irises. Where have I see her before?

She studies my face and gives a nod of approval. "I can see why Clay's taken a shine to you. Feisty, bold. Just like his mother."

I cock my head. "You know Clay's mother?"

"Yes." Dr. Vandewater smiles faintly. "Quite well."

The Sheriff snorts again. He slouches against the wall, his belly folding over his belt buckle. He's bored with this whole exchange and cranky, like he's being forced to be here. Is she in charge? How much power has been handed to the Sheriff by this blue-eyed woman? No wonder he's staring at the back of her head like he could smack it.

I point to my mama asleep on the bed next to me. "What about her?" I say, touching her hand. Her skin feels like brittle paper. "What's going to happen to her?"

Dr. Vandewater turns her graceful neck and gazes at my mother placidly. "Nothing's been decided. This batch of plan B pregnancies aren't going well. We've had to change plans." Her tone tightens and her hands claw around each other for a moment. Then she takes a deep breath and continues. "With the right treatments, she can be saved. Not the fetus, unfortunately. We weren't able to stop the mutations."

"What?" I snap my eyes to her.

Her head snaps back, eyes wide as if she's revealed too much. "Nothing." She smoothes a hand over her hair and forces a smile. "What happens to your mother is going to be up to you and Clay."

"To me and Clay?"

She touches an index finger to the metallic disk inside her ear. "Location of Clay?" she asks and then waits for a moment and nods. "He'll be here in twenty seconds." She gives a little smile. "Perfect timing."

Ethan drops my hand and takes a step forward, fists clenched at his sides. "What're you gonna do to Clay?"

She leans down and smiles at him. "Clay will be fine, little Ethan. Don't you worry about that." When she smiles her teeth are straight and white as bleached tombstones.

The doors behind us swish open. Clay charges into the room. He squints against the blinding lights, throwing up a hand to shield his eyes. He stumbles over to me. "Riley, Ethan, what—" His eyes fall on his father and the woman in the suit. "Pa? What …" Shock creeps over his face. "What … the hell is going on?"

Dr. Vandewater claps her hands, her face unfolding into a giddy smile. "Oh, Clay, look at you." She rushes over to him. "When I saw you on the monitor screens, I said to myself, *Look how much he's grown.* Not a boy now, are you?" She pauses a few feet from him, admiring him. "A man." She looks to the Sheriff for confirmation. He frowns back, but she just keeps smiling like a rabid coyote. "Oh, I'm so glad you've come."

Clay mouth drops open, his eyes wide. "You … You're—"

"Yes," she says, clasping his hand. "I'm your mother."

CHAPTER TWENTY-FIVE

Now I understand. Clay has his mother's eyes.

Clay stares into her face, slowly shaking his head. "But, I—I thought you were dead or gone or … Right?" He lifts his eyes to his father.

The Sheriff shakes his head. "It's your ma, alright."

She nods, inserting herself in Clay's line of vision. "Sweetheart, darling, I wish you could understand why I've been gone for so long." Her tone speeds up. Her eyes are too wide. Her hands flutter like panicked birds. "It was *impossible* to have you here while I focused on my work. What would I do with a child running around the labs? You would've just gotten into trouble. But now, it can all be different." She reaches a hand out to touch his cheek and he steps back.

"You left when me I was a baby. Pa said he was forced to bring you here to breed." He points to his father who shrugs, drops his head and twiddles his fingers on his revolvers.

She clasps her hands together. "We couldn't tell you the truth, darling. It was better you thought I was out of your reach. I'll admit I did get a little obsessed. We were *so close* to perfecting the procedure." She looks up at Clay. "That doesn't matter. What matters is when I saw you on the monitors when you came to get Riley."

Eyes turn to me, then back to the doctor.

"I knew I had to see you. I asked your father to bring you earlier today, but he was unable." She shoots him a glance.

The Sheriff eyes Clay. "Gave me the slip, didn't ya, boy? Beat me back home to see *her.*" He nods to me, disgusted. "Yer ma and I figured you'd come after the filly. Guess we was right." He smirks, but Dr. Vandewater shoots him another glare.

"Clay, darling, listen. I've given so much of my life to this job. Now it's my turn. I need to connect with you again."

Clay blinks and shakes his head slightly. "I—I don't understand. You want to come back now?"

She takes a step forward, her hand outstretched. "I gave up a life with you and with your father so I could help them here at the hospital. It was the right thing to do, but I've given them eighteen years of my life and now it's my turn. I'm stepping down from the experimental program. I have time now. Time for you." She cups Clay's cheek. This time he doesn't pull away. "It's not too late for us."

A tense silence hangs, the only sound the delicate beeping of my mama's heart monitor. If my heart had a monitor, it'd be beeping out of control. I watch Clay in his dirty jeans and cotton t-shirt torn at the shoulder. His boots are grimy, his chin dark with stubble. He came after me today, risked angering his pa. Now he stands between his mother and I and doesn't look at either of us. His blue eyes, his mother's eyes, are locked to the polished tile floor. His hands twitch at his sides, but other than that, there are no signs of a war raging inside him. I want to close the gap between us, throw my arms around his neck and lean my head to his chest. Instead I stand stock-still and await his judgment.

He looks up at his mother. "What'll happen to them?" He points at Ethan and me.

"That's the best part," she says, smiling too wide. "They can stay here at the hospital. Your father has already agreed to move the two of you to town so we can all be together. You can visit Riley as often as you like. She'll be safe here, free from disease, war, enslavement. She'll have the best food and medicine. And you two can still be together. It's perfect."

She makes it sound too good to be true. But as I look into her eyes, I don't see a future free from pain and torment. I see imprisonment, plain and simple. Yet, it's not my decision to make.

"What about her ma? And Ethan?" he says, shooting him a glance. "What'll happen to them?"

"We'll use every technology available to save Janine Meemick's life. Out there, she might survive, but …" She looks at my mother. "It won't be pretty. Ethan can stay with you and your father and visit his family on weekends. When he's old enough, we can get him a job. There are perks to knowing someone in the upper offices." She smiles slyly, raising her perfectly rounded eyebrows.

Clay frowns. "And what if I say no?"

Dr. Vandewater stiffens. "Why would you?"

He locks his jaw and stares at her. "What if I say no?"

Dr. Nessa Vandewater lifts a slightly trembling hand to smooth her hair. "Well, things could go *rather badly.*" She enunciates each word as she shoots eye daggers at me. She softens as she turns back at Clay. "I don't want it to come to that, Clay. Please."

Clay turns and walks toward me, reaching for my hand. I slip my fingers into his. I love the feel of his calloused palm in mine. But his eyes are so anguished. Will I be able to forgive him if he chooses his mother? I chose mine. I feel like I'm swallowing a throat full of cotton as I think about what I've set into motion.

"Riley," he says, leaning in until I can smell his aftershave, "could you be happy here? Your family would be here."

Dr. Vandewater leans over his shoulder. "We could even bring your Auntie in. She'd make an excellent nanny."

He ignores her and stares into my eyes. Emotions zap through me like lightening. I don't want to be a prisoner here, but what's the alternative? Death? Being put back in plan B? And if it will keep Mama and Ethan safe and give Clay what he wants? I can give up my freedom for them. A tear wells in my eye, blurring Clay's features for a moment. Can't I?

I try a smile. "If they were safe and you were happy, I'd be happy."

He steps closer. My eyes trace over the hollow at his throat, the stubble on his chin. "You'd do that for them?" He cups his hand around my cheek. "For me?"

A tear traces down my nose as I rest my cheek in his palm. "All I really wanted," I say looking deep into his eyes, "was to be with the people I love."

He pulls me to his chest and wraps his arms around me. I throw my arms around his shoulders and press into the warmth of his chest. His heart thuds against mine. I have wanted this so long. Now it's so bittersweet.

His arms drop from around me as he twirls around.

His guns are silver blurs. Before anyone can move Clay points both revolvers at his parents. Clay's blue eyes narrow. All emotion is gone. Only the gunslinger remains. "We all walk or none do. Your deal may sound sweet as candy, lady, but I've made deals with your kind before. They turn sour real quick."

His mother steps toward him. "Clay, I—"

He gives her a hard look. "You may a birthed me, but you weren't never a mother to me. No sense in starting now."

Dr. Vandewater starts a shrill protest, but the Sheriff's chuckle cuts in. His belly shakes as he strides around the doctor and stands in front of Clay.

"You was never a one to make a good choice, was ya, boy? Shoulda taken your ma's deal. My deal won't be so sweet." His nasty grin widens to reveal missing teeth. "Not sweet at all."

Clay doesn't waiver. "One more step and you'll be leakin'. I ain't afraid of you no more, pa."

The Sheriff grins and clomps forward. "You don't really think I'd leave bullets in them shooters, do ya?"

Confusion darkens Clay's face. He looks at his guns. "You're bluffing."

The Sheriff laughs, his belly jiggling. "I'll jist give you a minute to check."

"Marlin, stop it," Dr. Vandewater says shrilly.

"Shut up, woman," the Sheriff snaps, pointing a finger at her. "I did what you said and look where it got us. Now we do this my way. He's grown too big fer his britches and I'm 'bout to shrink him down." The Sheriff takes another big step forward.

Clay holsters his guns and steps in front of me. He juts his chin, his fists tightening at his sides. "I don't need guns to take you on, old man."

The Sheriff cackles again. He brings his fists up to his chin. "Try me, boy."

At first, they circle around, fists up, eyes cold. I grab Ethan and Betsy and take a step back.

Dr. Vandewater claws the Sheriff's arm as he steps past her. "Boys, that is enough!"

The Sheriff shrugs her off, never taking his eyes from Clay.

"Throw the first punch, Pa." Clay waves him forward with four fingers of his raised hand. "Or you afraid to get knocked ass-over-tea-kettle by your boy."

The Sheriff snorts and takes a practice jab at Clay. "'Fraid of a little pisser like you? You think you're an awful big bug, huh. Well, let's see."

The Sheriff steps forward and throws a solid right cross. His meaty arm snaps out as the blow grazes off the side of Clay's head. Clay bobs back, shuffles around and jabs twice into the Sheriff's ribs. There's a dull crunch. The Sheriff hunches, moaning. He stumbles back, rubs his ribs. Then he straightens and chuckles darkly.

"Big bug, alright. Who taught you to box, boy?"

Clay narrows his eyes, his fists hovering in front of his chin. "You did."

"That's right." The Sheriff charges, arms spread wide, and tackles Clay around the waist. Clay folds as his wind is knocked away. Their boots scrape on the floor as they struggle and stagger around, a raging monster with four legs. The Sheriff locks his hands around Clay's chest and squeezes. Clay gasps for air, clawing at the Sheriff's arms, trying to wrench free. There's a *pow pow* as the Sheriff lands two punches into Clay's kidneys. Clay's head drops forward like a broken doll's.

"Stop!" I step forward. Ethan tugs me back and shakes his head. I stand stiffly, my hands clenched at my sides.

Clay's up and scrambling. Slowly he wiggles out of the Sheriff's straining fingers and then he pushes his father off. Both men stagger back. They puff and spit. Is it over?

The Sheriff digs into his pocket for something, his eyes dark. Clay face drops in alarm as if he knows what the Sheriff will pull out. He runs, winds up and smashes his fist into the Sheriff's jaw.

There's a snap as teeth shatter. A crack as the Sheriff's head jerks back. A trail of blood arches from his mouth and the splatters on the floor. The Sheriff's legs unhinge. He goes down on the tile like a sack of bones.

I stare at the Sheriff slumped on the ground. Clay pants hard, his fists now at his sides. His knuckles are bleeding, his jaw swelling. He swipes the back of his hand across his mouth and takes big breaths.

Slowly the Sheriff props himself up on his elbows and shakes his head drunkenly.

Clay stands over him, panting. "You done, old man?"

There's a long pause. Slowly the Sheriff pushes himself onto his feet and licks blood from the corner of his mouth. As his grimace turns into a sneer, his hand digs for his pocket. This time Clay's too slow to stop him. He draws out a slim black pipe like a narrow flashlight. What's he doing?

"No," he says, popping his spine into place. "Not done."

The Sheriff snaps his wrist. Smaller sections slide out of the handle until the Sheriff's holding a two-foot baton, shiny and lethal.

Dr. Vandewater screams, "Marlin, stop!"

He draws it back and smashes it into Clay's knee.

The crack is sickening, like snapping a dry tree branch. Clay screams and tumbles onto the tile, reaching for his smashed kneecap.

"No!" That's it. I'm not watching anymore. I run forward.

The Sheriff raises the baton.

I spring on the Sheriff and claw for the baton. He shrugs me off. I stumble back and he turns. His smile's gone, replaced by one of the angriest sneers I've ever seen. I grab again for the baton, my fingers slipping over the smooth surface. The Sheriff swings his free hand. There's a blur in my periphery and then his fist cracks into my cheekbone.

There's an awful pop deep in my head. Stars explode across my vision. Then I'm falling. Falling. Falling.

Next thing I know I'm face down on the tile. Heat spreads across my cheek. I can't focus my eyes. Someone's crying. The Sheriff's face bobs before me. My eyes lock on the puckered C-shaped scar that keeps dancing in front of my eyes.

"No meddlesome piece of trash tells me what to do."

The pain throbs through my cheek, but I glare into the Sheriff's eyes. "Looks like a woman's been telling you what to do all along."

The Sheriff raises the baton. He'll crack my skull with it. I try to cover my head with my hands.

Nothing. No blow. Just some grunting, like someone's struggling. I look up.

Clay's and the Sheriff struggle over the baton. Clay's fingers grip the end. The Sheriff yanks on the handle. Clay spins and suddenly he's at his father's side. He draws a revolver from his father's holster. There's familiar click of the safety as Clay thumbs it down.

"Knock it off or I'll shoot." Clay digs his father's revolver into his back.

The nasty smile creeps slowly over the Sheriff's face. He turns around, his hands up. "You won't shoot yer pa." He reaches for the revolver.

When the gun explodes, I don't know who's more surprised, me or the Sheriff staring at the bloody hole in his chest.

CHAPTER TWENTY-SIX

"That is enough!" a voice screams from behind us.

I blink and see Dr. Vandewater striding to the doors. "Get out of the way, you idiot!" she says as she pushes past Dr. Rayburn. The doors slide open.

The Sheriff staggers back. He pokes one fat finger at the three-inch hole in his shirt. The wound beneath is ragged, red and pulsing blood. "Nessa." He looks at her pleadingly. "Help."

She gives him a cold stare. "You made your own bed, Marlin." Then she stomps out the door, Rayburn scuttling in her wake.

The room is still. Then both Betsy and Ethan erupt in talk that I can't hear since there's a buzzing in my ears, but I'm striding to Clay and putting my hands on him before I realize it. He shivers a little as if coming out of a dream and blinks at me.

"You okay?" I ask.

He looks at me, his face drained of color. He limps to face me and puts his hand delicately on my bruised cheek. "You?"

I nod, ignoring the pain flaring in my cheek and the dull ringing in my ears. Our eyes flick back to the Sheriff who staggers back to the wall and slumps against it. One hand leaves a red smear against the white paint. The man who used to terrify me looks small and helpless as he stares at his bloody hand in amazement. His shirt is sticky red. Blood puddles on the floor around him.

"Boy," he says, his voice trembling. "Help ... me." He reaches his hand out.

Clay drops his father's revolvers into his holsters as if they weigh a hundred pounds. He stares at the hole he's made in his father's chest. "She can save you."

The Sheriff shakes his head. A trail of blood dribbles from the corner of his mouth, down his neck and spreads into the collar of his shirt. He slumps to a sitting position with is back against the wall. "Your ma ..." he draws a gurgling breath, "is a spiteful bitch. You ... gotta help me."

Clay opens his mouth to speak and then closes it. When he forces words out, his voice is flat. "That's done. I can't help you no more."

Clay reaches for me. I take his hand and lace our fingers together. We watch the Sheriff take a few straggling breaths. Finally Clay speaks, soft and low. "I bin standin' here trying to think of what to say before ya die. Most would tell their pa they loved 'em, but I just can't. Would be a lie and I can't lie with you like this." He gestures to his father's slumped body. "Best I can say is thanks for not throwing me to the coyotes when you found out I was a boy. Other than that, well ..." He sniffs. "Not much else I can thank you for."

The Sheriff's head bobs up and down. He forces his head up and looks into Clay's eyes. "I gave you everythin'."

Clay shakes his head. He squats down on his haunches. His hands tremble as he grasps his knees. "You used me for your own gain. That's all you ever did, Pa. Use people. And you taught me to use people. I've been trying to unlearn that lesson for a while."

"I ..." The Sheriff's voice is thick with fluid. Blood pools at the corners of his mouth. His breathing sounds like a clogged pipe.

Clay shakes his head. Tears wet the corners of his eyes. "It's done, Pa. Let it go."

The Sheriff keeps his eyes locked on Clay. His mouth forms words, but no sound follows. He gurgles a few times, more blood spilling from his mouth and pooling under this chin. A couple of wet breaths and then his head rolls to his chest.

Clay crouches, letting his lean shadow cover his father's body like a shroud. Finally, he puts his palm softly on his father's chest just above where the gunshot wound still dribbles blood. Then he stands up and wipes his hands on his jeans.

I can't believe the Sheriff is dead. I want to comfort Clay, tell him it'll be all right, but my throat is dry. I reach my hand out. Clay takes my hand and pulls me away. "Come on," he says. "We gotta go."

Clay leads me to Mama's bed. I help him push it to the door. The bed's bulky, but with all those cords and wires I don't want to risk unhooking her. Betsy and Ethan gather beside us. I put my hand on Betsy's arm. "What're you going to do? Go or stay?"

She gives a little frown, but then plasters on her chipper smile. "Course I'm going, puddinhead. Can't really stay here now, can I?" Her curls bob back and forth lightly.

By helping me, she cut herself off from this life forever. I owe her big time. I give her hand a pat. "Glad you're coming."

"Let's save the happy reunion for later," Clay says, drawing his father's revolvers. He hands me one of his father's guns. "You can shoot?"

I nod, looking over the revolver.

"Good," he says. He holds up a box of shells he's dug out of his father's pants pockets and starts loading his two guns.

The four of us exchange our last looks. Ethan puts his hand on my arm. "Let's get the hell out of dodge," he says. It's a perfect imitation of my stepfather. I almost smile. We walk to the door and it slides open.

I'm the first to step into the hallway. I skid to a stop. The hospital bed crashes into my back. Ten yards down the hall, Dr. Vandewater stands with her arms folded across her chest. Her long red fingernails look like bloody talons. Behind her, guards line the corridor, guns slung across their arms, bullet-proof vests strapped on their chests. My mouth drops open. Betsy lets out a little squeal.

"No more deals," the doctor says, her face a cold emotionless mask. "Come with me, Clay, or die with them. You have one minute to decide."

I stare for a moment, unable to move. This? This is what we've come down to?

Clay turns and pushes us back into the room. We fall in. Ethan's hand gropes for mine. Silent tears trace Betsy's face. My eyes flick from the open doorway to Clay's face. He stares back in shock.

"What'd we do?" I ask.

Clay looks to the door, then back at me. He shakes his head slowly. "I don't … I don't know."

A sob breaks from Betsy. Ethan's whole body begins to tremble. I pull him to me. I squeeze him hard, trying to hold back my own tears.

"This is all my fault," I say, pressing my face into Ethan's hair. "We can't go against that many guards. We're done." My eyes flick up to Clay's stunned face. "I should've listened when you said not to be reckless. I had to run here with no thought, no plan." I wrap my arms around Ethan. My hand finds my mother's arm on the bed. "It's all my fault."

Clay grabs me by the shoulders. I press my face into his chest, my angry tears seeping into the fabric of his shirt. Is this my last moment with him? I try to memorize the smell of his neck, the flex of his arms, the touch of his hand on my cheek. This can't be the end. He lifts my face to his. His sky blue eyes stare deep into my own.

"No," he whispers, brushing his fingers against my cheek, "you were right. Sometimes you have to be reckless for someone you love."

He draws me to him, his lips pressing into mine, first soft, then harder. Passion rips through me, heating up my chest, my arms, my hands. I fold into him, drinking up this moment of sweetness. Our first kiss. Our last.

When he pulls away, I'm light-headed and breathless. "Clay."

He gives me one more longing look. Then he draws his gun, strides through the doorway and opens fire.

CHAPTER TWENTY-SEVEN

"No!" I shout.

My voice is drowned out by the rattle of gunfire.

In the hallway bullets ping off the walls, lights shatter. A smoke grenade plinks off the tile and begins spewing gas into the air. Betsy and Ethan cower. I can't take my eyes off the spot where Clay was a moment ago. He sacrificed himself for me.

I can't let him die.

I grab his father's revolver and spin toward Betsy. "Get my mother and Ethan out. Clay and I will cover you." Her eyes are round, cow-like. I grip her arm hard. "Find a way, Betsy. Tell me you will."

She blinks and nods, her curls bobbing slightly. There's no perky smile now. "Okay," she says.

Ethan's hand snakes around my arm. "No, Riley!" He pulls me away from the door and the gunshots that crackle every few seconds. There's no time.

"I love you!" I hoist the revolver and run into the smoke-filled hallway.

I skid to a stop next to Clay, my eyes burning. He looks at me and frowns, but his attention turns to a bullet cutting through the smoke like an angry hornet. It zings past close enough to blow my hair back. Behind us a light shatters. I hear the whine of the gurney wheels as Betsy and Ethan push my mother down the hallway.

Everyone I love is in peril at this moment.

A guard rushes through the smoke, gray tendrils curling around him. I see the whites of his teeth before the barrel of his gun aims for my chest. Clay fires and the guard staggers into the wall, but not before he gets a shot off. There's a *thunk* and a spray of blood from Clay's thigh. He lets out a snarl of pain, but aims and drops the guard with a bullet to the brain. Clumps of red and gray splatter the pristine hospital walls.

A moment of silence. My eyes are streaming, but I lock them forward and peer into the smoke. Beside me Clay's fingers fly as he reloads. The silver chamber spins as the bullets drop in with quiet clicks.

Fifteen feet away, a head hops out of a doorway, then a gun. A guard rattles off a few wild shots. I duck. Plaster sprays into my already streaming eyes, patters against my face. Clay stands stock-still, raises his gun and fires. His bullet buries itself into the guard's shoulder. He disappears, screaming.

"Go!" he says, squinting through the smoke that seers his eyes like acid. He fires again, the bullet pings off something metallic in the distance. "Go, Riley!"

"Not without you!"

He opens his mouth to protest, but a bullet zings between our two heads, hitting a light fixture that rains sparks on our heads.

A guard pops up ten yards away behind a metal bench. My finger draws back the trigger and my gun explodes, rocking my shoulder back. The bullet cuts through the smoke and hits the guard's vest. The guard staggers back, his mouth open. When he realizes he isn't dead, he smiles tauntingly. He lifts his gun to finish me. There's a crack beside me. The guard's neck springs a leak. His gun clatters to the tile. Blood patters the wall as the guard topples over the bench and sprawls on the floor.

I squint through the haze toward the wall of guards. Our victories are a drop of water in the ocean. The guards keep coming.

I shoot a look down the hallway. Betsy and Ethan round the corner and disappear. *Thank God for that*, I think. Time to go.

A gun cracks. A cry of pain pulls me out of my thoughts. I look over. Clay's hand is tucked to his chest. The palm is such a bloody, shredded mess, I can't tell what's happened. His revolver clatters to the floor. I reach for him, but the guards smell their victory. Bullets fill the air like lead rain.

"Come on!" I scream, dragging him away. "Run!"

He turns and stumbles along side me. Bullets zip past, slicing through the smoke, spraying plaster and shards of light casings on our heads. Something punches into my calf. I stumble, but Clay's good hand on my arm steadies me. Then a bullet smashes into his shoulder and he goes down on the tile.

"Clay!" I scramble over to him and drag him forward. He's drenched in blood. One pant leg clings to him in a red sopping mess. His white t-shirt is soaked through from his shredded hand. He stares up at me, his eyelids fluttering.

"Go," he croaks.

I slip my arms under his and drag him backward along the tile. His boots leave two red tracks on the floor. Ahead the pounding of footsteps sounds like a giant crushing wave. We're about to drown.

I grunt and tug, but it's no use. They'll soon be here. My eyes are already streaming, but the sobs that shake from my chest are new. "We gave 'em a good fight," I whisper. I lean down and kiss the top of his blood-speckled head. Beneath the blood and smoke and gun powder, there's still a trace of his familiar scent. I'll take it with me wherever this path ends.

A door pops open across the hall. Through the haze, I can just make out Dr. Rayburn's shocked face behind his bleary glasses.

"Good God," he says. Then his eyes flick to where the guards are breaking through the smoke. "Come on." He waves me over. I heave Clay over with all my might, but my wounded calf has stiffened and doesn't seem to work. Ray scuttles out, put his hands under Clay's armpits and drags him into the door. I limp after.

The door slides shut. Dr. Rayburn mutters over the keypad, frantically punching buttons until the lock clicks. He stands against the door, breathless. His white lab coat is streaked with Clay's blood. He adjusts his smeared glasses and runs a trembling hand through his greasy hair. "Door won't hold them for long." He nods toward the back of the room. "We got a truck."

We're in the same storage room where Rayburn handed me off to Clay and the Sheriff. There's an idling supply truck by the open garage door. I stare out into the fresh night air on the other side of the door. Can that really be freedom? My mother's lying in the back of the van, still hooked to her IV. Ethan sits beside her, holding her hand. When he sees me he waves and then frowns. He starts to climb out but I shake my head and hobble forward. Betsy, who's busy chucking supplies into the van, stops when she sees me.

"Oh my heavens, are you hurt?" She waddles over and reaches.

I shake her off. "Help me get Clay into the van!"

Her eyes go wide at the sight of him. She grabs Clay's bloody boots. I take his arms. Rayburn jumps in the van's driver's seat. The engine revs.

Fists pound on the door. Rifle butts slam into the metal, denting it. If Rayburn was right, they'll be here in seconds and my legs won't move any faster.

My wounded calf throbs, but Betsy and I double-time it to the van. It seems like a million miles. My back finally bumps into the van's bumper. I hoist myself up and then reach down for Clay's arms and draw him inside. He's so heavy and my arms so weak. Ethan reaches down and takes an arm. Together we heave Clay upward. Betsy pushes on his legs, her pudgy face red with strain.

The door flies open. Guards pour in like insects. They're coming.

"Come on!" yells Rayburn, looking in the rear view.

It's a swarm of guns and arms and angry faces. And black gun barrels. Hands reach out and grab Betsy's pudgy arms and legs. They drag her backward into the mound of guards. Rayburn hits the gas.

"Betsy!" I scream.

I drag Clay into the van as we bounce out of the storage room and into the parking lot. I get a glimpse of Betsy's terrified face in the sea of guards. So frightened. Then Rayburn takes the corner.

She's gone.

I scramble toward the van doors. I gotta go back for her.

Ethan's hands grab my waist. I turn my tear-filled eyes toward him. "Let me go!"

Then I see them, Clay and my mama both unconscious on the van floor. Ethan's terrified face is speckled with blood. "Riley," he says quietly. "We need your help, too."

I fold into his arms. He holds me as we speed through Albuquerque's darkened streets.

Now it's my turn to cry.

CHAPTER TWENTY-EIGHT

We drive for eight straight hours.

Rayburn and I take turns driving and tending to the wounded. Clay is in the worst shape. He's lost so much blood. Rayburn stops the bleeding and administers antibiotics, but without blood to give, it's hard to tell if he'll make it. When I'm not driving and gripping the steering wheel so tight my fingerprints embed in the wheel, I'm sitting in the back of the van holding Clay's and Mama's hands. She has yet to wake up. Rayburn just shrugs, but from what Dr. Vandewater claimed, Mama's life is in as much jeopardy as Clay's now.

We run out of gas next to an abandoned church down a long driveway. I look up at the bleached adobe building as Rayburn pulls slowly behind the back wall with the last of our gas. Some of the colored glass windows have a few panes intact. The giant wood cross aims skyward from the roof like a conduit straight to God. I sigh. It's as good a place as any to see who lives and dies.

I hobble through the old church, scouting out a room for Mama. In the sanctuary, with rows of sagging wooden pews, I scare a flock of birds out of the nest they've built in the organ pipes. They fly up out of a hole in the roof. Two tattered banners drape from the walls on either side of the little stage in the center. One says *Peace* with a silk dove sown below it; the other says *Hope* with a large brown cross. I grab a few crusty pew cushions and carry them down the hall.

I find the room a few doors down. This quiet little nook must've been the church's small library—stacks of yellow books lie in piles where they've spilled out of the tilted shelves. I push them out of the way. A book called *The Fiddler* loses its binding and cracks in my hands. The pages flutter out like tattered moth wings. *The Heaven Answer Book* must've had better glue because it stays intact. I turn the crackling book over in my hands. Maybe I'll try to read it if I have time. I could use some answers. Like why Betsy and not me? And what will happen to my mama if she dies? I set the books down and make a cozy nest for my mother. Then I walk back out to the van and help carry her in.

Rayburn and I settle her on the cushions. They smell faintly of bird droppings but it's the best I can do. I lay her veined hands over her stomach. She looks lovely with the dim afternoon light filtering in through the cobwebbed windows. Her burned face is set as in a peaceful slumber. Suddenly I have a vision of her inside one of the plushy coffins from before things fell apart. I shake the image away.

"Mama," I whisper, pushing a few strands off the burned part of her face. "Wake up," I say, running my thumb over her hand. "Ethan needs you." I choke back a sob. "I need you."

When she doesn't stir, I set her hand down and limp out to the van to help bring in Clay. I find Ethan and Rayburn hauling him out. In the sunlight, Clay's face looks like the pages of the books in there, pale, worn and fragile. There are large grayish circles under his eyes. The apples of his cheeks flare bright red in the white of his face. His eyes flutter open and he groans as they ease him into the small sanctuary. In one corner I've made a bed for him out of pew cushions. As they settle him onto the cushions, puffs of dust swirl through the triangles of light streaming in from the ceiling. Rayburn and Ethan go back to the van for supplies. I sit beside Clay and tuck the cushions around him.

Clay's eyes flutter as he reaches for me with his good hand. His bandaged right hand lies lifelessly on his chest. I'm too afraid to look at what's underneath. Will he ever draw from the hip again?

He runs the back of his hand over the bruise where his father hit me. I lean down and touch my lips to his parched ones.

He gives a delightful moan. "Is that all I get?" His voice is gravely and weak. "No sugar after I shot our way out?"

I smile wanly. "You'll get plenty of sugar when you're better." I brush the sweaty clumps of hair out of his eyes. His lids flutter again. He swims out of sleep and his face tightens in pain.

I start to stand. "I'll get you some of Rayburn's magic pills," I say. "Thank god for those supplies Betsy got us."

And there it is, the wave of pain that punches me in the stomach every time I think about Betsy. I haven't slept since the hospital. When I do, I know I'll see her face as those guards closed in like piranhas on a chunk of meat. Her terrified eyes greet me from every darkened doorway. Her cries echo from every quiet corner.

I jump as Clay's hand closes over mine. I offer a weak smile.

"It wasn't your fault," he says. "Nothing you could do to save her."

"Nothing?" I ask. I picture Betsy's face. I've spent the hours since going over every detail. If I'd had Clay's feet instead. If I'd been a second quicker. If I'd jumped out of the truck instead of hesitating. There were lots of things I could've done.

"Stop torturing yourself." He reaches for me again, but this time I don't fall into his arms. I like torturing myself. Maybe someday I'll stop, but not today.

"Riley!" Ethan's shrill voice calls from down the hall. I snap my head around.

"Go," Clay says, his eyes wide with fear.

I bolt from the sanctuary into the little library where we've tucked my mother. I scramble to a stop, knocking over a pile of books, sending up a cloud of dust.

"What?" I ask, stepping over the books to get to Ethan. "What is it?"

He doesn't answer. Instead he moves aside.

Mama's eyes are open. "Riley?" she asks.

For weeks, I'd been racking my brain to remember the color of Mama's eyes. I remembered they were brown like mine, but what shade? Chocolate? Mocha? Coffee? Where there flecks in the center? How did they look when they fell on me? How did I feel at that moment when my mother saw me and liked what she saw?

I kneel down, my trembling hand reaching for hers. Her cracked lips draw up in a smile. "Baby," she whispers.

I look into my mother's deep brown eyes. Now I remember.

***

In the light of an electric torch, I lean over Clay's sweat-flecked face as Rayburn readies the scalpel over Clay's exposed thigh. I look into Clay's eyes.

"Are you ready?" I whisper. I offer a leather bible cover. Clay folds it in half and nods. His face tightens, sweat streaming down in rivulets. He places the cover in his mouth and bites down.

I take his hand. "Squeeze as hard as you need." If only I could take the pain for him.

He nods again, but his eyes trace up into the rafters of the church as he readies himself.

I watch his face as Rayburn takes the scalpel and presses it into the bullet hole in Clay's thigh.

Clay's grip tightens on my fingers. His teeth pierce the leather. Rayburn begins muttering as he digs.

"Hurry, Rayburn," I say, as Clay's back arches and a little moan escapes his lips.

"I'm, uh, trying," Rayburn says. He swipes his forearm across his sweaty brow and goes back to searching for the bullet. Clay's hand tightens around mine again. The smell of blood and antiseptic makes my stomach churn, but I clench my jaw and fight the sickness. Clay needs me. Finally, Rayburn sighs and holds up bloody tweezers. At the end is the red slug.

I let out a puff of air. "Over," I say, patting Clay's hand. He gives a slight nod, but his face is still twisted in pain. He's more pale than usual. A shiver runs through him, though it's still nearly eighty degrees inside the church. I press my lips to his sweaty forehead. "You did great."

He leans into me and tries to smile. "Nursemaid, too," he says. "Nothing you can't do, hmm?"

I smile and wipe sweat from his brow with the hem of my shirt. "Can't keep you from getting shot up. Can't do that, can I?"

Rayburn finishes bandaging the wound and packs up his med kit. "I'll, uh, go out to the fire." He looks at me, adjusting his bleary glasses. "I gave him some morphine. He, uh, he needs to rest."

Clay nods, his eyes drooping. "You go out to the fire," he slurs. "I'll be fine."

I kiss his hand, the one that's not a giant, bandaged mess. I tuck the ratty curtain he's using as a blanket around him. Before I'm out the door, he's breathing evenly.

In the barren churchyard, Ethan's built a small fire. Rayburn sits Indian-style on the ground, digging into a can of food from the van. Mama and Ethan sit hip to hip. She's got her arms around him and he leans into her embrace. It's so good to see them sitting there together. Now it's my turn.

"I told her everything," Ethan says as I walk up to the fire.

"Lord, I hope not," I say smiling. She smiles back. It's so good to see my mother smile.

"He told me all the best parts," she says, her voice lilting, musical. "He saved the gory details for later." She pats the curtain she's spread over the dust. "Come, darling. Fill in the rest."

I fold myself into her.

Ethan pokes a stick into the blaze and then uses the burning end to trace red shapes in the darkness. "Mama knew Clay's mother. You know, the lady at the hospital."

I turn to Mama. "You knew Clay's mother?"

Mama nods. She's still weak, almost frail, but her mannerisms are all the same as I remember. The corner of her mouth lifts just before she speaks. "When I knew her, Nessa Vandewater wasn't such a fancy pants. She was just another patient like me at the Breeder's hospital. That was the year before you were born," she says, touching my knee. Her eyes trail back to the fire.

"They brought Nessa in already pregnant and big as a house." She rounds her arms out to mimic a giant belly. "I guess that was your friend Clay." She looks up at me. I blush and turn my eyes to the glowing embers.

"Anyway, Nessa always told us she was some sort of genius. All us girls on her floor thought she was crazy. Some girls come in that way, baked in the head." She looks down at Ethan who's writing his name in the dust with his stick. "Then they came for her one day and we didn't see her for a long time. We thought she'd been taken down to the experiments. Later we found out she was in charge of them. Turns out she was a genius after all."

I study the fire, considering this. "So she experimented on the same girls she'd been friends with?"

Mama shakes her head. "Nessa never had friends. She didn't care if she ruined girls' lives, killed people. Never was right in the head." My mother shivers. She lifts her eyes to mine. "I'm sure your friend Clay's not like that."

"He's not," I say. I think about him alone in that dark church and frown. "What about Clay's brother, Cole? He was born four years after Clay."

Mama shrugs. "That was after your Auntie broke us out of the hospital, sweetie. What happened to Nessa after that is anyone's guess."

I ponder this while the fire crackles and the bugs chirp shrilly around us.

"What'd we do now?" Ethan asks, chucking his stick into the fire. It crinkles and pops as the blaze eats it up.

We all look at him as if it hasn't occurred to us to ask this question. Of course it's occurred to us. Just none of us are sure of how to answer it. I open my mouth to speak, but then my eyes flick up to my mama.

She nods at me. "Don't stop on my account. What should we do, Riley?"

I sigh deep. "I think we should go back for Auntie. With the Sheriff dead, Clay's got claim as leader of that town. The Warden won't give up easily, but we can't leave Auntie behind."

Mama nods. Her eyes shine as she pats my hand. "I couldn't have said it better myself, darling."

Above the stars are a handful of sparkles toss across the night sky. The fire pops and crackles. The night insects sing their shrill melody. Beside me Ethan hums a little tune under his breath. Even Rayburn's shuffling and sniffing blends in until, if I closed my eyes, the scents and sounds could transport me home. With my eyes still closed, I lean in and rest my head on my mama's shoulder and inhale her earthen scent.

For a moment I almost say, *Let's go home*, but I stop myself. Here in the dark, with my family and Clay not too far, I realize home isn't a building or a place we'll travel.

I'm already home.

***

Three Weeks Later

"Get a move on, slow poke!" I yell down the hallway. Yelling in a church is probably a sin, but I'm not sure anyone's up there counting. If they are, I owe them big time.

Ethan comes loping around the corner, caring one of the hospital supply bags over his shoulder. It looks like it weighs more than he does. I grab it for him and heft it up. "Is this the last of it?"

He nods, his hair far too long now, brushing the bridge of his nose. He tosses his head to move it out of his eyes. "All the other supplies are in the van."

Ethan and I walk out to the church's dusty front lawn. Rayburn loads the gasoline he purchased in the closest town over. He won't stop belly-aching about the sores on his heels from the six-mile walk, but I think he's pleased with himself. He should be. It's no slouch bartering in town when you look like a pudgy seventeen-year-old with glasses and loafers.

I toss the heavy bag in the back of the van. Gentle footsteps tread up the gravel. I can tell it's my mama without turning around. She walks up, folding a blanket in her arms. She wears a hospital gown, which she's stitched to make it snug and a pair of scrub pants we found in the van. She looks solid, more like the mother I knew everyday. I note the slight swell of her tummy as she pads toward me. We haven't talked about what Dr. Vandewater said about the mutated fetus she's carrying. That'll wait until the time comes. For now I try not to think how hard it'll be for her to be pregnant on the run. It doesn't matter, I tell myself. She's tough. And, so it turns out, am I.

I walk up the path and lean in for a hug. I've been doing this all too often. I wake each morning in a panic that she's gone. Only when I roll over and see her sleeping on the floor beside me does my heart slow its patter.

"Are we ready, darlings?" she says, as I release her. Ethan comes over and slips his hands around her waist. She rests her hand on his shoulder.

"All set, except Clay." My eyes trace back to the open door. It takes him longer to do most things now, though he doesn't complain.

My mother pats my cheek. "Go get him, my love."

She doesn't have to tell me twice.

I stride through the open archway and into the interior of the church. The wooden floors creak under my footsteps. My eyes trace past the little enclaves in the wall where decaying saints watch. I pass a giant wooden cross, tilted to one side. For a moment I wonder if these relics are why we've been so lucky, left alone here in the desert for so long. I touch the rough wooden cross. It's about time we had some damn luck.

I stop at the entryway to the sanctuary and take a deep breath. Even though Clay and I have been boyfriend and girlfriend for the last three weeks, I still get butterflies every time I stand here.

I rap my knuckles twice on the ancient wood as I enter. I hear a shuffling in the shadows beyond, but can't see him until he steps into the streamers of light from the busted window. Dimples form in the corners of his cheeks as he smiles. "Come in, madam." He gives a mock bow. "You'll have to excuse the mess. It's the maid's day off."

I stride down the aisle and into his arms. The stubble on his cheek rubs deliciously against mine as he nuzzles my neck.

I run a hand over his cheek. "No shave?"

He leans in to my touch. "Can't manage without slicing my own throat. Gonna need some help 'til I work out being a lefty."

He holds up his bandaged hand to illustrate. It's wrapped in gauze, but I know what's underneath: a ragged bullet hole straight through his palm. He's got all his fingers, but right now they're useless. Rayburn says he might be able to get some function back, but it'll be slow. The pain is nothing compared to the ache of knowing he'll never draw from that hip again. He looks down at his hand, frowns and then uses it to pull me to him.

His breath is hot and sweet on my neck. "Do we got a sec for that sympathy lovin' you promised me?" He runs his nose along my jaw. I shiver as fire surges through me.

Everyone else is at the van. Being alone with him sends tingles to all the right parts of my body. His arms slide around my waist and pull me to his chest. The heat from his body burns against mine. I look up into this eyes, steel blue with flecks of gray. He runs his hand through my hair, traces the pads of his fingers down neck, across my collarbone. I'm breathless. My head's spinning.

"Everybody's outside, right?" he asks, leaning in to kiss the hollow of my throat.

Blood is rushing to my head. "Mmm hmm."

"Good," he says, letting his lips trail up my neck to my chin. My heart's thrumming like an electrical wire. His left hand grips the back of my head.

He pulls me closer. I smell the sweetness of his breath on my mouth. My heart pounds a crazy rhythm in my chest when our lips meet.

Kissing him is letting cool water slip over your body on a scorching day. Like the charge that crackles in the air after a lightening storm. Like the eating the last chocolate on earth, the sweetness melting on your tongue. I don't have words for this feeling. I forget comparisons. I lean into his chest and wrap myself around him.

Outside the horn beeps. We pull apart, breathless. He kisses me on the forehead and then takes my hand. "Time to go."

So much of me wants to stay here in this room with him and let the hours and days spin out around us. We're heading back into dangerous country where every day something will threaten to pull us apart. I lace my fingers through his and but don't take a step forward. I don't know if I'm strong enough to face what awaits.

He tugs on my arm. "You ready?" His understanding eyes seem to realize what he's asking.

I shake my head.

He nods and pulls me to him. I rest my head on his chest. His voice is low and reassuring. "Riley, I'm going to protect you."

"I know," I whisper into the fabric of his shirt.

"We'll be okay," he says, pulling back so he can look in my eyes. "We will."

"How can you be so sure?" I glance out his little window to the dusty landscape. It looks extra harsh and uninviting now.

He takes my hand and pulls forward. "Because," he says smiling, "we'll be together."

A ghost of a smile touches my lips. I follow Clay out the door. I don't know what troubles lay in wait like hungry animals, ready to claw us to pieces. I don't know if we'll be safe from the forces that will threaten us. But I know we'll be together. I grip his hand tighter as we step into the sunshine. Right now, being together is enough.

ABOUT THE AUTHOR

Katie French imagined herself an author when her poem caught the eye of her second grade teacher. In middle school she spent her free time locked in her room, writing her first young adult novel. Though her social life suffered, her love for literature thrived. She studied English at Eastern Michigan University, where she veered from writing and earned an education degree. She spent nine years teaching high school English. Currently she is a school counselor, doing a job that is both one of the hardest things she's ever done and the most rewarding. In her free time she writes, reads great books and takes care of her two beautiful and crazy children. She is a contributor and co-creator of Underground Book Reviews, a website dedicated to erasing the boundaries between traditional and non-traditional publishing. She lives in Michigan with her husband and two children. You can find her at www.katiefrenchbooks.com, at www.undergroundbookreviews.com or on Facebook.

ACKNOWLEDGMENTS

Many thanks go out to the people who made this dream a reality. I want to thank my first readers, Brian Braden, A.B. Riddle and Kimberly Shursen. You took a chance on a stranger joining your writer's group and somehow let me stay. You read chapter out of chapter with an unfailing honesty and constant support that made feel like my story was indeed worth telling. You are my writer's soulmates and I am better for having met you.

Thanks to my Author Salon team, Amy Grossklaus, Fran Kefalas, Jackie Krah and Ingrid Seymour. Girls, you were the support team I needed when making the choice to send my baby into the world. I've learned a lot from such talented writers, but it's your friendship and kindness that keep me going when the road seems impossible. Thanks go out to Michael Neff, who's tough love taught me a lot about a high concept idea and how to make sure I had one.

Many thanks go out to my writer's group partners, Nancy Brown and Greg Warner, who met mostly for my benefit. You shared stories, laughs and a few glasses of wine. You listened to me ramble on about writing many summer nights. Those are good times I will always remember. Several other friends read pages along the way, so thanks go out to Marlena Bravender, Trista Dymond, Greg Martin and Amanda Kimosh. Your friendship is without measure.

Thanks to my cover artist, Andrew Pavlik, who put up with my constantly changing mind. Thanks to Catherine Adams, editor extraordinaire. You helped me find Riley's path back home and the books is so much better because of your insight. If I only learn half of what you know about the English language, I'll be in good shape.

Finally, thank you is not a big enough phrase to tell my family how much I appreciate their love and support. Without my parents none of this would have been possible. They fiercely believed I could do anything and made a geeky, self-conscious kid believe it, too. Thank you for making me the (semi) well-adjusted member of society I am today. To my children, you are the light in my life. And lastly, to Ryan: It doesn't get any better than spending my life with you.

If you enjoyed The Breeders, please leave a review on Amazon, Barnes&Nobel or GoodReads. For updates on book two of the series, like me on Facebook or visit my website at www.katiefrenchbooks.com.

Made in the USA
Middletown, DE
28 September 2018